...ing, because dreams do come true...

FEATHERS AND FLAMES

Simona Pellegrini

Design by www.paulkayley.co.uk

All characters and events in this publication, other than
those clearly in the public domain, are fictitious and any
resemblances to real persons, living or dead, is entirely
coincidental.

ISBN 978-0-9929681-0-6

D'Angio Publishing

Simona Pellegrini studied Foreign Languages and Literature in Italy and moved to England in 1999. She lives in Lancashire and is currently preparing the *Feathers and Flames* sequel for publication while working on the third book of the series. The story of *Feathers and Flames* began to take form during a visit to York Minster. From that day all she could think about were angels and demons. Within a fortnight, she had created a world populated by mystical yet credible characters. Three months later, she had drafted the whole series from beginning to end. If you want to find out more about *Feathers and Flames*, visit www.feathersandflames.co.uk

To my mother, Maria Rosaria,
the angel in my life.

Acknowledgements

My biggest thank you goes to my family.
Without their support and love
I would never have believed that
I could achieve whatever I set my heart on.
They always believed in me and
encouraged me to pursue my dreams.
Also to my patient and understanding friends,
who stuck with me
even when I deserted them
to spend every free moment I had writing:
thank you for your support and for helping me bring
Feathers and Flames to life.
Last but not least, a huge thank you
to my book editors,
Debi Alper and Martin Ouvry,
who have helped me shape my novel into
the best story I could tell,
and to the amazing team of people responsible
for making this happen.
It's been hard work, endless weekends hibernating
in my room, and, at times, a hell of a rollercoaster ride,
but I have loved every minute of it.
I'm so grateful for all the love and support
I've had during this incredible journey.

Thank you

CONTENTS

For he will give his angels charge over you,
to guard you in all your ways.
On their hands they will bear you up, lest you
dash your foot against a stone.

Psalm 91: 11-12

1. MIRACLE

Rome traffic is dreadful. I squeezed my eyes shut as my cousin dodged in and out of lanes, manoeuvring round cars at full speed. I could taste the stink of exhaust fumes at the back of my throat. It was too warm to wind up the window, and the air con in Mia's car wasn't working. Blasting horns, and scooters flying past within an inch of my door, had given me a headache. I pinched the top of my nose to relieve the pain. It didn't work. I breathed a sigh of relief as we pulled up at the airport in one piece.

"You have time to grab a coffee before you check in," Mia said, looking at her watch.

We sat down at the first empty table we found. I ordered a coffee and a bottle of water.

"It meant so much to me that you came, you know?" Mia's voice broke as she fought back tears.

I smiled at her, placing my hand over hers and squeezing it tight. "I know."

"It must have been hard for you to come back after all these years," she said.

Hard? Hard was an understatement. I was eight when I left Italy and moved with my Nana to Featherstone, England. This was the first time I'd been back to Rome since that day. It had been far from easy.

"I'm OK." I shrugged. "I just wish it didn't have to be for your dad's funeral."

Me and my big mouth. Tears welled up in Mia's eyes.

"I'm sorry, cuz. Sometimes I forget to switch on my sensitivity button."

"Don't worry," she sniffed. "How about you? You feeling OK?"

"I'm good," I lied.

"Did you ring Nana?"

"Yeah, this morning. She's still upset she couldn't come."

"There's no way she could have travelled. She's too frail. Mum was right to stop her."

"You know Nana Holly. She's as stubborn as a mule." I forced a smile.

"Reminds me of someone else I know," Mia said, raising one eyebrow. She peered at me. "Are you sure you're all right?"

I must have looked as awful as I felt, judging by her expression.

"Yeah, yeah. I'm just a bit tired, that's all."

"You've been feeling tired a lot." Mia narrowed her eyes at me. "I know I've said it a million times, but I really think you should see another doctor."

Mia's Italian accent was more noticeable when she was fretting. She was only a couple of years older than me, yet sometimes she worried more than my Nana.

I sighed. "I'm fine. It's my anxiety attacks. I'm used to them. Can we talk about something else?"

We sat, finishing our drinks in silence. Dealing with feelings had never been my forte.

I glanced at the clock on the wall. "Will you look at the time?" I said. I threw a handful of euros on the table and sprang off the chair. "I promise to visit again soon, hand on my heart." I smiled, but I knew I'd just lied to her.

"Don't wait another ten years." Mia hugged me tightly. "Say hello to Nana Holly for me."

I turned and strode towards the check-in queue. I didn't look back.

I glimpsed my reflection in a shop window and couldn't

help noticing the dark circles around my eyes, compliments of months of insomnia. The pain in my chest was still troubling me. A sudden sting behind my ribs at that very moment almost took my breath away. My anxiety attacks were getting worse. No doctor had been able to fix me, and the medication seemed to make no difference whatsoever. The last shrink I saw reckoned the cause was my parents' death. I wasn't convinced.

As I rushed through the security gate, I felt a strange sensation, as though I was being watched. I'd had that same feeling, on and off, the whole time I'd been in Rome. This time, I put it down to being nervous about travelling alone. The last thing I needed to add to my list of mental disorders was paranoia. By the time the plane was in the air, the pain in my chest had eased off a little, just lingering in the background. I rested my head against the seat, falling asleep pretty much instantly, until a violent shudder of the plane woke me up.

I gripped my seat in horror. The lights went off, and the plane started to descend, nose down, at a terrifying speed. People were screaming, and the oxygen mask dropped in front of me.

Oh God. This was it. I was going to die. I wasn't even going to make it to my eighteenth birthday. The plane would hit the cold sea with a mighty blast. Salt water would fill my lungs. I would drown, or even worse, burn alive. I pictured my Nana's distraught face as a police officer gave her the news. She wouldn't be able to handle another upset. This would kill her too.

The overhead compartments burst open, bags and cases flying around, creating more chaos. The man beside me was trembling, sweat dripping from his face and landing on the collar of his shirt. He glanced at me but said nothing, then stared forward with his eyes wide open, shuddering.

I closed my eyes and started praying. I had never prayed so hard in my life. Couldn't even remember the last time. When Nana used to make me go to church every Sunday, I pretended to know all the words by moving my lips like a fish. Yet now I remembered every single one of them. Perhaps, in a weird kind of way, dying like this made sense. After all, I had been lucky enough to escape death once already. Maybe I wasn't meant to survive this time. At least I would see Mum and Dad again.

No. I wasn't ready to die. Not yet.

Oh God, please stop this plane from crashing. I'll never ask for anything again, I swear.

The juddering stopped. I opened my eyes. The lights were back on and the plane had levelled out. The Captain announced in a shaky voice that we'd hit severe turbulence, but we were out of danger and would be landing shortly. The cabin crew walked along the aisle, putting back the overhead luggage and checking that everyone was OK. They were trying to reassure us, forcing smiles, but I could see the shadows of panic still on their faces.

A passenger walked past my seat, the only person looking calm and in control. I caught his eyes.

As we stared at each other, I felt as though I was in a trance. His hair was raven black, slightly longer than I normally like in a guy, but it suited his defined jaw; he was wearing a black T-shirt and jeans. A shiver ran down my spine. The longer he looked at me, the faster my heart pounded. There was something magnetic about him, and I shuddered as he brushed past.

After we landed, the crew escorted us off the plane. I guess miracles do happen. I'd managed to escape death – again. Getting my luggage, however, turned out to be another challenge. Together with the other passengers, I hovered by the conveyer belt for fifteen minutes but nothing moved. Great, that was all I needed to end the day in style.

I had decided to sit down and wait when the guy from the plane reappeared out of nowhere. He kept his gaze level with mine as he took a seat opposite me. My heart started to race.

Now he was closer, I could see the colour of his eyes. They were blue. But not just any ordinary blue. The irises shimmered like clear waters in sunlight. I felt drawn to them, as if he was hypnotising me. I lowered my eyes and looked at the floor, embarrassed.

I was certain I had never seen him before. So why did he seem so familiar? And why did he make me feel so self-conscious? I'd never been impressed by good looks, but this guy had grabbed my full attention. He was still staring at me. I could feel his penetrating gaze even as I looked down, avoiding its full force. His mobile started ringing in his pocket. He answered, finally shifting his attention away from me. I couldn't make out what he was saying, but his voice sounded husky and incredibly sexy.

He looked about my age, maybe a bit older. After a minute, he stood up and walked towards a corner of the room where I couldn't see him anymore. I took a deep breath and tried to relax. It felt as if my lungs couldn't pump air fast enough. I found myself looking around for him.

Get a grip, for crying out loud! What was up with me?

My attention was caught by a girl with dark hair standing in the opposite corner, biting her nails nervously. She lifted her head and looked over at me, and for a second I could have sworn her eyes were scarlet. I blinked a few times, and when I looked again, she was gone.

After twenty more minutes, the luggage started to come through at last. Thank goodness: Nana had pre-booked a taxi for me and it was still waiting outside.

As I closed the cab door, I glanced out the window. He was standing at the side of the road, staring at me intensely. It seemed as if his eyes were sparkling in the dark. Although I hated how he made me feel, I couldn't deny how mysteriously attractive he was. There was something spellbinding about the way he looked at me. His presence lingered as we drove off.

I felt a surge of relief when I saw my cottage. During the drama on the flight, I thought I'd never see it again. I tried to be quiet as I pulled my suitcase inside, though I was never the quiet type.

I checked on my Nana; somehow, I'd managed not to wake her up. I gently stroked her silver hair and placed a kiss on her cheek before heading for my bedroom. As usual, it was nearly daylight when, exhausted, I finally drifted off to sleep.

Hissing noise. Darkness swallowed me. Smoke clutched at my lungs. A warm breath brushed against my cheek, sending shivers along my spine. I froze with fear. Scorching flames flickered around me. Whoever that breathing belonged to, it didn't sound human.

2 . STRANGE THINGS

The next morning I dragged myself out of bed and opened the curtains, letting the feeble sunlight filter into the room. Nana was already in the garden, watering her roses. She jumped as I shouted through the window.

"Good morning, Nana."

"Morning, dear. Come down for breakfast."

She was buttering some toast when I walked into the kitchen.

"How is my beautiful grand-daughter this morning?" she said as she caressed my cheek.

"I don't feel beautiful, Nana, but thank you. I'm OK." I poured myself a coffee. "Have you missed me?"

"I certainly did, my darling." She sat next to me. "How is everyone bearing up?" It sounded as if she was afraid to ask.

"Aunt Mary is putting on a brave face, and Mia is trying to be strong for her. They seem to be coping OK," I said, my voice sounding a little flat.

"What about you? How did you find Rome?"

I shrugged and carried on nibbling my toast.

"Your mum and dad loved Rome dearly. It's a shame you don't." There was a hint of sadness in her tone.

I stared at the crumbs on my plate. "It's not that I don't like it, Nana – I hate the place. I know it's where I come from and I should feel a connection, but I don't. I don't belong there. I belong here in Featherstone, with you."

I couldn't help the way I felt. It wasn't my fault if every memory I had of Rome was painful. Rome had stolen everything

I loved the most from me. How could I cherish such a place?

We finished our breakfast in silence. Nana knew me well enough not to push certain buttons too hard. She wisely changed the subject.

"Are you going back to school straightaway?"

"No, Nana, not until tomorrow. You have me for the entire day. We can bake muffins, do some gardening, or go for a walk in the countryside. What do you fancy?"

Nana stood and moved around the kitchen at her usual snail's pace. "Anything you want, my dear, as long as I don't have to walk far."

She'd lost more weight. There was a definite tremor in her hands too. Nana was using the furniture around the room for support, as if her legs were too weak to carry her on their own. Not a good sign.

"Has Jill been taking good care of you?" I asked, trying to sound casual.

Nana looked at me, annoyed. "I've told you before, Arianna, I don't need a carer." She shook her hand in the air, bolshie as always. "I can manage on my own just fine."

"I know, but it makes me feel better knowing that someone is here to look after you while I'm away." I walked over and put my arm around her shoulders. "Please, do it for me?"

She sighed. "OK. I'll put up with her for a bit longer. She's not that bad, I suppose. She makes a good cup of tea at least."

I couldn't help but giggle as I drained my coffee. I placed my cup in the sink and went back up to my bedroom.

The pain in my chest was starting to niggle. I'd forgotten to take my tablets – again. What was the point? I took two with some water anyway, even though I knew it would make no difference. I rummaged through the suitcase. Everything was jumbled, which wasn't surprising. But there were things missing. Where was my camera? My diary? I clearly remembered packing them. I double checked, but they definitely weren't in the case. I massaged my chest nervously, trying to ease the pain. Somehow, I must have left them in Rome. I grabbed the house phone and called Mia. She checked the room and said there was nothing left behind. Deep breaths. Must stay calm.

Trying to put my anxiety aside, I had a quick shower and spent the best part of twenty minutes drying my wild, dark hair. I pulled on a pair of skinny jeans, a white vest top, and zipped up my favourite hoodie, before looking at myself in the mirror. There was no denying I looked tired, but that was nothing new.

When I came down, Nana was waiting for me in the kitchen.

"So, what do you fancy doing today?" I asked.

"I thought we could go to Mass together first. We haven't done that in a while. Then maybe go strawberry picking at Holt Farm, like we did when you were little. We could stop there for a picnic. What do you think?"

She looked so hopeful I could hardly refuse. Though the prospect of spending an hour listening to Father Chris's preaching wasn't appealing in the slightest.

"Great, Nana. Ready when you are." I forced a smile.

The bells were ringing in the square and all the villagers were making their way into the church. I knew everyone in Featherstone. It was a small place, way too small according to most of my friends. One church, one bank, one local store; no cinema, not even a bowling alley; and it was miles away from anywhere lively and exciting. It had a huge library, though, and that suited me just fine.

I walked into the church with Nana's arm tucked under mine, feeling light-headed and shaky. The smell of incense was intense, more powerful than I remembered. I hadn't attended Mass in a while, and the villagers stared, clearly surprised to see me.

As Father Chris reached the altar, I felt a rush of heat, starting in my chest and rising all the way to the top of my head, like a flame. Every sound was amplified in my head. All through the service, I felt fuzzy and disoriented. What was happening to me?

I couldn't wait to get out of that claustrophobic place.

At the end of the service Father Chris stood outside, shaking hands with his parishioners as they left the church.

"Mrs Blight, you look radiant as always." Father Chris shook Nana's trembling hand. "Arianna, how lovely to see you. It's been a long time." He smiled, reaching out his hand to me.

The moment our skin touched, I felt a strong, prickly current run through my arm, sending shivers down my spine. I snatched my hand away. Whoa. What was that?

I wasn't the only one who felt it. Father Chris gawped at me, stunned.

"It was a beautiful service, Father," I managed. I lost hold of Nana's arm as she stopped behind to talk to one of our neighbours.

"Thank you, I'm glad you're pretending you enjoyed it." He knew me far too well. "Are you going back to school right away?"

"Tomorrow." I looked away, embarrassed.

"Arianna, please be careful. Make sure you keep safe, and stay out of trouble, OK?"

"I will. Thank you, Father." I nodded, though I found his words a bit odd.

I tucked Nana's arm under mine again, and we started walking towards Holt Farm. I spent the rest of the morning strawberry picking with the Hamilton family, while Nana sat under a shady tree. The Hamiltons lived a few cottages down the road from ours, and I used to baby-sit for the children. Courtney was a sweet six-year-old, while eight-year-old Cameron was always getting into trouble. Today, his mission was to climb every tree on his path. The kids and I had walked a bit further away from the others.

"Be careful, Cameron," I warned.

He was clambering up the tallest tree. His foot slipped and he almost fell.

"Cameron, I won't tell you again. Come down." I doubled over as I felt a sharp pain in the middle of my chest. When I looked up, Cameron was hanging in the tree, swinging from a branch.

"Cameron!" I shouted as I ran towards him.

He struggled to hold on to the branch, but his fingers slipped, and he plummeted down.

I couldn't explain what happened next. All I knew was that, as I reached up and stretched my arms out to catch him, he began floating in the air like a falling leaf, slowly dropping into my arms. Courtney was running back towards her parents, and Cameron's eyes were shut. No one had seen what happened.

Cameron's mum ran towards us.

"He's OK. I managed to catch him." I was trembling.

What was wrong with me? Why did these things keep happening? I tried to find a rational explanation and came up empty. How on earth did I do that? All I knew was that it wasn't normal. I wasn't normal.

I thought about it all through the picnic, and in the end I decided that the chemical imbalance in my brain was making me hallucinate. Yes, that was it. It couldn't possibly be real. I had never told anyone about the *strange things* – but Nana understood. She knew I was a mental case, and loved me anyway. Each time I caught her eye she nodded and smiled at me; but I felt shaken for the rest of the afternoon.

Back home later, I helped Nana sit down on the couch before closing the curtains and switching on the side lamp.

"Are you all right?" she asked.

"Uh huh." I gave her a quick nod.

"Do you want to talk about it?"

"When have I ever wanted to talk about it?" We both knew what she was referring to.

By the time I brought her tea, she was fast asleep. I'd used the last of the milk, so I decided to cycle to the shop while she was resting. I got there in the nick of time, just before they closed. I was the only customer. I had picked up the milk and was walking towards the till to pay, when I had that weird sense I was being watched again. I looked round. No one was there apart from me and the guy behind the counter. My chest was burning as I walked back to my bike. I looked both ways before pedalling across the road.

It all happened so fast. By the time I saw the car, it was already too late; no time to react. There was a loud screech of brakes. One second I was on my bike, the next I'd hit the pavement hard.

My head was spinning. I tried to get up, but my legs gave way. I closed my eyes tightly and lay back on the pavement. A male voice came from somewhere, but I couldn't make out what he was saying. Each time I tried to open my eyes, waves of nausea overwhelmed me.

"Can you hear me?"

I opened my eyes at last and almost fainted. It was impossible. This had to be a dream. It couldn't be the same guy from the airport. Could it?

"I – I'm OK." I shuddered as he put his arm round my waist to help me sit up.

"Are you sure you're all right?" His piercing eyes were on me. He was so close I was finding it hard to catch my breath. His jaw looked tense, his lips pressed together. I stared, hypnotised.

"What happened?" I blinked fast as my vision blurred.

"I'm so sorry. I didn't see you," he said. "Are you sure you're OK? I can take you to the hospital."

"No, no honestly, I'm all right. I just need some help to get up."

He lifted me off the pavement as if I was as light as a feather. My hands were scratched and my jeans were ripped and dirty. I leaned against the bonnet of his flashy car and watched him pick up my bike and put it in the boot. I couldn't take my eyes off him.

"Honest, I'm fine. I just need to go home." I was still feeling dizzy, but there was no way I was going to get in his car.

"I insist. It's the least I can do. You look like you could faint any minute. I won't take no for an answer. Please?"

He looked genuinely concerned, making it impossible for me to refuse. Somehow, I felt I could trust him, though for all I knew he could have been a total weirdo.

I staggered as he helped me get in the car. The warm touch of his hand on my elbow sent a tremor along my arm. As he sat in the driver's seat, his aftershave filled the air and I felt a wave of heat. I was positive it was the guy from the airport, but he never let on. Surely he must remember me?

"Where do you live?" His voice was husky and low.

"Just past the church on the right." I pointed at the road ahead. My hand was shaking.

He drove very fast, as if he knew where he was going, even though he'd asked. It was scorching in the car. I was drenched in sweat. Yet, as I checked the dashboard, I noticed that the heating wasn't switched on.

As he pulled up outside the cottage, he turned to look at me. "Are you sure you're going to be OK?"

He was even more attractive close up. I couldn't hold his gaze. I needed to get out of the car.

"Positive, thank you. I'll be fine."

I followed him around the car and stared at his toned arms and chest as he lifted the bike out of the boot.

Stop it now, Arianna. You're acting like a silly teenager. How can you be so shallow?

I took the wrecked bike off him and was about to walk away, but I couldn't hold back the question that had been going around my head.

"Have we met before?" I blurted out.

"I don't think so. Maybe in another life?" He flashed me a

charming smile.

Before I could reply, he was back in his car and disappearing fast down the street, leaving a trail of musky aftershave behind.

I was still in shock when I closed the front door behind me. Nana wasn't in the kitchen. Good. I put my hands under the cold water so she wouldn't see the blood. The cuts were stinging, but weren't too bad. I still couldn't believe what had just happened. I was certain it was him, but he'd denied it. Why? And why did he have this weird effect on me? Muscles and big eyes had never impressed me much; yet, when he looked at me, my knees turned to jelly and my palms became sweaty.

I touched the side of my leg and winced. That was going to be a nasty bruise in the morning.

"Everything OK? Where have you been?" Nana's voice made me jump.

"To the shop. Have I got time for a quick shower before dinner?" I folded my arms to hide the blood stains on my shirt.

"Sure, darling." She turned to click the kettle on, so I ran upstairs. Nana didn't seem to have noticed anything wrong.

My head was pounding and every muscle in my body was aching. The shower didn't help. As I looked at my bruises in the mirror, the bathroom light flickered a few times, before going off and staying off. I gasped as I stared at my reflection. A beam of light was shining from behind my shoulders, like a golden ray of sun upon my head. I squeezed my eyes shut, my heart thumping in my chest. Don't freak out, Arianna. Must stay calm. No need to panic.

This wasn't the first time I had seen that freaky glow, but it shook me every time. I took a deep breath and opened my eyes slowly. Oh thank God. The bathroom light was back on and the golden beam had vanished.

When I returned downstairs, Nana was serving dinner. I forced a couple of mouthfuls down, but my head was hurting and I felt queasy.

"You look tired, dear. Maybe you should go to bed." Nana placed her hand against my sore head.

"You're right, Nana. I'm not feeling great. Sorry I couldn't finish it." I grunted in pain as I stood to leave the table.

"Don't worry, darling. Night-night. I'll see you in the morning before you set off. I love you."

"I love you too, Nana."

Once my head lay on the pillow, I started to feel a bit better. But I couldn't get the mysterious guy out of my head. It was him. I was sure of it. Maybe I was mistaken, or perhaps I didn't have the same effect on him that he had on me. I couldn't stop thinking about his intense eyes, the warm touch of his hand, his voice and his perfect body.

Stop it, right now. I shook my head vigorously. This was getting ridiculous.

I spent most of the night tossing and turning, and my head was still pounding when I saw the sunlight peeping through the curtains. When I dragged myself out of bed, I didn't feel any better – worse, in fact.

"Good Morning, Arianna." Nana's voice sounded like a pneumatic drill boring into my head.

"Morning," I murmured as I kissed her cheek and poured myself a cup of coffee.

"All packed and ready to leave?" She placed some toast on my plate.

"Yep. The guys should be here to pick me up shortly." I pushed the plate away. The smell made me feel sick.

I heard Julian's car pull up outside. He honked the horn twice. I waved through the window and Megan and Kayla waved back as they got out of the car.

Leaving Nana was always hard. We stood outside the house and she hugged me yet again.

"I'm going back to school, Nana, not to prison," I said as she cradled me in her arms.

"Call me as soon as you get there."

"Don't worry, Mrs Blight, we'll look after her," Megan said, pushing a red curl away from her face.

"I'll try and keep her out of trouble, Mrs Blight," Kayla added.

"As if that's remotely even possible." Julian's comment cost him a punch from Kayla.

"Just try and keep it under control, OK?" Nana whispered in my ear.

I decided to ignore her last remark. As I placed my last bag in the boot, I felt dizzy and light-headed, and leaned on the side of the car. Kayla and Megan rushed to my side, grabbing me just in time to stop me collapsing on the ground.

"I think I'm going to be sick." I held my hand against my mouth.

"You look as if you've had a bump on the head."

I blinked at Julian as he touched the swelling on my forehead. My vision was becoming blurry. It looked like he was wearing two pair of glasses.

Kayla wrapped her arms around me. "Aw, come here."

I relaxed with my eyes closed, feeling the heat of her body against mine.

"You always make me feel better," I said. And it was true. She did.

"Good, that's exactly what I'm here for." She kissed my head where it hurt, and then let go of me.

In the back seat of the car, I rested my head on Megan's shoulder. Amazing. My headache had gone completely and I wasn't feeling queasy anymore. Even odder, the scratches on my hands had disappeared, and I couldn't feel the pain in my leg.

"Everything all right?" Megan asked.

"I think so." I nodded, feeling confused.

An hour later, Julian parked the black Clio outside St Nicholas' Boarding School. The courtyard was already crowded with students.

The House Master walked over to us. "Welcome back," he said. "I hope you're excited about being a House Tutor this year, Megan."

I couldn't help but giggle at the expression of horror on her face.

"Erm, I think you mentioned something before I left," she mumbled.

"Good, that's settled then. I need you to come with me to greet the First Year students."

"B-but…" Megan protested, but Mr Taylor ignored her and dragged her by the arm towards the main building.

"See you later, Meg." I tried to suppress another chuckle. Her face looked like thunder.

I said goodbye to Kayla and Julian, whose rooms were in different houses. Thistle House was already swamped with loud students running around. You could spot the First Years. They all looked really excited, big grins on their faces. That would soon wear off. On the first floor, I stopped outside my room, turned the key in the door and flung it open. This room had been home for the last seven years. This would be my last one. The bed was made with pristine white sheets, the citrusy fragrance in the air suggested the carpets had been cleaned, and there wasn't one speck of dust on the bare, white furniture. I sat at my desk by the window and looked out into the thick forest, already missing Nana.

By the time my things were delivered, I'd had something to eat with the guys and put my stuff away. It was time for bed. The curfew at St Nick's was seven o'clock sharp – every night. I was wide awake. After reading three chapters of quantum physics, I still wasn't tired. When I eventually drifted off to sleep, it was worse than lying awake.

There was a picture on the wall behind me: a young woman in a red dress, holding a child wrapped in a white blanket. The flames rose high around me and a warm breeze swept across the room. It was hot, so hot it took my breath away. Smoke began to swirl towards me, choking me. Loud footsteps were approaching. Two red sparks moved in the dark, and the hissing noise grew louder. The flames were at my feet, burning my flesh as if it was paper. I was going to be burnt alive. I screamed.

3. STATIC ELECTRICITY

My first day back, and I was already late. I grabbed my bag and ran out of the room without even looking in the mirror. As I raced through campus and across the immaculately-kept lawn, ignoring the reprimands of passing teachers, I could hear the choir practising in the chapel. Damn. Nine o'clock already. Dodging past groups of students, I finally made it to the main building.

"Stop running, Arianna Morelli! At least in your final year," I heard my English teacher shouting from across the corridor as I reached the assembly hall.

I eased the door open, hoping to walk in unnoticed, but all eyes were on me instantly.

"Sorry," I said in a feeble voice.

"Take a seat, please." Joya was my Science teacher and guardian. She always hosted the Welcome Back meeting. She stood by her desk, her arms folded across her chest and her brow furrowed.

The room was full. I spotted a space behind Megan and rushed over to it.

"Now that we're all finally here, shall we start the presentations?" Joya turned her head to the side.

As I followed her eyes, I almost fainted. A dark-haired guy stepped forward. No way. It was him. Here. In my school.

"This is Keaghan Blake, a new student," Joya said. "He moved here from London and will be joining us at St Nicholas for his final year. Welcome, Keaghan."

He looked straight into my eyes as he walked past me to sit in the back row. His tanned skin was glowing under the light, and he was taller than I remembered. He was wearing a casual white T-shirt and jeans and a pair of unlaced Dr Martens; his hair was messy around his face. His gaze sent a shiver through my entire body, making me twitch. I heard a group of girls giggling as they ate him up with their eyes. It occurred to me that I was behaving exactly like them. I was turning into the shallow teenager I detested so much, and I seemed powerless to control it. That was so not like me.

I dragged my attention back to what Joya was saying. "Could the students assigned to me for the quantum physics project stay behind. I need to have a word with you, please." She looked in my direction as people started to get to their feet.

"Why didn't you wake me?" I hissed at Megan.

"I tried. I banged on your door for ages. I must have sent you a million text messages."

Kayla peered at my face. "What's up with you? You look like you've seen a ghost." She picked up her bag from the floor. "Must dash. See you in class, guys," she said as she rushed off with Julian.

I glanced behind me, furtively. The new guy was talking to Clarissa, a pretty blonde girl, who was visibly slobbering.

Megan jabbed me in the ribs and said something. I wasn't listening. I was too busy staring at Keaghan.

"Hello? Earth calling Arianna?" Megan waved her hand in front of my eyes.

My head was all over the place. Who was this guy? Wherever I looked, he was there.

"Sorry. I'm so tired. I'm hardly sleeping these days." I massaged my temples.

We climbed down the steps to go and speak to Joya.

"Hello, girls. How's it going?" She smiled at us.

"Very well, thank you, Mrs Francis," Megan said.

Joya turned to me. "I'm sorry about your loss, Arianna. How are you?"

"I'm OK, thanks."

A waft of aftershave reached my nose, making me dizzy, and a rush of heat spread over my cheeks. The new guy was standing beside me. My legs felt unsteady and my heart was pounding in my chest. For God's sake, get a grip.

"Arianna," Joya said to me, "I hope you don't mind being Keaghan's chaperone while he gets his bearings around campus. He's on the quantum physics project with you." Joya picked up her folder and handbag from her desk. "I'll leave you to get to know each other," she called over her shoulder as she left.

I couldn't avoid looking at him this time. His eyes glinted at me.

"Pleased to meet you, Arianna." His voice was entrancing.

"Erm... I'm... pleased too... I mean, to meet you too." Why was I mumbling this nonsense?

Megan introduced herself. Keaghan greeted her with a friendly nod.

"So, how much more do you need to do with your final piece?" he asked me.

Unable to hold his piercing gaze, I stared at my feet, out of the window, at a corner of the ceiling. Everywhere but at him.

"Arianna won't need any help, she's a genius," Megan said on my behalf.

I winced, embarrassed.

"I hope you're feeling better than the last time I saw you," he said.

Megan stared at me, her eyebrows raised.

"Erm, I'm fine, much better, thank you." I stuttered the words out, sounding pathetic.

"Glad to hear it."

Did he just wink at me?

Megan looked at Keaghan, then back at me, frowning.

Finally she shook her head. "We need to go." She tugged my arm. "We've got a class in five minutes."

"I guess I'll see you later, then?" Keaghan said before I was dragged away.

Megan yanked me out of the room. "And how on earth do you know him already?" she demanded.

"I – well, he kind of... ran me over."

Megan's mouth dropped open in shock. "You what? When?"

"Calm down, I'm fine. He didn't do it on purpose – I hope."

"That explains why you looked so freaked out when you saw him. What happened?"

"Not much, actually. He seemed genuinely worried though." We reached the end of the corridor and headed down the stairs.

"What do you mean? Why wouldn't he be worried? He ran you over, for crying out loud, Arianna."

Kayla and Julian appeared from the side corridor. I ducked inside the classroom to escape Megan's interrogation.

As Mrs Parker droned on about the influence of social networks on today's society, I couldn't stop thinking about Keaghan. His face. His smile. The way he looked at me with those piercing eyes. Combined, they all made me feel as if I was under a spell. I realised I'd been staring at the pen on my desk too long. It was floating in mid-air in front of my eyes. I gasped, and grabbed it quickly. Ever since I'd come back from Rome, the *strange things* were happening more and more. This couldn't be a panic attack, or another hallucination. I saw the pen float, and I grabbed it. Whatever it was, it didn't make any sense. It was crazy. Was I losing it? I didn't want to end up in a mental institution, but it looked like I was heading that way.

It's all in your head. I kept repeating it to myself, silently, over and over.

After lunch I had physics. I was supposed to be chaperoning Keaghan but I hadn't seen him around school since we met first thing. I had to admit I was disappointed.

Nobody had arrived in the lab yet, so I sat at my desk, reading my book on today's topic. I heard steps down the hallway, and froze. My heart started pounding, even though I couldn't see who it was yet.

"You're early this time." Keaghan's voice was becoming more familiar.

"I like to be early for this class." I tried to sound relaxed. It didn't work. His stare made me nervous and self-conscious.

"May I?" He pointed at the desk next to mine.

I gave him a quick nod and he sat down.

"You like physics then?" He looked at the pile of books on my desk.

"I like anything to do with science." I lowered my eyes, trying to focus on the page in front of me.

"Likewise. We're going to get on fine, I can tell."

I could hear the beating of my heart as if it was a ticking bomb in my chest. Thankfully, the other students started rolling in. The spell broke.

"Good afternoon." Joya walked in and sat at her desk. "Is this everyone?"

There were more empty seats than students. Physics wasn't a popular class, which was another reason why it was my favourite.

Three girls walked in, dressed in tight jeans and pink tops, swishing their beach-blonde hair as they walked past Keaghan's desk.

"Sorry we're late, Mrs Francis," one of them said.

Keaghan paid no attention to them and started setting up the electroscope in front of him. They weren't in this class last year, but it wasn't hard to work out the reason for their sudden interest.

"Right. Static electricity. Who can tell me what that is?" Joya said, looking around.

I put my hand up. "It's a phenomenon created when two

surfaces of opposite electrical charge come into contact and separate."

"Correct." Joya smiled at me, nodding. "Static electricity requires a separation of positive and negative charges."

"So it's true, opposites attract?" I heard Clarissa's voice from the back. Giggles spread around the room.

"Definitely. Care to tell the class what a conductor of static electricity is?" Joya stood, waiting for an answer.

Clarissa turned bright red.

Joya glared at her before turning away. "Keaghan?" she said.

He slouched in his seat. "Most conductors are metal. Copper is the most common. But you can create static electricity just by contact." He glanced at me and gave me a sidelong smile. He sounded so confident.

"Correct. I'm glad some of you are in this class for the right reasons."

I was disappointed when the bell rang at the end of the lesson. The hour had gone so fast.

"Hi, Keaghan." Clarissa stopped by his desk, smiling at him in a way I guessed she thought was sensual. "I'm Reese." She fluttered her eyelashes and swished her blonde hair to one side.

"Charmed, I'm sure," he said.

"Brilliant class, eh?" She sounded overly keen, for someone who'd never shown the slightest interest in science before.

I could hardly suppress a smirk, wondering how much of the lesson she had actually understood. I collected my books and made my way to the door.

"Arianna? Can I talk to you for a minute?" Keaghan called over.

I was inches from the door. "Sure." I walked back over to him, trying not to blush under his scrutiny.

Clarissa hesitated, then stormed out the room when she saw Keaghan was focusing his attention on me, not her. It was the first time Reese had been ignored by a guy in school. Ha!

"Great class. You clearly have a talent for physics," he said.

"Thanks." I smiled shyly. Weird. I wasn't the shy type.

"I think you'd like this." He reached in his jeans' back pocket to pull out a small book. "Read it and let me know what you think."

As I stretched my hand to take it, my fingers touched his. A current shot up my arm and across my body like an electric shock. It was so intense that I dropped the book as I snatched back my hand. What the hell was that? It was like being flicked with a big, thick elastic band. Keaghan picked up the book, held it out, and this time I made sure not to make any contact. The cover was worn and the pages yellowed.

"Gravitation?"

"It's one of my favourites," he said. "It's about the force that attracts objects towards each other. I think you'll enjoy it." His smile turned my knees to jelly. "You like Galileo, right?"

"I do." How did he know?

"You could show me around campus, if you've got time?"

"Erm, now?" I didn't see that one coming. "I – I'm a bit busy, actually. Maybe later. Thanks for this." I put the book in my bag and rushed out of the room.

I could still feel the heat in my fingers where I'd touched his hand, as if I'd been burnt. My arm was tingling and I couldn't stop shaking. That was taking static electricity to a whole new level, and I had no idea how it happened. I forced my feet to walk along the corridor.

"Here comes *brainiac*." Megan was waiting for me by the admin office with Kayla and Julian. "Already impressing the new guy, are we?" Megan nudged me with her shoulder, grinning.

"What are you talking about?" I grimaced.

"Clarissa was fuming in the corridor before. You should have seen her face."

"Why? What did she say?" I could feel my cheeks burning.

"Apparently, today's physics class was more like a one-to-one between you and Keaghan Blake." Megan raised her eyebrows.

"I can't help it if we were the only ones who knew the answers."

We walked into the canteen and I picked up a tray.

"You mean you can't help being a nerd?" Julian laughed as he squeezed past me and Megan to grab a tray.

"Ha-ha. You're so funny." I faked a smile.

There was just one table left, on the other side of the room. We had to walk past Clarissa and her friends to get there. They glared at me as if they wanted to scratch my eyes out.

"Ari-Einstein is gracing us with her presence, girls," Clarissa said.

I tried to ignore her, but she pushed her chair out to stop me passing.

"Have you finished sucking up to the new guy?" Her eyes were twinkling with jealousy.

"That's your speciality, Reese," I said, pretending to smile.

"Move out of the way, Barbie." Megan pushed Clarissa's chair back under the table so we could pass.

"Try not to choke on your food," I muttered as I squeezed past.

We sat down and had started eating when I heard coughing coming from Clarissa's table. I looked round to see her friends patting on her back.

"Oh, God. Is she choking?" Megan gasped.

I brought my hands to my mouth, guilt eating at my stomach. What had I done? Oh God, help me, what had I done? "I didn't mean it. I really didn't mean it."

The House Master was rushing over. Clarissa was red in the face.

I squeezed my eyes shut, and prayed for her not to choke, repeating the words in my head, over and over. Clarissa stopped coughing and collapsed on the chair, exhausted. The curious crowd dispersed, and everyone sat back down.

"Are you all right?" Kayla was looking at me from across the table.

I nodded, and stared down at the food on my plate.

"It wasn't your fault, Arianna. It was just a coincidence," Megan said.

Was it? Megan stroked my hand, but it was no good. I had nearly killed someone. I was out of control. I had to be stopped. This was going too far – whatever it was.

I couldn't finish my food, and told the others I was going to bed. I felt sick. As I left the canteen, I saw Keaghan. He was standing by the door, looking at me intensely. I could hardly catch my breath as I ran across the muddy lawn in the pouring rain, desperate to get to Thistle House and hide away in my room.

4. DISASTER

The first couple of weeks of term went incredibly fast. I had three assignments to hand in the following Monday, and I still had tons of work to do. It didn't help that Kayla was nagging me to give her a hand with her project, which was how I found myself sorting through canvases in the store room.

"I told you I'm rubbish at this, that's why I need your help." Kayla pouted at me, looking for sympathy.

I shoved a canvas with my foot, and an enormous spider ran across the floor. We both shrieked. The store room was crammed with all sorts of useless stuff, and the paintings were buried under a thick layer of dust.

"So why did you offer?" I said. The Annual Exhibition Show was due to take place at the end of the week and Kayla was in charge of all the organisation.

"I didn't. Joya said I should take charge this year, remember? You agreed to help me before we broke off for summer. Please?"

"That's so typical of you, Kay. We've been back for weeks and you only remind me about this now?" I ground my teeth in frustration.

"It's not as bad as it looks. We just need to get cracking. Pretty please?" Her begging smile looked more like a demonic grin.

"So what's actually ready?" I gave in, as usual, and looked at the poster she'd handed me earlier.

"The work to exhibit is all in here. We just need to organise it in the Gallery and make it look perfect by Friday."

She made it sound easy, but Friday was only four days away.

"Help is on the way!" I heard Julian's voice in the corridor. Megan was right behind him.

"Thank God." Kayla kissed him on the lips with such force that she almost knocked the glasses off his nose.

"What do you need me to do?" Megan rubbed her hands in anticipation.

"A miracle." I couldn't help resorting to sarcasm.

"Well, we're the right people then." Julian and Kayla both smiled.

I decided to take charge. "Right, I'm going to check the room to see what needs doing before we move all the paintings in. Can you start sorting through this mess?" I pointed at the boxes covered in cobwebs.

When I arrived outside Milton's Hall, there was bad news from the caretaker.

"There was a leak in the night," he told me, leaning on his mop. "We've had to close it to the public. It's a hazard. Health and Safety first, I'm afraid." He pointed at the green patches spreading over the walls. The stained curtains didn't look good either; the room was certainly unusable.

"What's happened?" Kayla arrived just in time to see part of the ceiling crumble down.

"Disaster, that's what's happened," I replied. "You can't use this place for the Exhibition. You need to find somewhere else, and quick. Otherwise you'll have to call it off."

Kayla's eyes widened with panic. "First of all, it's *we* need to find another venue; and second, we *can't* call it off. This goes towards my final grade. I can't cancel it."

Julian crowded in behind her, looking round in horror. "She's right. It's our most important project this year."

Megan raised an eyebrow. "So important you decided to leave it to the last minute?"

She had a point. I wanted to help but didn't know how.

I sighed. "I suppose we can try and talk to the Admin Department, see if they can find us another room?"

Kayla shrugged. "It's worth a try."

The assistant was no help whatsoever. After we'd spent ten minutes begging, she still gave us the same answer.

"I'm sorry, guys. I really want to help you, but I've nothing available for this weekend. Every student has a project on. The rooms are all booked."

"But it's not our fault the Gallery has been closed. What are we supposed to do now?" I said. I was losing patience with this helpless blonde bimbo.

"You'll just have to postpone the event." She looked at her nails, sounding like she couldn't care less.

"Oh, no, that's a disaster," Kayla moaned.

"What's a disaster?" Keaghan's voice came from behind me.

I turned to look at him. "Where do I start?"

I told him what had happened as he leaned against the door. I tried to keep an even tone but I felt as if everyone in the room could hear my heart thumping in my chest.

"Maybe I can help," he said, arching his brow. He looked so handsome.

He walked towards the desk, flashing a charming smile at the assistant. "Hi," he said.

"H-hi. Can I help you?" She looked at him, her eyes soft with fascination.

"I truly hope so." Was he flirting with her?

"I'll try my best. What can I do for you?" She was definitely flirting with him.

"My name is Keaghan." His smile was disarming. "I'm a new student here and I really want to make a good impression on the House Master."

The girl carried on drooling over him.

"We need to find a new venue for the Exhibition this weekend. Do you think you can help us?" He pinned her with his intense, blue eyes.

"Erm, let me have a look." She tapped at her keyboard and then bit her lip. "It's not looking good, I'm afraid."

"Please, try again." His voice was low and sensual.

She gazed up at him as if she was in a trance. "OK, Keaghan." She blushed and stared at the screen, shaking her head. "I'm afraid I don't have any free rooms big enough to host the Show. It's a very busy weekend. I'm so sorry. I've tried."

"It's Wendy, right?" He had obviously read her name on the badge, but it felt personal. "Wendy, I'm sure you can try a bit harder for me. It's really important." Oh my goodness. Could he have sounded or looked any sexier?

"Of course, Keaghan. Let me try one more time." She made puppy eyes at him.

Glancing over my shoulder, I saw Kayla and Julian rolling their eyes. Megan pretended to throw up.

"Thank you, Wendy. I really appreciate what you're doing. Don't we, guys?" He finally acknowledged our presence.

We nodded, faking smiles.

"I'm not really supposed to, but the Theatre isn't being used. It's waiting to be refurbished. Maybe I can see if you could use that." She looked at him with adoring eyes.

"You're a star, Wendy. Can we go take a look now?"

"Sure – and I can take you if you like. You won't be familiar with the grounds yet."

Pass me a bucket, please. She sounded desperate.

"That's fantastic. Thank you so much, Wendy. Can you make sure it's all sorted with the Headmaster?" He was oozing sensuality.

"I shouldn't really but... I'll break the rules this once." Yuck. She was pathetic.

"After all, what are rules for, if not to be broken, right?" He winked at her and she giggled. He had her wrapped around his little finger. Their flirting was almost obscene.

"Arianna, shall we go?" I jumped as I realised Keaghan was talking to me.

"Erm, sure," I replied with a sarcastic smile.

The rest of us trailed behind them. Their bodies were nearly touching as they walked along together. I glared as she laughed at his jokes, gazing at him with adoring eyes. Why was I so bothered? I was the pathetic one.

"God, it makes you want to puke," Megan whispered in my ear. At least I wasn't the only one who thought so.

The Theatre looked OK. It wasn't an art gallery, but with a little project management on my part and Kayla's designing talent, it could possibly work.

"It's sorted then." Wendy batted her fake eyelashes at Keaghan. "I just need you to complete some forms for admin purposes."

"I'll make it worth your while, I promise."

The way he looked at her triggered a surge of jealousy in my gut. They turned to leave the Theatre together. As he walked past, I caught a wink from the corner of his eye.

"Looks like the new guy has the power to make people do exactly what he wants." Kayla shook her head in amazement.

"Apparently so." I tried not to look bothered. "What do you think then?"

"Looks all right to me," Julian said.

I took a look around. "We need to set it up to look like a gallery, clean up the place, move the seats out of the way and use that space for the dance floor. I suppose we can make it work."

I knew I didn't sound overly enthusiastic. My thoughts were elsewhere.

***

Later that day, I walked to my next class, arriving early – which didn't happen very often. Keaghan was sat at his desk. A small smile spread across his lips when he saw me.

"Hi," he said.

I sat down, keeping some distance between us. "Hi."

As I pulled my things out of my bag, I could sense his eyes on me. The students started rolling in. The room was full, no empty seats. The female attendance rate for physics had considerably gone up. I didn't have to ask myself why.

When the bell rang at the end of the class, I waited for everyone to leave before I turned to look at Keaghan.

"I meant to return this last week." I placed the physics book on his desk.

"Did you enjoy it?" He smiled at me and I felt the familiar knee-wobble.

"I did." I wished he would stop staring at me.

"What's your favourite part?" he asked.

I had to think for a moment. "I guess Galileo's law of free fall always fascinates me. Although the story of his dropping cannonballs from the Leaning Tower of Pisa is questionable."

"Wow. You're questioning Galileo's theories? You're brave." He grinned.

He gathered his books and we walked to the door together. "I hope the Theatre is OK for your exhibition?"

"It is. Thanks for helping." I glanced at him, feeling more relaxed.

"I'm glad I could help."

Students were crowding the corridor, swapping classes. Keaghan and I were squashed against each other as people swarmed past. The spicy scent of his aftershave overwhelmed me. A sudden weakness in my knees made me stumble. I would have fallen if he hadn't caught me. He grabbed my arm and pulled me towards him. I landed with my face on his chest.

"Wow, is that a new dance move?"

I recognised Megan's sarcastic tone, and pushed myself away, my cheeks on fire. Keaghan was still holding my arm. The warmth of his touch penetrated my clothes.

"Are you OK?" He finally let me go, leaving numbness along my arm.

"Yeah," I mumbled. I excused myself and followed Megan into the classroom.

"You two looked cosy just then." She sat next to me, looking curious.

"Don't be silly, Meg. Keaghan is definitely not my type." If only I could make my racing heart believe that too.

"Oh, definitely not," she whispered, her eyebrows lifted, just as Mrs Parker started her class.

"Quiet at the back, please." I was glad someone had shut Meg up at last.

5. TAKEN BY SURPRISE

Once again, the following morning I didn't hear the alarm and was late, thanks to another horrible night. I felt exhausted. I gulped down my anxiety tablets in the hope they would stop my chest pain, even though I knew they wouldn't. I pulled on my clothes, and as I looked outside the window, I wished I hadn't. Rain was pouring down and it looked bitterly cold.

As I ran across the lawn, I heard the caretaker shouting, "Off the grass!" I ignored him and ran into the building, drenched from head to toe.

"You're making a habit of being late, Arianna," Joya said, looking annoyed as I sidled into the room.

Keaghan was already in the seat next to mine.

"I'm sorry, Mrs Francis." I hurried to my desk and slid into my seat.

"I've just told your fellow students I want you to complete a test." Joya walked to my desk and handed me a paper. I caught Keaghan gazing at me out of the corner of my eye. I dried the rain from my face with my sleeve in an attempt to hide my red cheeks.

"Arianna, as I already know you'll be first to finish, do you want to go and dry off? We don't want you going down with pneumonia."

Joya was right. I did finish first, even after spending fifteen minutes in the toilets with my head under the drier. The test was easy – a selection of twenty multiple choice questions about atomic structure, electric fields, kinetic theories and gas laws.

A walk in the park, basically. Keaghan's eyes followed me as I walked over to Joya's desk, handed her the paper and left the room. When I heard footsteps behind me, I guessed he'd come a close second. Halfway down the corridor, I turned and was glad to see we were going opposite ways. Why was I running away from him? I wished I could stop acting so edgy around him all the time.

I texted Kayla as I headed towards the Theatre.

On my way x

When I got there, Julian was up a ladder with a painting in his hand. Megan was cleaning the stands, and Kayla was arranging the canvases into piles.

"Grab a painting. There's another ladder over there," Kayla instructed.

"Looks like you've almost finished," I said as I started climbing the steps to hang up a painting on the stand.

"Almost." Megan sneezed as she blew the dust away.

As I came down the ladder, I caught my hand on a nail that was sticking out of the wood.

Kayla pulled my hand towards her. "Let me have a look."

I felt queasy. The sight of blood didn't normally bother me, but it was dripping from my finger.

"It looks deep. We should put it under cold water."

Kayla dragged me through the back and pushed my hand under the tap. The blood splashed onto the ceramic tiles and my stomach churned.

"Look at me, not the blood," Megan said.

I felt a sudden heat over my hand and the pain disappeared.

"There you go, all done," Kayla said.

I tried to look at my bleeding finger but Kayla had already placed a blue plaster over it. It didn't hurt at all.

After we'd gathered all the empty boxes, we pushed the

trolleys to the store room on the other side of campus. The rain had stopped, at least. Just as we got to the building, I noticed a guy with a goatee beard lurking outside the school gate. He was wearing a leather jacket and smoking a cigarette. When he noticed that I'd spotted him, he walked away, disappearing down the path leading to the forest. I swallowed hard, the familiar pain stabbing in my chest. A rush of heat rose over my head like a fever. It took my breath away for a moment. Deep breaths. Calm down. No need to panic.

The store-room door was wide open. I pushed the trolley inside, and as I turned to shut the door, it moved before I even touched it. Huh? How odd. I couldn't feel a draught. I was distracted by Kayla's voice shouting my name from the other room. We put away the boxes and headed back to the main building.

Keaghan was standing in the middle of the Theatre when we got back. It was odd the way he seemed to appear out of nowhere, like a ghost. Wherever I looked, he was there.

"Looks good," he said, his eyes darting around the room.

"Thanks." I turned to the others. "Guys, you remember Keaghan, right?" They gave him a quick nod. "You don't think it's too over-the-top?" I gestured at the room and realised how much I wanted his approval.

We had separated the paintings into two categories, portraits on one side and landscapes on the other. The decorations consisted of flowers and papier-mâché sculptures. They worked perfectly with the subtle light of the crystal chandeliers, and there was plenty of space in the middle of the room for the students to dance after the exhibition was over. It did look good, considering the tight deadline.

"You've done an amazing job." He sounded sincere.

"We couldn't have done it without you. I can't thank you enough." I realised I was holding his gaze for once, without having to look away embarrassed.

Megan broke the hypnotic spell. "Right, we should go for lunch, Arianna."

"Yeah, you should." Kayla darted a frosty look at Keaghan. Keaghan left the room without saying a word, as if she'd spoken to him not me. I had a feeling my friends didn't like him much.

After lunch, I didn't see the girls or Julian for the rest of the afternoon. They weren't replying to my text messages, and they didn't join me for dinner either – which was unusual. After sending one last text, I decided to spend a few hours in the library working on my assignment.

The time sped past until I looked up to see the librarian standing next to me. She was wearing her coat and holding her bag, ready to leave.

"Oh no," I said, "is it curfew time already? I still have a good hour on this. Can I lock up? I promise I'll be as quiet as a mouse," I begged.

The librarian sighed. "All right, but this can't happen all the time, Arianna. We'll both be in trouble if we get caught. Lock yourself in once I've gone." She handed me the keys and turned all the lights off, leaving only a small lamp on for me.

I closed the door behind her and turned the key in the lock. After a while, I lifted my head and checked the time. Only a few more pages before I finished. A dull thud came from the other side of the library and I jumped. I peered across the dark but couldn't see anything. I lifted up the lamp and used it like a torch to scan the room. Nothing. I carried on typing faster, desperate to finish and get back to my room.

"What on earth are you doing here at this time?"

I let out a loud squeal. Keaghan stood opposite me, with his arms folded.

"You scared the hell out of me!" I held my chest, my heart pounding.

"Sorry, I didn't mean to make you jump. Are you OK?" He

sat on the chair next to me, his eyes glowing in the dim light. I gawped at him, stunned.

"How did you get in? The door was locked."

"It was open, I can assure you. Maybe you forgot to lock it."

"No, no. I clearly remember locking it," I insisted. I was sure of it.

"Anyway, do you know how dangerous it is to be around campus alone at this time? Not to mention the detention if the House Master finds out," he said.

"You won't say anything, will you? I was working on my assignment. Please, don't tell Mr Taylor, I'm already on my last warning," I begged.

He pursed his lips. "Mmm, I don't know. You're breaking the rules by being here at this time without authorisation." Was he being serious or sarcastic?

"Isn't that what rules are for, to be broken?" I quoted back at him, and he laughed.

"Touché. We better go before we both get caught."

I closed down the laptop, put the books away and switched off the lamp. Keaghan followed me outside and waited while I locked the library.

"What are you two doing here after curfew?"

Mr Taylor's voice made us both jump. Keaghan and I slowly turned to face him.

"Erm... I..." I looked at him, my eyes wide open, speechless. Speak. Say something, fast.

"It was my fault, Mr Taylor." Keaghan stepped forward. "I got lost, and if Arianna hadn't found me, I would still be locked in the library."

"Right." The Master looked at us, his brow raised in suspicion. "You better get going. As you're new here, I'll let it go this time."

"Thank you, Mr Taylor. It won't happen again." Keaghan tugged my arm, pushing me down the corridor.

"Phew, that was close," he said relieved as we stepped outside.

"Thank you for covering for me. I'd have been in deep trouble if he'd caught me again."

"Don't mention it," he said with a grin. "Let's say you owe me a beer and we can call it quits."

He walked with me through the grounds and over the forbidden grass. A chilly breeze swept through the air, but I wasn't cold. There was a cloud of heat around me, keeping me warm.

As we arrived outside Thistle House, my phone started to ring in my bag. I stared at the flashing name on the screen before I answered, turning away from Keaghan.

"Hello, gorgeous. I hope it's not too late. Am I disturbing you?" Marcus's voice was unchanged, even though I hadn't heard it for ages.

"Is everything OK? Where are you?" My voice trembled.

"I'm coming back to England. I wanted you to hear it from me."

I swallowed hard. "When?"

"I'm flying out on Monday." He sounded nervous.

"I have to go, Marc. Curfew's at seven. Bye." I hung up, not knowing what else to say. The call had taken me by surprise.

"Sorry about that." I looked at Keaghan. He was standing against the wall with his hands in his pockets, staring at me.

"Are you all right?" he asked.

"Yes. Thank you for walking me back."

I felt tears filling my eyes, but I managed not to cry until I walked inside and closed the door behind me.

Hearing Marcus's voice had brought back all those feelings I thought I had buried deep down in the remote corners of my heart. Clearly I hadn't buried them deep enough.

6. DUTY

It was already Thursday – the day before the Annual Exhibition Show – and we still had heaps of things to sort out. I also had a Maths test today. I couldn't have picked a worse day to be late.

I was trying to put my hair in a ponytail, but my hands were shaking as I hurried. Megan was shouting and banging on my door.

"Sorry, Meg." I opened the door to let her in. "I don't feel so good. I need to catch up on some sleep. I'm starting to hallucinate." I took two tablets and swallowed them with some water.

"Are you still taking them?"

"Yeah. I don't see the point, though. They don't work. Maybe I should go and see a shrink again." I slammed the door shut behind us.

We arrived late for class. We could have been a bit quicker but Megan refused to walk across the lawn and we had to go all the way round the building. English was my least favourite subject, and I fell asleep twice. I caught Keaghan's eyes from across the room. He was chuckling at me, clearly amused.

Kayla and Julian were already tucking into their food when Megan and I joined them for lunch.

"Have you heard the latest?" Julian said. "Guess who's back in town soon."

I bit into my burger, trying to act casual.

"Who?" Megan asked.

"Marcus," Kayla replied, her grin giving away her excitement.

"No way. When?" Megan dropped her sandwich on the plate.

"Monday," I said, acting disinterested and carrying on eating.

"You know? Why didn't you say anything?" Megan looked at me, stunned.

"I was going to. I forgot." I shrugged. "He rang me last night to tell me."

"Oh, did he? And are you OK with that?" Kayla said.

"Yes, it's great news. I'm over him, OK? We're better just as friends." I could tell I sounded defensive. Damn.

"Sure, as long as you're all right." Kayla didn't look convinced.

"Yes, I'm perfectly fine about it," I lied. Why couldn't she just drop it?

"Busy day tomorrow. What time are we opening the doors?" Julian was smart enough to change the subject.

After lunch, we all got up to leave the table when I felt lightheaded and the room started to spin. I lost my balance and fell back on the chair.

"Whoa, are you OK?" Megan grabbed my arm. "I'm starting to get really worried about you."

"You seem worse lately," Kayla said, looking at me with concern.

"I'm just tired, I think," I said, standing up again. "I'll go and see the nurse tomorrow. Maybe she can give me something to help me sleep." I rubbed my eyes, swaying with exhaustion.

"Shall I walk you to your room? A lie-down might do you good," Megan said.

"No, I'll be fine. I have a maths test this afternoon. I don't want to miss it." I picked up my bag.

"You truly are a geek. There's no hope, no hope at all." Julian messed up my hair playfully.

As I walked down the corridor, the dizziness hit me again. Something weird was happening to me; my head felt as if it was on fire. This couldn't just be tiredness. Everything started to look blurry. A sting in my chest doubled me over and I felt a rush of blood to my head. I forced myself to walk in the classroom, and as I caught Keaghan's eyes, I felt my breath drawn out of me. My legs folded under me, and I fell to the floor.

"Welcome back."

Keaghan's eyes were the first thing I saw when I opened my own. Had I fainted?

"You gave us a big scare. How are you feeling?" His face was inches from mine.

I was lying on a single bed. There was a drip in my arm, and I recognised the Infirmary by the pungent smell of disinfectant.

"What happened?" My voice was just a whisper.

"You walked into the classroom and fainted. You're making a habit of passing out every time I'm around, Ms Morelli." He stood up from the edge of the bed as the Nurse walked in.

"How's our patient? Any nausea, headache, stomach pain?"

"No." I cleared my croaky voice. "Not anymore."

"Good. I've given you something to help you sleep. The drip is a solution of vitamins and minerals to get your strength up. What you need is a good night's rest." She turned to look at Keaghan. "You should get going, young man."

"I'll stay a bit longer, if that's all right," Keaghan said. "Mrs Francis asked me to make sure she's OK. You can check, if you like."

The Nurse narrowed her eyes, but agreed to let him stay, and left the room.

"I feel fine, now." I struggled to sit up.

"Don't you even think about it," Keaghan ordered.

He gently pushed me down, pulling the covers up to my chin. I shuddered as I felt his warm breath on my cheek.

"Where are Kayla and Megan? Do they know I'm here?"

"They were here for about an hour while you were still unconscious. It's past curfew now. They said they'll come and see you tomorrow."

"But tomorrow is the Exhibition! I need to help them set up." I looked at him, aghast at the thought of letting my friends down.

"Calm down. You will, after you have a good rest and a long sleep." He sounded genuinely concerned. "You heard the nurse. You're exhausted. You need to take it easy."

"What about you? You'll get into trouble for being here after curfew."

"Nah, I can pretty much get away with anything." I could believe that. "Now try and get some sleep."

He relaxed in his chair.

"Easier said than done. I'm wide awake now." I stared at the ceiling.

"Shall I read to you?"

I couldn't help but laugh. "What am I, six?" I turned serious. "You don't have to stay, you know."

"I know. I want to. Why? Do you want me to leave?" He sat forward, ready to stand up.

"No, no!" I cursed. My voice sounded pathetic. "I mean – it's up to you."

"I can talk to you about quantum physics or the theory of relativity if you want?" He stretched his legs out, placing his feet on the edge of my bed. He ran his fingers through his raven hair and smiled in his casual way. He looked so sexy. Stop staring at him!

"That's not what sends me to sleep."

"I can quote you Shakespeare, Wordsworth, Blake?"

"God, no. That would send me suicidal," I said. He chuckled.

My eyelids were suddenly heavy, and to my surprise I felt like I was about to drift off. I blinked a few times, but couldn't keep my eyes open.

"Just close your eyes and go to sleep, Arianna." His voice was feeble and distant – then nothing.

It was pitch black in the room when I woke up. The drip was still in my arm and I was desperate to pee. I had no choice but to pull the needle out. My stomach churned. To my relief, hardly any blood spilled. I carefully climbed out of bed and used the toilet. When I walked back in the room, I saw two red sparks in the dark and screamed.

"Shush, it's me, Keaghan."

He turned the light on, and I realised the dots must have come from the phone he was holding in his hand.

"You've got to stop scaring me like this." I couldn't catch my breath. "What are you doing still here?"

I felt self-conscious in my hospital gown and climbed into bed, pulling the covers up to my chin. He sat on the chair.

"Have you been here all night?" I asked, feeling uncomfortable about the thought of him being so close while I was asleep.

"Yep." He didn't look tired. "Do you want some water?"

He poured me a glass before I could answer. I gulped it down. The room was so hot. I hadn't realised how thirsty I was, and asked for another glass.

"Do you have any chocolate?" I couldn't believe I'd just asked him that.

"No, but I can go and get you some," he said with a grin.

"Nah, it's all right."

I was amazed at how caring he was being towards me. Although we'd only met a few weeks ago – and he'd made my knees wobble with just one look – I was starting to feel more comfortable around him.

"How are you feeling?" His voice was less croaky.

"I'm OK." I bit my lip. "You don't have to stay, you know. You must be sleepy." I looked at the clock on the wall. "It's four in the morning."

"I'm nocturnal. I don't sleep much." We had that in common.

"What are you, a vampire?"

"Much worse." He laughed, his eyes glued on me.

"I'm going to be a famous physicist one day." I changed subject in an attempt to hide my embarrassment.

"Sounds like hard work to me. Why do you like science so much?" He looked at me with genuine interest.

"Because it's real, it's tangible, you can't make it up. There's no mystery about science, just facts, proof. And for every question there's a plausible answer," I said with conviction. "Like maths: two and two is four, it can never be five."

He looked intrigued by my response. "I get that. But even the most tangible of sciences hides a mystery, don't you think?" He leaned forward.

"No, I don't think so. Fire is made by the combustion of fuel, oxygen and heat. There's no mystery about that."

"That's not entirely true." He stared at me, pensive. "Did you know that there's a river in Thailand that spits fireballs from its waters?"

"That's clearly just a legend," I said.

"It isn't. No one has been able to scientifically explain it."

I shook my head. "Nah. People like to believe in mystical things so they have something to blame their misfortunes on. I don't buy it."

"I see. You're truly rational, Arianna." He nodded, looking smug. "I like it."

There was a brief silence while we stared at each other.

"Right, I'm going to leave you to rest. I'm keeping you awake and you need to sleep."

As he stood up, I realised I didn't want him to go. "Thank you for the company." I smiled.

"It's my duty." He walked over to the door, but then he stopped and turned to look at me one last time. "Sleep tight."

He kept his eyes on me a little longer, before switching the light off and closing the door behind him. The heat in the room left with him.

7. LIKE A PRINCESS

First thing in the morning, Kayla and Megan came to visit. They looked worried, and Kayla wouldn't stop fussing around me, propping up my pillows and asking me over and over if I was OK. Megan seemed to think it was her fault, and kept apologising profusely for no reason. I was annoyed that I would be missing the morning Exhibition, but Kayla reassured me, telling me I could still help at the party tonight.

"Well, we're off to class. Not everyone gets to have a day off." Megan stood up. "By the way, I picked up a dress for you to wear tonight."

My eyes snapped open. "Please tell me it's not pink."

They both laughed. As they left the room, Keaghan walked in. Kayla's face turned cold when she saw him.

"How's Little Miss Faint this morning?" His smile was captivating and utterly gorgeous. For God's sake, I must stop staring at him.

"I feel great, thanks," I said.

He sat on the same chair he'd spent most of last night on. "Has the nurse said when you can leave?"

"I should be all right to go by lunchtime. I can't wait. I'm so bored." I shook my feet under the cover.

"I thought you might be. That's why I brought you this." He handed me a book.

I read the title out loud. *"Thirteen Things That Don't Make Sense: The Most Intriguing Scientific Mysteries of Our Time."* I drew my brows together. "Not funny."

He laughed. "It was either that, or *Twilight*. Tough choice. Anyway, I'd better get to class. I must say, it'll be boring without you." His smile sent my pulse into a frenzy.

As he left, the room grew cold again.

* * *

A few hours later, I was standing in Megan's room, holding the dress she expected me to wear for the party.

"I'm not wearing that, not in a million years."

The baby-pink chiffon dress was still wrapped in its cover. The fitted corset was covered in sequins, and the silky, puffed skirt reached down to the floor, like a pink cloud.

But that was nowhere near as frightening as the shoes I was supposed to wear. They were the highest platforms I had ever seen. How would I walk in them?

"Don't be so miserable, Arianna. It'll make a change from leggings and sweatshirt for once." Megan held out a pearl necklace and matching earrings. "Come on, in that bathroom, *now*." She bustled me in there, ignoring my protests.

As I stepped into the dress, I heard Kayla's voice as she walked in the room.

"Is she wearing it?" She sounded surprised.

"Yes, if I have to force her. I curled her hair as well, and she's wearing make-up." They both giggled.

"I can hear you both, you know," I shouted through the bathroom door.

Megan gasped as I walked back into the room. "Aw, you look stunning."

"You look like a princess," Kayla added. She picked up one of my curls between her fingers and smiled.

I groaned. "I'll never be able to walk in these." I wriggled my feet into the shoes.

Megan was wearing a beautiful black dress, which brought

out the natural red of her hair. Kayla's long dress was a soft blue, with silver ruffles round the shoulders; her blonde hair was pinned up in a sophisticated bun.

"OK, can I get changed now?" I wasn't kidding.

"No way. You look amazing," Megan said, sniffing.

"You're not crying, are you?" I looked at her, shaking my head in disbelief.

"Oh, give over, of course not." I definitely saw a tear.

I had to hold on to Megan the whole way there, tottering on the platforms. Kayla looked nervous as we stepped onto the red carpet outside the Theatre.

"We did a fine job, girls." I nodded in approval as I looked around the room. The place was packed with students and guests admiring the exhibits.

"Wow, Arianna, is that you?" Julian walked over, pretending to look stunned. "You actually look like a girl."

"Julian!" Kayla jabbed him in the ribs.

"Thanks. You actually look like a penguin." I grinned, pulling his dicky-bow tie.

Someone dragged Kayla and Julian away, saying that the Headmaster was really impressed and wanted to talk to them.

"If they don't get an A for this, I'll be surprised." I smiled at Megan, looking round at the paintings.

I caught a few boys from my year gazing at me with stunned eyes. I ignored them.

I was still talking to Megan when Keaghan made his entrance. He looked gorgeous and all the girls turned to stare at him. A shiver ran down my spine as my eyes met his.

"Oh my God, who's the sexy minx hanging off Keaghan's arm?" Megan whispered.

I hadn't noticed the girl standing next to him until now. She was nearly as tall as him, with long bright-red hair. Her gorgeous figure was squeezed into a long black dress, very low cut on the back. She looked like a *Victoria's Secret* model.

"Wow, that's what I call an entrance," Megan hissed in my ear.

I felt a sharp, irritating sensation in my chest. Not the pain I usually had. Jealousy. My emotions were out of my control. I had never behaved like this before, but I wanted to scratch her eyes out as I watched her sensually walk alongside Keaghan.

Get a grip, Arianna. You're sinking to a whole new level of pathetic.

Julian and Kayla reappeared from somewhere. "Megan, we need to talk to you for one minute," Julian said.

I tore my eyes away from Keaghan and noticed that Julian and Kayla both looked really worried.

"What is it, guys?" I asked.

"Oh, nothing, just a minor hiccup." Kayla's smile looked unnatural.

They left the Theatre. I tried to grab a glass of champagne from a waiter walking past with a tray.

"Sorry, students are not allowed alcohol. Adult guests only."

I grimaced in frustration. My mobile beeped in my handbag, and just as I was about to pick it up, I heard Keaghan's voice behind me.

"Hello, Arianna."

I froze. I took a deep breath and turned round slowly, trying not to stumble in my ridiculous shoes. He was looking at me with his usual breathtaking gaze. His lady-friend wasn't with him.

"You look incredibly beautiful, may I say?" he whispered, his voice husky. His eyes were level with mine.

"Thank you." I knew I must be bright red: my cheeks were on fire.

"How are you feeling?" He was wearing a black suit and shirt but no tie, his hair gelled back. Smart yet sexy.

I stared at him, hypnotised. "Much better, thank you. Isn't this great?" I tried to make conversation, wishing I didn't feel so nervous.

"Everything looks absolutely stunning."

He looked me up and down before his eyes came back to mine. Was he staring at me, or was it the other way around? I wasn't sure. I could hardly breathe. The foxy redhead girl walked over to us, and I sensed Keaghan tense up. She smiled at me. I had never seen so many teeth in a mouth.

"Baby, aren't you going to introduce us?" She spoke with an American accent. That explained the teeth.

"Donna, this is Arianna. Arianna, Donna."

We nodded politely at each other.

"Would you excuse us, please?" Keaghan took her by the arm and they walked towards a corner of the room.

Damn. I tried to see where he'd gone, but I was distracted by Mr Taylor, who started talking to me about Caravaggio and Michelangelo's influence on British artists. If only I could tell him to shut up. I knew everything about the subject, and it didn't interest me in the slightest. My focus was elsewhere.

While he was chatting, I sensed Keaghan's intense look upon me, and caught his eyes from across the room. I had to look away, feeling flustered, but a force out of my control made me look over again. As Mr Taylor walked off, I felt a huge thud in my chest, which nearly threw me off my feet.

"Arianna?" Kayla and Megan walked over to me. "You look really pale," Megan said.

"It's the dress. So bloody tight." I took a deep breath. "How's the night going?" I asked, trying not to think about the chest pain.

"A total success. Julian is about to start the real party." Kayla pointed across the room to where Julian was announcing the DJ. The music blasted out and people started to dance.

"I'm going to have to leave you, I'm afraid." Keaghan appeared from behind.

"Already?" I hated the sound of my pathetic voice.

"I'm afraid so."

His foxy friend was waiting for him by the door.

"Thank you for helping us," I said. "We couldn't have done it without your help, could we, Kay?" I nudged her.

"Right, sure." She shrugged, and forced a smile.

Keaghan directed his smile at me. "I didn't do anything, it was all you. You've put together a great event."

He turned to look at Kayla, the smile disappearing from his face. "Are you all OK to get to your houses safely?" he asked.

"Of course. Arianna will go with Megan. We're all sorted."

Kayla sounded cold. It was clear she didn't like him at all. She moved away to join Julian on the dance floor.

"I'm sorry. That was so rude. I don't know what's up with her," I said.

"It's OK. Make sure you get back to your room safely, Arianna." He extended his hand to grasp mine, bringing it towards him for a kiss.

The moment was brief, but so intense I felt a rush of heat across my body as his lips touched my skin. At the door, he turned to look at me one more time before walking out the room with the sleek, flame-haired girl hanging off his arm.

The rest of the evening passed without incident, and, with Keaghan gone, I lost interest in the party. I was pleased when it finally came to an end.

Megan and I were the last to leave. We began walking towards our houses, the chill of the night biting at my bare shoulders. If only I could make a jacket magically appear out of my handbag. My handbag!

"Damn. I forgot my bag inside," I cursed.

"I'll come back with you," Megan offered.

"No, there's no point both of us going. I'll catch you up."

I took my shoes off and gave them to her, turned round and started running back to the main building. The corridors were deserted and dimly lit; the floorboards creaked under my feet; my dress swished as I ran. I opened the Theatre door and turned the lights on. I looked everywhere for my bag, trying to remember where I last saw it. Couldn't find it.

The door slammed shut, and I jumped. I ran over and tugged at it. It didn't move. My chest pain flared up again and my heart was pounding in my ears. I began shouting and banging on the door in panic. No one came.

8. FLAMES

I'd always felt different from everyone else I knew – and not always in a good way. I knew I was super-smart, there was no hiding it. I could read a book within minutes. Solve the hardest equation within seconds. My brain sucked up knowledge like a vacuum. But what freaked me out the most was how I could open and close doors without touching them, turn lights on and off without flicking a switch, or move random objects just by looking at them. I was different all right, and after being in therapy for most of my life I had convinced myself that my weirdness was the result of a severe mental health disorder. They say there's a fine line between genius and madness. But even that couldn't explain what happened next.

The lights went off and a deadly silence fell into the Theatre. The only sound was the floor creaking under my feet as I ran over to the window. Maybe I could get out that way.

An agonising pain shot through my chest and a chill ran down my spine as a breeze rose from the floor towards me. The heavy door opened, and a waft of hot air entered the room. I spun round as two men walked in, wearing dark suits. One of them crossed his arms and leaned against the wall, smirking. He stared at me, his head tilted. The man's eyes sparkled in the moonlight coming through the window.

The room seemed immense around me. Though they were standing on the other side of the Theatre, I could see a cloud of heat moving towards me. It looked as if their bodies were surrounded by wavy, invisible lines. The door slammed shut behind them. I started to shake. My chest was getting tighter, making it hard for air to get in.

Don't panic, Arianna. Stay calm. Breathe.

"So this is her, Aiden?"

"Indeed it is. Didn't expect her to be so gorgeous, eh?"

"Who are you? What do you want from me?" I gasped, holding my chest, my heart in my throat.

"She sounds petrified, Aiden, doesn't she?"

"You better let me go. My friend will be looking for me right now." I tried to sound tough, but the quiver in my voice betrayed me.

They both laughed, still keeping their distance.

"I'm afraid no one is looking for you, Arianna. Not after receiving your text messages."

How did he know my name? I gaped at him. He was waving my mobile phone at me.

"They all think that you're in bed fast asleep, Princess Arianna," the other man said.

As they began walking slowly towards me, the pain in my chest intensified, and I gulped for breath.

"I can't believe how easy this is, Malyse. Not one Feather in sight. They don't suspect a thing."

My phone came flying across the room, missing me by an inch before smashing against the wall behind me. I screamed and fell to the floor.

"Sorry, did I frighten you there?" This one was shorter but bulkier than the other man. He was holding something in his hand – like a lighter. A flame was sparkling on and off in his palm.

Oh God. Panic set in. I couldn't move.

"This is going to be fun." The taller one threw something at the chandelier above my head, setting it alight. The crystals shattered to pieces as they hit the floor below. Flames crackled into life, lighting up the room around me.

"What do you want?" I cried.

"Just a slow, painful death, that's all."

My blood went cold, my legs frozen. What do I do now?

"How shall we do it, Malyse?"

A flame was burning in the palm of his hand. Not a lighter or a candle. The fire was coming from his skin. Maybe this was just one of my dreams. That's right. It must be a dream. A nightmare. Couldn't possibly be real.

"Mmm, I reckon we should burn one finger at a time."

The one called Malyse threw a flame at me. I sensed the heat blasting close to my skin and ducked just in time. The flames consumed the painting behind me. This couldn't be happening. I was dreaming or hallucinating.

"How about we start with her feet so she can watch herself burn?" They began to pace around me, as if I was the prey and they were lions.

The one called Aiden threw more fire, setting alight the floorboards in a ring around me.

"Why are you doing this?" I shouted.

The flames licked at my feet. A spark landed on my dress. I flapped at the flames with my hands, my palms stinging from the burns. My breathing was ragged. Adrenaline rushed through my blood. Instinct told me to get up. Run. At the very least I had to put up a fight. Think, Arianna. Think quickly. A blast of heat shot from my chest to my head; an overwhelming energy washed over me. As I shifted, I felt a shard of glass pierce my foot.

Flames were billowing round the Theatre. The heat was intense, the room filling with black smoke. I gasped for air, but there was hardly any left. No way out. I was going to die. Tears sprang into my eyes as Kayla's beautiful paintings were devoured by flames. Only one remained intact on the wall opposite me.

I brought my hands to my mouth, stunned. It was a lady in a red gown, holding a child wrapped in a white blanket. Not possible. My mind was playing tricks on me. I coughed as smoke filled my lungs. I heard the sound of steps getting closer. Then a hissing noise reached my ears. I wasn't dreaming. This was reality.

The door looked so far away. The flames were leaping around me but I had to try, I had to run. I launched myself forward, jumping over the flames. Glass tore through my feet but I couldn't let the pain stop me.

"Where do you think you're going?"

Aiden stood in front of me, his arms out wide. I panicked, tried to dart round him, but he was quicker. He grabbed me by the hair and threw me on the floor with such force that I heard my bones crack on the boards. I screamed in agony. Blood gushed from my chin. I coughed, and spat more blood.

"She's got guts, I must admit."

They stared down at me.

That was the moment I realised their eyes were scarlet. I started praying, but this time no miracle could save me. Tears welled up. Nana Holly.

"No use in praying, gorgeous. He's not listening."

Malyse picked me up by the throat and lifted me off the floor. His scorching hand choked me, stopping me from screaming. My vision blurred; I was losing consciousness.

Through the roaring in my ears, I heard Aiden's chilling words. "Malyse, don't spill too much of her blood. He'll want the pleasure of it."

A blast. A loud explosion. Something had blown the Theatre door open, and cold air flooded into the room like a stormy wind.

Malyse released my throat, and I fell to the ground, gasping. He reached down and grabbed me by the waist.

"Let go of her now, Malyse."

The voice was deep, sharper than I'd heard before, but I recognised it immediately.

I blinked and my vision cleared. Keaghan was standing in the middle of the room, tall, hard-faced and angry. A boy was on his left: dark curly hair and a goatee beard. On his other side, a stern-faced brunette. I was sure I'd seen both of them before, but where? The flickering flames blurred my sight.

Keaghan stepped forward, looking directly at me. His eyes shot bolts of terror through me. They were scarlet. There was a circle of heat swirling around him like a wave. How was this possible? Malyse's grip got tighter, and I gasped in agony.

"Did you hear? Let her go before I turn you to dust." Keaghan's voice was controlled, but his anger burned.

Unbearable pain shot through me as Malyse pulled me closer to him. I felt my ribs being crushed, and I screamed.

A scorching wind started from somewhere, as if a hurricane was moving across the room. Something yanked me away from Malyse's hold and I found myself in a vortex. I kept my eyes shut until the spinning stopped. When I opened them again, I was on the other side of the room, pressed against someone's chest.

I was in Keaghan's arms. I could smell his aftershave.

"You thought you could beat me?" Keaghan's voice resounded in my head, his lips close to my ear.

In the seconds that had passed since Keaghan had arrived, everything had changed. The boy and the girl who had come with him now held Aiden and Malyse by their throats. They too had flames burning in their palms. They shot them at their victims. The flames around Aiden and Malyse turned from red to blue and purple. They screamed as their bodies turned to dust in front of my eyes. They had vanished, gone, like they never existed. I buried my head in Keaghan's chest, tears of fear and pain flowing down my face. I wasn't sure what had happened; all I knew was that it wasn't real. It couldn't be real.

"Brue, you and Nero clean this place up and get rid of the evidence. I need to take her somewhere safe. She's too exposed. Let's move."

His voice echoed in the room. I didn't look at any of them. Their red eyes still terrified me.

"I'll meet you at the church," Keaghan said.

"You're kidding, right? I'm not stepping into another church." The goatee guy sounded alarmed.

"No, Nero, I'm not kidding. It's the safest place for her right now. They should be on their way; I hope – for their sake."

I was still too shocked to speak. I lay in his arms, listening to their weird conversation. The unbearable pain should have rendered me unconscious but I was managing to stay awake.

The brunette spoke next, in a soft northern accent. "Come on, Nero, let's just get on with it. We always end up cleaning up their mess anyway."

"Yeah, a mess the Feathers should be cleaning up, not us," Nero growled.

Keaghan carried me from the Theatre down the dark corridor and onto the deserted street. He ran across the lawn with me cradled in his arms. It felt as if we were flying, he was going so fast. I moaned. My ribs were throbbing, and the pain in my chest was getting worse. He ran on and on until he stopped. I looked up. A church. Keaghan didn't touch the door. He didn't need to: it opened the moment he stepped towards it.

9. CAN'T BE TRUE

I'd always felt a bit funny in churches, though I never knew why. The woody smell of burning incense made me dizzy and light-headed. The cold, dark spaces used to make me shiver, and I found the flickering candles creepy. Now here I was, going into a church with a guy who had just saved my life after I'd been attacked by red-eyed men. I should have been petrified. I barely knew Keaghan, and he certainly wasn't who I'd thought he was. His eyes could turn red, his hands could hold flames, and his skin-prickling voice was still ringing in my ears. Yet I had never felt as safe in my life as I did at that moment, encircled by his arms.

The church was dark. The powerful scent of incense filled my lungs. Keaghan lit the candles with his fingertips, as if they were matchsticks. He laid me down, very gently, on one of the benches and leaned over me.

His eyes were back to their normal colour. He dried my tears with the back of his hand and I shrank back from his touch. He stood up and shook his head, massaging his temples, but said nothing. A couple of times I thought he was about to speak but then he seemed to change his mind.

He pulled a phone from his trouser pocket, pressed a button and swore. Whoever he was trying to call clearly wasn't picking up. He glanced over at me and I looked away. Could I trust him? What did I know about him, really? Nothing. I knew nothing. I still wasn't sure if this was an illusion, the rotting fruit of my twisted imagination – a creation of my madness.

I couldn't speak, although I wanted to; every breath was agony. Now he'd moved away, I felt the freezing cold, the pain in my chest and the stinging from the cuts on the soles of my feet. I touched my chin, and my fingers came away sticky with blood.

"Here, let me."

Keaghan moved to my side. With a tug, he ripped a chunk off the hem of my dress and dabbed the cut with it. Was the heat coming from his body? It was overpowering, like an invisible energy whirling around me. At least I wasn't cold anymore.

"Stay still. Keep pressure on it."

I pressed the fabric against my chin, feeling a strong, prickling pain. His phone rang.

"Is it sorted?" He sounded agitated. "Good, make your way straight here." He waited for a reply. "No, I can't get through to them, damn it. I can't believe they were so stupid. This is the last time I let them do things their way. I'm taking charge now." Another pause. "Not yet, but I'm sure she will soon. I'll check now." He knelt in front of me and touched me above my stomach, just under my breast, and pressed firmly. I grunted in pain. His hand moved to check my arms and legs.

"What are you doing?" I yelled.

My face was burning with embarrassment and anger. Keaghan stood up and walked away again.

"Not good. She's badly hurt. Nothing she can't fix – if she gets here soon. They need to be quick. I could wring their necks for being so stupid and thoughtless." He waved his hand in an angry gesture. "They got way too close this time. We do things our way from now on. I've been more than reasonable up to now. And Bruna – bring a bottle of water or something." He hung up and turned to look at me.

"What's going on?" I panted. Every time I breathed or spoke, the pain shot through me.

"I don't think I'm the best person to explain that to you, Arianna." He dialled another number on his phone.

Rage boiled up inside me. "I don't care what you think. I want to know why I was attacked tonight." I took a few short breaths. "Who were they? They knew who I was. How?"

"You'll have your answers soon. Try not to worry. You'll make your injuries worse. Really, you don't want to hear it from me."

His voice sounded casual, infuriating me even more.

"Look at me. I'm in agony and I don't know what the hell is happening. I have a right to know what's going on. Look at me!"

I managed to shout out the words. My voice echoed round the church. I tried to sit up but dizziness overwhelmed me and I fell off the bench.

"Arianna." He ran towards me and knelt by my side, trying to pick me up, but I shoved him away. "Arianna, I know this must feel weird to you but –"

"Weird?" I panted. "This is beyond weird. What's going on, Keaghan? Where's Megan? She could be hurt too. Call Kayla and Julian. Now." I was shaking, tears flowing down my cheeks. The pain in my chest was unbearable. "Who are you people?" I whispered, my lips trembling.

He dried my tears with his fingers, closing his eyes. For a moment I thought he looked hurt.

Footsteps. Someone entering the church. I twisted to see who it was, wincing, and saw the brunette from earlier.

"They're on their way. They were in Featherstone," she said.

"What the hell were they doing over there?" Keaghan shouted, shaking with rage.

"Apparently they were tricked."

She walked over and I saw that the goatee guy was with her too. He looked around with an expression of disgust, covering his nose and mouth with his hand. "Why do they always have to smell like this?" he said, retching.

The girl ignored him. "They received text messages from her phone to say she was safe in her room and tucked up in bed."

She looked down at me. I must have looked pretty bad, judging by her expression. "Arianna, hang in there," she said. She sat on the floor next to me, talking as if she knew me. I had no idea who she was.

She raised my head to help me drink from a bottle of water, but I couldn't swallow. I coughed instead, sending fresh daggers of pain across my body.

"It's OK, slow down." Her eyes were black now. She was really pretty. Hard to believe she was capable of turning a man to dust. "You must be wondering who the hell we are, you poor thing," she said. "I'm Bruna, and this is Ranero, but you can call him Nero."

"No, she cannot," he snapped.

"I'm afraid you've already had the pleasure of meeting Keaghan." She winked at me.

Bruna seemed friendly and warm. Yet I'd just seen her throwing fire with her hands, her eyes devil-red coloured, and hissing like a snake.

"Will you please explain to me what's going on?" I asked, my voice feeble.

Keaghan shook his head, stopping her from saying anything.

"Who the hell *are* you?" I whispered, unable to control my rage.

"Hell is the right place to start, actually." Nero sneered; but Keaghan wiped the smile off his face with a daggers look.

"It was a joke." He shrugged.

Keaghan's phone rang again, making us all jump. He answered it.

"What took you so long? Yes, she's safe now, I took her to St Nicholas Church... Malyse and Aiden... yes, we cleared all the tracks leading to us. It'll look like the fire was accidental. She's asking questions, and lots of them. You need to get here now, or I'll tell her myself."

I was trying to make sense of his words, but I was slipping in and out of consciousness.

"Stay with me, Arianna. Don't fall asleep." Bruna patted my cheeks.

"I need to get out of here." I heard Nero say. "This place is giving me the creeps. I'm itching all over."

My eyes flickered open to see Nero twitching in discomfort, scratching his arms and neck.

"Well, you can't, Nero," Bruna said. "So just grin and bear it. It's only a church, for crying out loud. And if it's working on you, it'll keep the others away, for sure."

"I don't even want to be here. I can't understand why we have to risk our skin for her." Nero looked at me with hatred. My flesh crawled.

"Shut your mouths, the pair of you," Keaghan snapped.

I had to get away. I didn't know who these people were and what they wanted from me. They seemed to have saved my life. But could I trust them? Were they even human?

What was I thinking! This was a dream! Had to be. So why did it feel so damn real?

Keaghan was still talking on the phone; Nero and Bruna were arguing intensely. I braced myself. Somehow I had to break through the pain to get to the door. If only I could have called Kayla and Julian; and where was Megan?

No one was watching me. I took a deep breath and hauled myself to my feet, then staggered from the altar to the door. Every step was agonising. The glass was stabbing into my bare feet; my heart was pounding and I struggled to breathe. But somehow I found the energy to keep going. Almost there. The door was inches away now.

"Nero!" Keaghan had spotted me from the corner of his eye. Damn!

Nero grabbed me by the arm and stood between me and freedom.

"Let me go," I shouted, ignoring the pain.

I somehow managed to shake him off, lurching back towards the altar, but Bruna was already there. I felt a rush of adrenaline coursing through my veins.

"Arianna, don't be silly, you're hurt. Please, stop," she begged.

I raised my hands and pushed her away with all my strength.

To my amazement, she flew across the church and smashed into one of the stone pillars, cracking it down its entire length. I couldn't believe my eyes. Did I do that? I turned to run towards the other side, but Keaghan was there to block me. My efforts to push him away were in vain. I collapsed, the energy draining from my battered body. I was growling in pain and anger as he gathered me in his arms again.

"Why are you doing this to me?"

"I'm sorry, Arianna, I know this is hard for you. Trust me. It'll all make sense soon." He put me down on the bench again, placing a velvet cushion behind my back.

"I can't breathe. I'm hurt, and none of you seem to have any intention of taking me to a hospital. Who are you? You have no right to keep me here against my will." I tensed. The pain was excruciating.

"Keaghan, you need to tell her something. Can't you see she's only making herself worse?" Bruna walked towards us, limping slightly.

Keaghan turned to me, looking intense. "All you need to know, for now, is that you mustn't be scared of us. You're safe here. They'll be here soon to explain everything. It's best if you hear it from your friends rather than me." His voice was gentle. As his hand dried my cheeks, I felt that now familiar current passing through my skin.

"Those men who tried to kill me. They didn't look... human," I gasped through the pain.

"They were Flames, you idiot! Demons." Nero smirked. "Haven't you figured that out yet? I thought you said she was smart."

"Nero, shut your mouth before I shut it for you, and for good this time." Keaghan's eyes flickered from blue to red and then back to blue again. "It's not what you think, Arianna," he said.

"It can't be true, this isn't true." I kept on shaking my head. "I'm in a dream, right? This is one of my hallucinations." My breathing was short and fast as I tried to control a rising tide of pain.

"Arianna, listen to me, you need to calm down..."

I shuffled away from him, shuddering. Once again, I rolled off the bench.

"Please, Arianna, you have to calm down. You're bleeding internally and your broken rib may have pierced your lung," Keaghan said.

"Don't come near me."

I held on tight under my chest, struggling for breath. I felt as if I was going to pass out, but I was too afraid of what would happen to me if I did. But I wasn't sure how much longer I could resist.

"Your eyes were red too... You... you had fire in your hands... Oh my God, you... demons?" My jaw dropped. "Stay away, or I swear..." All of a sudden, I felt a huge energy rising above my head, taking me over.

"Arianna, you're seriously going to hurt yourself. Please," Keaghan begged.

"We won't hurt you, Arianna. We're different." Bruna looked agitated. "But you need to control your breathing. You can do it, please, Arianna. Breathe."

"You're keeping me here... against my will. How's that different?" I wheezed.

"We're here to protect you, Arianna, not to hurt you. Please listen to me." Keaghan's voice was starting to fade away.

A wave of dizziness flooded over me. I couldn't make out

what they were saying. Their faces were becoming a blur. I had to let go. Can't… stand… the… pain… anymore…

"Arianna!"

That was the last thing I heard Keaghan say.

10. FEATHERS

I was familiar with near-death experiences. As a child, I'd already seen that light shining bright, luring me; the levitation, the total serenity and warmth. But even though I wanted to follow the light, I never could. And even now something was stopping me from moving towards it.

The light began to move away. It was no longer blinding me. My chest pain was receding too. A warm sensation passed through my body, as if something was drawing the agony away. My breathing was back to normal. My feet weren't burning; my back and ribs were no longer sore. Instead, an overwhelming sensation of wellbeing was flowing over me.

What was happening to me? Was I dead?

I heard voices, but couldn't make out what they were saying. Then I had a sudden urge to cough, and as I did, I felt the last atom of pain drain out of me.

"Arianna? Can you hear me?"

I knew that voice. I opened my eyes, blinked, and saw Kayla's sweet blue eyes.

"Kay," I whispered. Sighs of relief echoed around me.

"Thank God, I arrived in time. You're OK now, everything's fine. You're safe."

"Am I in hospital?" I tried to get up but Kayla restrained me.

"Wait, don't get up just yet. You're not completely healed."

I heard Julian's voice. "You gave us all a fright," he said. If he and Kayla were here, it must mean everything was all right, mustn't it?

As I looked up, I saw the frescoes on the ceiling. I was still in the church. Keaghan was sitting on the bench opposite me. Bruna was standing behind him, and Nero was leaning against the door. Oh God. I was still dreaming. It wasn't over.

"No, no, no." I shook my head frantically, throwing myself into Kayla's arms.

"It's all right, Arianna, we're here now. You'll be fine." She stroked my head.

She didn't know. She wasn't aware of who they really were. We were all in danger. I had to warn her.

"Kayla," I whispered. "Keaghan is not who we think he is. I know it sounds weird, but you have to believe me. We need to get out of here." I looked into her eyes, but she didn't appear to be worried.

"It's OK, Arianna. We know." She sounded calm, which just made me more confused.

"No, Kayla, you don't understand. Something really scary has happened tonight. We need to call the police. Julian, we have to leave now." Why weren't they listening to me? Why weren't they reacting?

"Arianna, we know exactly who Keaghan is." Kayla's eyes looked sad. "We should have been there for you. Not them. We let you down. I'm so sorry. Because of our stupidity, you almost died tonight."

"W-what are you talking about?" I tried to fight down the panic. "And where's Megan?"

"I'm here, Arianna. I'm so sorry too."

I turned round to see Megan sitting on a marble step by the altar, tears running down her cheeks. A bright light was shining above Kayla's head.

"I think it's time for you to hear the truth," Kayla said. "We can't keep it from you any longer. You need to know."

Wow. My friend was surrounded by a golden glow hovering around her head and shoulders. I'd seen that light before, above my head, but never this bright. I looked down at my body. Not one scratch on my legs and arms, no wounds anywhere, no burn marks on my skin. I could breathe without pain. How could that be possible? The blood stains on my dress were the only evidence of the ordeal I had been through.

"I don't get it. I had cuts and burns all over my body, and broken ribs."

"I healed you," Kayla replied.

Healed? I couldn't have heard her properly. A terrible thought hit me.

"Oh my goodness – you're like them." I shrank away from her, terrified all over again.

"No, Arianna. This is what I do. I heal. I'm a Healing Angel." Kayla smiled at me, the light around her head shining brighter.

Did she just say *angel*? I stumbled to my feet and backed away from them all.

"This isn't real, right? Can someone please wake me up? Because if this isn't a dream, either I've gone completely insane or you're all barking mad."

"Arianna, this isn't a dream," Kayla said. "I'm sorry it had to happen like this. We planned to tell you differently; but Keaghan is right, you must be told. We put you in more danger than ever before. He insisted we tell you tonight, though I wish we could have done it differently." She darted a look of disapproval at Keaghan.

Nero stepped forward. "If you'd done your job properly, we wouldn't even be here right now, would we, Feather girl?"

Bruna joined in. "And if it wasn't for us, she'd be dead. So you better start sounding more grateful."

"We were tricked, you idiots," Kayla snapped. "They used Arianna's phone. Julian had overseen the location before leaving. It was fine."

Megan groaned. She looked devastated, as if this was her fault. "I was with her. I didn't sense any demons. I don't know how they managed to get past unnoticed."

Demons? What the hell…?

Keaghan butted in then. "Will you shut up? Can't you see how confused she is? We owe Arianna an explanation, and fast. You'd better start telling her the truth, Kayla, or I'll tell her my side of the story, shall I?"

Kayla sighed. "Sit down, Arianna." She pointed at the bench.

I grabbed handfuls of my hair. "This is ridiculous. I'm definitely hallucinating. That's it! I'm having a psychotic episode. That's what it is."

"I said sit down, Arianna." Kayla's voice echoed in the church. "Please."

I had never seen her look so serious. I sat down. Maybe I'd get some answers at last.

"I don't know where to start." She squeezed her eyes shut.

"Why don't you start by telling me what the hell happened tonight?" I demanded.

She took a deep breath and started speaking. "When Julian and I left the Theatre, Megan was in charge of taking you back to Thistle House. We were convinced you were OK, because I rang Megan and she said you'd texted her to say you were in bed safe. I received the same text too, so we all thought you were fine."

I had a sudden flashback of Aiden's face, twisted with evil, his hand waving my phone at me. The memory made my skin crawl.

"It wasn't me. I didn't text you," I whispered.

"We know that now," she sighed. "I rang you to confirm you were OK, but you didn't answer. We were already on our way to Featherstone, so I called Keaghan and told him to check on you."

I stared at her, confused. "What's this got to do with him?" I looked over at Keaghan; he was leaning against a pillar, keeping quiet.

"Keaghan is in charge of your protection." Kayla threw a swift glance in his direction. "We all are."

"Protect me from what?" I glared at her. She might be talking at last, but this still wasn't making sense.

"Aiden and Malyse were demons, Arianna. Keaghan and his fallen angels were the ones who saved you tonight. We were all assigned to protect you quite some time ago. You weren't supposed to know until you were ready. But things have changed now. It's getting too dangerous, and you need to know the truth."

"Kay, you're not making any sense. This is insane. Why would I need protecting?"

Fallen angels? Impossible. The *brainiac* in me was refusing to accept this nonsense.

"This is real, Arianna. I'm not making this up, trust me."

I searched her face and she certainly looked serious. "So what are you?" I dared ask.

"We're angels." She glanced at Julian.

"You're an angel?" I looked at Julian, in disbelief.

"Hard to believe, I know." He was trying to joke about it. I didn't laugh. He got the message and turned serious. "I'm an Overseer Angel, Arianna. My job is to control the area where angels are, and make sure it's safe."

"You're not very good at it then, are you?" Bruna chuckled under her breath.

"Enough, Brue," Keaghan said, silencing her with a look.

"Hold on a second. I'm still not getting this. Who's after me?"

Julian cleared his voice. "Morfran." The name meant nothing to me. "He's one of the Princes of Darkness and he's after the Angel of Light."

"And who's that?"

Kayla touched my arm. "You, Arianna. You're an angel, just like us. But we couldn't tell you before, because if you knew, you would have exposed yourself to danger, and it would have been impossible for us to protect you and keep you hidden."

I tried to rationalise her words in my mind, but it was impossible. They made no sense.

Kayla continued. "Now Morfran knows who and where you are, and we have to act fast. The Celestial Order would have told you this on your eighteenth birthday, but we don't have time to wait till then." She massaged her temples. "The Order arranged for Keaghan to get closer to you so he could protect you better. But we let you down. We failed to protect you tonight."

The Order? Celestial Order? What were they talking about?

Keaghan butted in. "Hang on a minute, Feather girl, *we* didn't fail. So from now on we do things my way."

"I don't think so," Julian replied.

"Hold on," I cut in. "So you're not just my friends by chance? Megan, are you in this too?" I looked at her, struggling to make sense of it all.

She nodded. "I'm not an angel like you, or a fallen. I'm a Lightworker. I have supernatural powers too, but I'm not a celestial being. The Order brought us all together to protect you after your parents died."

The world tipped sideways. I looked at her in shock. "What on earth are you saying, Meg?" I trembled.

"You were meant to die in that fire, alongside them." Megan's eyes held mine.

"I don't understand, this is crazy. What the hell is this... Order?" I rubbed my hand on my forehead in frustration. Somebody wake me up. This had to be a nightmare.

A new voice came from the direction of the altar. "Maybe I should explain this to Arianna."

"Joya?"

"Yes, dear. Let me start from the beginning."

11. SOMETHING
WE ALL AGREE ON

Despite all the bad things that had happened in my life, I had always felt lucky. At least, I'd been surrounded by people that cared about me. Kayla and Megan had been there to wipe away my tears, or laugh at my jokes – even when they weren't funny. Julian always knew the right thing to say to cheer me up. Joya was always kind and protective of me. She had supported me, even when I was wrong. I assumed this was a personal favour to my Nana, or because she'd taken a shine to my talent and passion for science. Nothing had prepared me for the real reason.

"I am a member of the Celestial Order."

Joya walked down the altar steps. Her slender figure was wrapped in a bronze-coloured cloak. She pulled down the hood. Her blonde hair was perfectly styled around her face, her skin glowing in the light shining above her head. She gazed at me with her blue eyes.

"You shouldn't be here, Joya. It's dangerous tonight," Kayla said.

"It'll be fine, Kayla, I need to be here. If there's anyone she should hear the truth from, that person is me."

I heard Keaghan snicker under his breath, but he turned serious when everyone stared at him.

"Hello, Keaghan. I see you haven't changed," Joya said with a smile.

"It's a good job I haven't, or she would be dead right now," Keaghan replied.

"You're absolutely right. And we're very grateful to you and your fallens. You proved your value." Joya turned to look at me. "Your head must be spinning. Come, sit with me and let me tell you everything."

I sank down next to her on one of the benches. She was right: I was more than confused. I tried hard to focus on her words.

"Your mum and dad weren't the ordinary parents you thought they were, darling. I was your dad's best friend for many centuries." Did she just say *centuries*? "Your father was a powerful and magnificent angel. He was the best Angel of Judgment Rome has ever had."

I gawped at her. "You knew my dad?" A chill travelled down my spine. "He was what?"

"The Archangel Moriel was an angel of Rome, Arianna." Joya's eyes shone with pride. "He was, of course, known under the name of Alfredo Morelli to the human world. And your mother – beautiful, sweet Rose – she was a Lightworker, just like your friend Megan. Your parents' death wasn't an accident, Arianna." My fists clenched. "Do you remember the night of the fire?" she asked.

I tried, as I had so many times before, but my mind was a blank. It was as if those memories had been removed. "Very little. I remember the flames around me, and the kind nurse who looked after me at the hospital." I tried to swallow the lump in my throat. "Nothing else."

"Arianna, that nurse was me. You were the one Morfran wanted, and he's never stopped looking for you ever since. We managed to hide you from him all this time, and that's why we are here. Kayla, Julian, Megan and Marcus were assigned to protect you."

I shot up, "Marc? He's like you?"

Joya smiled. "Yes, he's like us, Arianna."

"Is this the reason he's coming back?" I turned to Kayla for an answer.

"Yes. We are all in this together," Kayla said. "Including the fallens." Her last words were uttered with distaste.

I twisted to look at Keaghan. "So that's why you pretended to be a student here, so you could keep a closer eye on me?" He nodded. My mind struggled to catch up. "You were in Rome at the airport that day, weren't you? But you denied it – why?" I knew I was right. I knew it.

"I couldn't tell you. I was under strict orders. I would have told you years ago if it was up to me. But I couldn't."

"What good would that have done, Keaghan?" Joya asked.

"It would have been the truth, for a start, and she'd have had more time to deal with it, and now we wouldn't be in such a mess, trying to fill her in as quickly as possible, before Morfran gets his claws in to her." His voice was thick with bitterness.

"Of course, 'cause you know all the answers, don't you?" Kayla snapped.

"I do, actually. I'm one of them, remember?" Keaghan moved in front of Kayla, challenging her. "No one knows how Morfran thinks, speaks or even breathes, better than I do. That's the main reason you need me, right?"

"Back off, Blake," Julian said. "We put up with you because we have to. We wouldn't have you anywhere near Arianna, otherwise."

"If I hadn't been anywhere near her tonight, she would be dead. You seem to keep forgetting that part." Keaghan strode away and sat back down next to Bruna.

"This isn't easy for us, you know," Bruna said. "We did our job tonight. It's more than any of you can say."

Keaghan lifted his hand to silence her. "Brue, leave it. I can fight my own battles."

She looked hurt but said no more.

Joya stood up. The light shone brighter above her head.

"Being at each other's throats isn't going to help anyone. We need to come up with a plan, and soon. I'll speak to Lucius in the morning. Arianna needs to meet the rest of the Celestial Order. She has to be trained as soon as possible."

Bruna cleared her throat to draw attention. "She's strong already. I was on the receiving end of her powers tonight."

A heated discussion followed as they debated the next steps, as if I wasn't there. I sat alone on the bench, watching as my so-called friends decided how my life was going to be conducted from now on. Hello? I'm still here, you know. They made it sound as if my life was no longer mine. Who was I, anyway? Had I really been living a lie all this time? I'm an angel. How could that be even remotely possible?

As I looked around, I noticed that Keaghan and Nero had disappeared. I stood up and walked towards the door, unnoticed.

As I stepped outside, Nero grabbed my arm. "What the hell are you doing out here?"

"Let go of me," I growled, pulling my arm away.

"Let her go, Nero." Keaghan appeared from behind me. Nero released me instantly. "Can't you stand the smell of churches either?" Keaghan said, a half-smile tugging at his lips.

"Something like that."

He sat on the wall by the side of the church.

"Do churches bother you?" I asked, sitting down next to him.

"Not as much as they used to. I had to adapt if I was to protect you." He shrugged. "Is it getting a bit too much in there?"

I nodded. "I don't get it. This stuff is unreal. It can't be true. I don't know what to believe anymore." I looked down at my hands. There were no wounds, but they were still covered in dried blood and black ash.

"You need more time for things to sink in, and unfortunately time is a luxury we don't have. You've just found out that you're not the girl you thought you were. Cut yourself some slack." He looked up at the dark sky.

"Maybe, but I just find it so absurd. I can't get my head

around it. I still think I'll wake up tomorrow and realise this was all a dream." I massaged my temples, feeling drained.

"Stop stressing, Einstein. You won't find a rational answer this time."

I turned to face him. His eyes looked less hard, so different from the red fire before. His gelled-back hair was all messy now.

Before I had a chance to reply, the church door burst open and Kayla and Joya ran outside.

"Arianna?" Kayla cried. "Oh, you're here. Girl, you're going to give me a heart attack."

"Do angels have heart attacks?" I stood and strode back inside.

Julian smiled as I walked past him. "Oh, she's better already. She's got her sense of humour back."

I didn't smile back at him. I felt betrayed by the people I thought were my closest friends. They weren't who I thought they were. They'd lied to me the whole time I had known them. I curled up on the last bench, hugging my knees to my chest.

"So, what's going to happen now?" I asked, knowing I sounded like I couldn't care less.

It was Kayla who replied. "I think she should come and stay with us in Featherstone."

The squeak of rubber soles on the marble floor caught everyone's attention.

"I thought I made it clear," Keaghan said, "I make the decisions now. After tonight, it's quite obvious she's not safe with you." Kayla opened her mouth to argue, but he talked over her, addressing Joya. "Arianna stays with me from now on, end of. Do it my way or I'm gone."

There was a short pause. "As you wish, Keaghan." Joya looked unhappy but she seemed to believe there was no choice.

"But, Joya you can't –" Kayla objected, but Joya cut her off.

"It's my decision," she said, her voice ringing out.

"I'm not going anywhere with anyone," I said. "I want to go

to bed. I'm exhausted. You're all busy dictating what I should do, without even asking what I want or how I feel. My life has been turned upside down tonight. I don't know who I am anymore, or who you are, for that matter, and you all seem to think you have a right to decide what's best for me. What about what I want?" My voice echoed round the church.

There was a long silence. My assertive outburst had brought them all up short. Then Megan walked towards me, taking me in her arms.

"I'm sorry, you're right. How insensitive of us. You must be so confused and shocked." She kissed my forehead and held me tight. I couldn't help relaxing into her warm hug.

"I want to go back to my room in Thistle House," I whispered.

"That's fine," Keaghan said. "If that's what she needs right now, that's what we'll do. Bruna and Nero will check out the location while I stay here with her." Keaghan didn't even wait for anyone to answer. He prised me from Megan's embrace and picked me up, lifting me like a child.

"This is starting to become a habit. I can walk, you know." I wriggled in his arms, embarrassed.

"With no shoes on your feet? If that's what you want." He lowered me a few inches.

"No, no. You have a point," I said.

He grinned and pulled me closer to him. His heat passed through my dress, making me shudder. How odd. I kind of liked that burning sensation. I was starting to get used to it.

"I'll take her back to Featherstone in the morning. Deal?" he said to Joya.

She nodded, though she still looked worried.

Julian wagged a finger at Nero. "Call us as soon as you get there and give me an update on the patrolling around Featherstone."

Nero replied with a sarcastic smile. "We have fallens stretching as far as the woods, overseeing the area. We'll make sure she's safe, don't you worry."

"Finally, something we all agree on." Keaghan smiled coldly and walked through the church doors.

The voices faded into the distance. The motion of Keaghan's walking had the effect of a rocking chair on my tired body and mind. I placed my head in the fold of his neck, my face brushing against his chin. Safe at last.

When I opened my eyes, it took me a moment before I realised I was in my room in Thistle House.

"It's OK. I'm here."

Keaghan's voice. I turned to see him sitting by the side of my bed. I sensed the warm radiations coming from his body. How could someone produce so much heat? Looking down, I realised I was still wearing my torn and dirty dress.

"I need a shower," I said. "I'm going to get changed and then I want some answers." I didn't feel tired anymore. It was time to talk.

"By all means have a shower," he said. "But then you need to sleep. We can have question time tomorrow." I didn't reply as I headed towards the bathroom and locked the door behind me. No way was I going to wait. I was ready now, whether he liked it or not.

I was shocked at my pale reflection in the mirror. My make-up was smudged and runny. Blood stains streaked my cheeks, chin and neck, and I was covered in black soot. I looked awful, and yet, as I checked my body, I could see no sign of cuts or bruises. Kayla had healed me. I still couldn't believe those words, but the truth was there to see.

Confused and overwhelmed, I stood under the shower and started crying, watching the water wash the dirt and blood down the shower drain.

A gentle knock on the door. "Arianna? Are you all right in there?"

"I'm fine. I'll be out in a minute," I shouted as I turned the tap off and grabbed a towel.

I pulled on my pyjamas and walked back into the bedroom. Keaghan was standing by the window. I sat on the bed, dabbing my wet hair with a towel. I was alone in a room with a demon; yet as I looked at him I felt a wave of gratitude, not fear.

"I'm alive because of you," I whispered.

"You need to rest, Arianna. We can talk in the morning."

He gazed at me with his smouldering blue eyes. It was hard to get away from them, even if I wanted to. And I didn't want to. His black hair was falling around his forehead; his smile was faint, but warm. A wave of exhaustion engulfed me, forcing me to tear my eyes away from him. Perhaps he was right.

"Fine." I climbed into bed, curling up under the covers.

"Night, Arianna. I'm here if you need me, OK?"

I closed my eyes. We could talk in the morning, like he said.

I'm running so fast I can hardly breathe. The shadow is right behind me. "No use in running anymore, Arianna." The voice is guttural and frightening, as if it was coming from the depths of the earth. The mocking laugh is growing louder. I fall over and the shadow catches up with me. My heart pounds as I slowly turn round. Warm breath on my face, red eyes staring into mine, a hissing noise buzzing in my ears. The wet touch of a forked tongue on my cheek. No! No, no, no!

My eyes flew open. The light was switched on and Keaghan was by my side, so close I could feel his body against mine. I shuddered, sobbing. Was I still dreaming?

"It's OK, Arianna. It's me, Keaghan, calm down. It was just a dream." I threw myself into his arms, letting him hold me.

That current of electricity travelled down my spine once again as he held me tight; the smell of his aftershave was intoxicating. I could have stayed in his arms forever. Oh God. What was I doing? We were in bed. Together. I pulled back, aware of the flush on my cheeks.

I cleared my throat. "Sorry. Really bad dream." I looked

away, embarrassed.

"Tell me what it was about." He put his hand on my arm, and I jolted at the touch.

"It's always the same. A black shadow in the dark. A hissing and breathing sound. A creature with red eyes. Flames. I've had the same dream lots of times, but I didn't know what it was until now." My voice trembled, hesitant. "It's *him*, isn't it?"

"Yes, and he seems to be getting closer." He pulled his hand away. "You have nothing to worry about, Arianna. I'm here. He can't get anywhere near you." He gave me a quick smile, and then stood up to turn the light off. "Go back to sleep."

"That's it? That's all you have to say? You expect me just to fall back to sleep like nothing happened?" If only. "Well, excuse me if I can't. You see, I'm just a bit scared and not so keen on seeing those eyes again."

He looked at me with a serious expression; then he sighed, shaking his head. "Come on then, move up a bit."

"What are you doing?" I started to panic as he climbed on my bed.

"I'm going to lie next to you. Maybe he'll sense my presence. That should hopefully keep him out of your head for a bit. Morfran can scare you, but he can't scare me."

I turned my back to him, pulling the covers up to my chin. The single bed was so small I could feel his breath on the back of my neck as he settled behind me. My heart was bouncing against my ribs like a tennis ball.

"Is that OK? You seem uncomfortable," he said in a husky, low voice.

"No, I'm fine, thanks, night." I spoke quickly, staring at the window.

I didn't know how long I lay awake, not daring to move a muscle. Keaghan's hot radiations kept on swirling around me, making me sweat under the covers.

"I guess the *heat* is a demon thing, right?" I said.

"Are you still awake?"

I heard him chuckle, and the next moment I was asleep.

12. MORFRAN

When I woke up, I was alone in bed. A wave of panic washed over me.

"I'm here."

The sound of Keaghan's voice instantly unknotted my nerves. I looked over to find him sitting on the chair, sipping from a plastic cup. He looked relaxed. A flawless face surrounded by raven hair. His eyes were on me and it was as if he could see right through me, to the very core of my soul. His gaze was breathtaking.

Enough, now, for crying out loud!

"Come on, I'm waiting. Start the grilling." Keaghan sat back, stretching his legs on my bed, a cheeky grin on his lips.

The time had come at last; but which was the most important question of the many crowding my mind?

"Who is he? And what does he want from me?" My voice shook a little.

"This is going to be hard to explain, Arianna, because it's not going to sound believable. Morfran is... He's the right-hand man of the Devil." His expression betrayed no emotion. "He's one of the seven Princes of Darkness. He is evil beyond imagination, and very dangerous."

Oh. Right. If he was trying to reassure me, it wasn't working. "Why is he after me?"

"You're the Angel of Light, the most powerful angel on earth, the only one able to kill him. Of course he's going to want you dead."

"So, I'm really supposed to believe I'm an angel?" Come on. I shook my head.

"You are. This is real, Arianna." Keaghan sat up, staring intently at me. He was serious. "And the sooner you come to terms with it, the better for all our sakes – not just yours."

"But this is crazy. Angels and demons? I don't believe in that stuff," I said, screwing up my nose.

"You are the Angel of Light, Arianna. Whether it sounds crazy to you or not. Your power is inside you and it's stronger than you can ever imagine."

I shook my head, stubborn to the last. "I don't feel like an angel. I'm just me, an ordinary girl with pale skin, muddled hair and a boring fashion sense."

Keaghan's eyebrows shot up. "You obviously don't look at yourself in the mirror very often."

His remark made me blush. "There's nothing special about me. I believe in science, in facts that can be proved, in things that can be explained. How can I make sense of this?"

"You can't. I can't make you believe you're an angel, Arianna. You'll have to see it for yourself."

"How? The last time I checked, I had arms, not wings."

"You have to earn those, I'm afraid. They don't come free," he said with a laugh. Then he turned serious again. "I'm not really the best person to tell you who you are, Arianna. The Celestial Order will do that when you go and see them."

He'd lost me there. "What?" I vaguely remembered Joya mentioning some "order" or something.

"Have you ever heard of the Angelic Hierarchy, Arianna?" He could probably guess the answer by looking at my blank face. "To think you go to such an expensive school, and they haven't even taught you that?" He shook his head. Preferring the facts of science, I'd never paid much attention during RE class. Now I wished I had.

"You'll learn about all that soon, anyway. All you need to

know for now is that the Celestial Order is made up of the Highest Angelic ranks. Joya is one of them. They're in charge of what you Feathers do, how you do it, and when. They make up the divine authority that regulates angels on earth." He didn't sound passionate about the subject. Not sure I was either. "You'll learn more details during your training. It'll all make sense to you then."

"I need to take notes. This is way too complicated." I nervously ran my hand through my hair, moving it away from my face. "What did you mean by *you Feathers*?"

"Angels. You're one of them, Feather girl." He winked at me again.

"If you say so." I nodded my head, no less confused. "I feel like I've met you before. Even before I saw you on the plane. Why is that?"

"Because you have – well, sort of. I was always there, protecting you, in the background. I wanted to tell you it was me that day, when you stopped the plane from crashing." He leaned back in his chair.

"What do you mean, *I* stopped it from crashing?" I gaped at him in shock.

"I don't know, angel, but whatever you did, it worked." He shrugged.

"Was it really me? But how?"

"You have powers, Arianna. Surely you've noticed?"

It was all starting to make sense now. "The *strange things*?"

"Thank hell we got to your luggage before the demons did. There was enough info in your diary to bring them straight to you."

"You read my diary?" A rush of blood flushed across my face.

Keaghan nodded, trying to suppress a laugh. "Don't worry, my lips are sealed." Just kill me now. "I'm kidding. But I'm afraid I had to destroy it, and your camera as well. We were kind of in a hurry."

"So, I'm not crazy? I'm not a mental case?"

"That's a matter of opinion." He laughed, and I threw a pillow at him.

"It didn't stop them from finding me though, did it?" I trembled as I remembered the faces of the demons that almost killed me.

Keaghan became serious again. "I know. We were caught by surprise. I can only apologise. I can't understand how they managed to find you. We thought we had it covered one hundred per cent." He sounded frustrated with himself.

"You saved my life, Keaghan, you've nothing to apologise for." I wanted to show my gratitude, but I still had more questions than answers.

"Go ahead. I know you've been dying to ask me," he said.

Could he read my mind? I sincerely hoped not. I stared at my feet, hoping he didn't notice my embarrassment. "Who... I mean, what are you, and why are you protecting me from one of your – kind?"

I swallowed hard, hugging my knees to my chest, waiting anxiously for his answer.

"I'm a demon, but I'm not the bad guy, Arianna. Though your Feather friends may disagree." He sneered. "I'm the leader of the fallen angels. I don't serve your God and I don't follow the commands of the Celestial Order – unless they pay me a hefty fee. That's the reason I'm protecting you." His last words hit me like a bullet. He sounded cold, like he didn't give a damn.

"So, I'm a job?" I didn't mean to sound hurt.

"Yes – and no. It's complicated, Arianna. You see, I don't serve anyone, I work for myself. Yes, the Order hired me to protect you against Morfran, but the truth is I want him dead as much as anyone else." His face registered no emotion.

"So you fight demons?"

"My fallens and I like to think that we defend whoever needs defending, doesn't matter who they are. We bring them our kind of justice. You see, we're not as merciful as your God." His eyes briefly turned red, then blue again.

"Bruna and Ranero are fallen angels, right?" My voice was croaky.

"Yes, they're my most trusted fallens. With us by your side, you've nothing to worry about." He reached over, placing his hand on my head and mussing up my hair.

Supposedly, I had no reason to be afraid of him, yet I couldn't help jolting every time his eyes turned red. His face seemed to harden when he was angry, almost disfiguring his otherwise flawless features. It terrified me.

Stop analysing everything. He saved your life, for God's sake.

"What about Mor – Morfre… you know who I mean. How do you know him?" I couldn't say his name.

"Morfran. I used to work for him, a long, long time ago, which means I know him inside and out. We can use that to our advantage. You need to concentrate on you, get strong and ready for when the time comes for you to fight him." He stared through the window into the forest. The sun was peeping up, rising behind the trees. "That'll be the Reaper's job, I guess."

"The Reaper? Who's that?" I followed him with my eyes as he sat back down.

"Your boyfriend, Marcus. He'll be in charge of your training." I sensed mockery in his tone.

"He's not my boyfriend," I snapped. I had to make that clear. Didn't want him to think I was with someone else. God, I was so pathetic.

Keaghan smiled as he turned to look at me with a more relaxed expression.

He wasn't off the hook yet though. Far from it.

"So, to you all, I'm just a job you've been assigned?"

"No, Arianna, you're not," he said. "The angels have a close relationship with you. There's nothing they wouldn't do for you, and they care about you very much. You may be a job to me and my fallens, but I know for sure that the angels see you as the best friend you've always felt them to be."

So he didn't feel the same as they did. My heart sank. "What's a Reaper?" I asked, trying to focus.

"His job is to train new angels. Marcus will explain it better than I can, Arianna. You just concentrate on becoming the angel that you are, as quickly as you can, and leave Morfran for me to worry about for now. OK?"

I looked into his beautiful eyes, hoping to find some comfort. "I'll try not to faint at your feet again, I promise."

He grinned. "Good. Now why don't you get ready? I'm taking you back to Featherstone. This place is no longer safe for you." His words brought me back to reality.

"So, what's going to happen next?" I dared ask.

"You're going to meet the Celestial Order. And I think it's time for you to have *that* chat with your Nana, don't you think?" It was like he knew me better than I knew myself.

"I'm ready," I announced twenty minutes later, as I walked back into the bedroom.

Keaghan looked at me up and down. "Back to your old self, I see."

I shrugged, looking down at my blue Adidas sweater, skinny jeans and sneakers. "The world will never see me in a pink dress ever again." I shoved the ruined dress into a plastic bag.

"Good, I prefer this version. But you did look amazing last night." His words sent my heart into a frenzy all over again. "Right, I've packed all your stuff and put it in the car. Is there anything I've forgotten?"

As I looked around my room, I realised all my things had gone. "Am I ever coming back?" I asked with a stab of regret.

"I don't think so."

"What about my A-levels?" Everything was happening so fast.

"You can finish them after your training. A genius like you should have no problem catching up." He winked. "Come on, are you ready to go?" He held the door open for me.

"As ready as I'll ever be." I took one last look at my room, trying to swallow the lump in my throat.

We were both silent at first as he drove at a ridiculous speed down the country lanes. I thought we were heading towards Featherstone; instead he took a different turn.

"Where are we going?" I asked, puzzled.

"Milton Abbey. The Order's waiting for you there." He kept his eyes on the road ahead.

"I'm meeting the Order now?" I felt a flutter of panic.

"Yes, I told you this morning."

Pain stabbed in my chest. I took several deep breaths.

"Relax, Feather girl. You've been giving your aura a hard time lately." He laughed.

"What?" I narrowed my eyes at him.

"Your aura is shining again. You need to keep it under control when you get nervous or scared."

"What the hell is an aura?"

"You must have felt it loads of times. Chest pains, short breath, heart pounding?" He glanced at me with a frown.

"That's my anxiety attacks." I touched the middle of my chest, feeling its warmth.

"That's what you thought."

"No, no, that's what I know. Trembling, heart palpitations, chest tightness and hot flushes – they're my nervous system responding to a panic attack." I wasn't sure who I was trying to convince, him or the *brainiac* in me.

"Sorry to burst your *scientifically-built* bubble, Einstein, but they're a sign that your angelic aura is trying to engage." He grinned sideways at me.

"That's ridiculous," I said, looking out the window.

I knew he was right though. I just didn't want to believe it. It was going to take a while to get my head around it.

The abbey was only an hour or so away, but with Keaghan's driving it didn't take long at all. He pulled up outside, and within seconds he was on my side of the car, holding the door open.

"Right, I'll wait for you here. Good luck, Feather girl."

"You're not coming with me?" Fear set in.

He smiled, holding my chin between his fingers. "Your eyes are the most amazing emerald green when you're scared, did you know that?"

Once again I was paralysed under his gaze, his touch sending a shock through my limbs.

"I'm not allowed in there, Arianna, but you'll be fine. Lucius is all right – compared to some of them."

I looked towards the front of the abbey, shaking. Its Gothic facade loomed upwards, dominated by three sculptured gargoyles in the entranceway and a crowning rose window uniting the two towers.

Keaghan grabbed my hand and squeezed it tight. His heat went into my skin like a flame. I jerked my hand away, even though I didn't want to.

"You'll be fine. Go." His blue eyes sparkled.

I forced my feet to take me towards the entrance. A middle-aged man dressed in gold robes had emerged and was standing by the door. I looked over my shoulder. Keaghan nodded at me, encouraging me to embrace my destiny.

13. THE CELESTIAL ORDER

The pungent smell of incense hit me as I stepped inside the abbey. Nana used to take me to church every Sunday without fail. The smell always made me woozy, close to losing consciousness. As a kid, I could be excused for holding my nose throughout the service, but as I grew older, people would give me funny looks. Eventually I stopped attending Mass altogether. But it looked like right now I didn't have a choice. This scent was going to be part of my life whether I liked it or not. I'd better start getting used to it.

"Welcome, Arianna."

The man's voice was calm and soft. The flickering of candles brought back vivid glimpses of the last twenty-four hours. I shuddered as I followed him across the hallway, my sneakers squeaking on the tiled floor.

He stopped by a heavy door. "You have to carry on by yourself from here, my child. Take the second turning on the right and go down the marble stairs. At the bottom of the corridor you will find another door. They're waiting for you there."

He opened the door with a silver key. I had no idea what to expect, and I had already forgotten his directions. As I entered, I heard the door shut behind me and jumped. Now what?

There were loads of corridors in front of me and I stared at them, baffled; it looked like a maze. After taking the wrong turn a few times, I managed to find some marble stairs. Once I reached the bottom, I walked down a long corridor before arriving in front of a wooden door. The door was ajar, so I pushed it open.

I swallowed hard before entering. My heart was pounding and my palms were damp with sweat.

The room was softly lit by more flickering candles. Bookshelves ranged along two of the walls, and a large oak table stood in the middle, laid with a fruit basket, a cake-stand piled with decorated cupcakes, and a tea set. Not what I expected at all.

"I thought you might be in desperate need of cake."

The voice came from behind me. I spun round and saw a man with a white beard and hair, smiling at me. As he moved closer, I realised I was taller than him. He looked old. Very old.

"Hello, Arianna. My name's Lucius. I'm here on behalf of the Celestial Order. Please sit down." He pointed at a chair. "You look surprised, child." He sat down at the table, facing me.

"I – I was expecting something different." I lowered my eyes, feeling nervous. In truth, I'd had no idea what to expect, but it certainly wasn't a tea party.

"We're not as scary as we may sound, Arianna. The Order is here to protect and guide you, not to frighten you." He smiled as he poured tea into two cups. "You must be confused and overwhelmed." Understatement of the century. "Arianna Morelli, Angel of Light. I'm honoured by your presence in my home. You're the daughter of the Archangel Moriel. It must have been a shock finding out that your parents weren't the ordinary people you thought they were, right?" His gentle voice relaxed me a little. "What do you remember from when you lived in Rome?"

"Not much. Practically nothing. It's all just a blur."

"Your father was in charge of the Celestial Court of Justice in Rome." He handed me a cup before continuing. "He was responsible for punishing those accused of atrocious crimes committed by Celestial Beings on earth. He was the best judge the Order has ever seen."

"I knew he was a judge, but not that kind of judge," I said, dubious.

I picked a cupcake from the stand. It looked too pretty to eat. I took a bite. Wow. The buttery sponge melted in my mouth, a hint of almond and chocolate hitting my taste buds.

"He met your mother in Featherstone. Your father was on a mission and Rose, being a powerful Lightworker, was the perfect match." He had to be speaking of someone else's family, not mine. "They fell in love with each other at first sight. Your Nana Holly disapproved at first, but she had no choice. Their union was predestined."

"Was their destiny also to die because of me?" My voice was hoarse from the lump in my throat.

"Their death was not your fault, my child. Their spirits have moved to the other side. You'll meet them again. I promise." I wanted to believe him so badly. "But their sacrifice was necessary. You had to live to fulfil your destiny."

"Which is?" My voice trembled.

"Once trained, you'll become the most powerful angel this century has seen. You'll have the power to destroy the Princes of Darkness, Arianna. Morfran knows that very well, that's why he needs to kill you before you become a fully fledged angel."

He couldn't have put it more bluntly, but there was nothing logical or rational in his words for me to cling onto.

"And when will that be?" I had a feeling it was going to be soon.

"Arianna, on your eighteenth birthday your angelic evolution will take place." I suddenly couldn't swallow. "You will receive a Celestial training until then, after which you'll be asked if you wish to embrace your Angelic Life." A bright light shone above his head. "If you accept, you'll be expected to fight Morfran and his demons, alongside your fellow angels." Was he for real? Me, fight a demon? He obviously didn't know me very well.

"This is a dream, right?" I breathed. "Either that, or I'm having a prolonged psychotic episode."

Lucius laughed. "I know it'll take you a while to process all this information, Arianna. The Order doesn't expect you to understand straightaway." His expression turned serious. "That's why your friends will be a great help and support through all this. Keaghan and his fallens will protect you until you're ready."

A doubt troubled my thoughts.

"What if I can't do it?" It was a very strong possibility.

"You have a choice, Arianna. Nothing will be imposed on you. Your father was clear on this. At the end of your training you'll have the chance to decide." My head was spinning. "I think I've given you enough information for one day."

We both stood up. Lucius moved to my side and reached out to place his hands on my shoulders. I had to bend my knees a little. A rush of energy surged from the middle of my chest all the way to the top of my head. I gasped. A golden light shone around me. My body was shuddering.

"Your aura seems ready. I know you'll do the right thing, Arianna." He gently tapped my shoulder. "Good luck, Angel of Light."

I couldn't speak. I just nodded, before walking towards the door. What a bizarre meeting. That must have been the weirdest conversation I'd ever had. I managed to find my way out without getting lost.

The moment I stepped outside the abbey, I started looking for Keaghan in the churchyard, scanning the area. He was somewhere close. I could sense him watching me.

There he was. Leaning against a lamp-post, waiting for me, just like he'd promised. He looked serious, but when he met my eyes his expression relaxed. I walked over and stopped just a few inches away, feeling an urge to throw myself into his arms and let him hold me tight. I managed to stop myself – just.

"Are you all right?" He gazed straight into my eyes.

"Think so. I'm not sure." I couldn't lie to him.

"Come on, let's get out of here. All this holy scent is driving me insane." He opened the car door for me.

"Was meeting Lucius as scary as you thought?" he asked as we drove away.

"Not really. It was actually quite peaceful. I was expecting to see someone dead tall with wings on his back, telling me to bow down to him. Instead, I found myself drinking tea and eating cake with Santa Claus."

Keaghan laughed out loud. "Stereotyping a little, aren't we? Lucius is sound. He's what we call a *retired* member of the Celestial Order. Wait till you meet the rest of the CO officially. That's scary."

"Thanks for reassuring me. I'm starting to think this is going to get worse, not better."

"You'll be fine, Feather girl. I'm relieved you know the truth at last. I don't have to hide from you anymore." I was glad about that too.

After a while, I looked out the window and my stomach flipped when I realised where we were. Keaghan stopped outside Nana's cottage.

"You best go in. Your Nana's waiting." He didn't switch off the engine.

"Are you going to wait for me here?" I couldn't explain why, but I really didn't want him to go.

"I can't stay. There's somewhere I have to be. I'll pick you up in a few hours. Don't worry, you're safe. There are angels and fallens patrolling the area." His smile reassured me a little, though "a few hours" seemed like an awfully long time.

I stood outside my front door for a few seconds. Time to face the truth. A moment I had been putting off for far too long.

"Nana?" I popped my head round the door.

She was sat at the table, waiting for me. "Come and sit with me, my little cherub." Her voice was soft and gentle. I did as she asked. "So, you know, at last," she said.

"You've always known?" I couldn't help the resentment leaking into my voice.

"Yes, and so have you, my darling. You just didn't want to see it." Nana looked at me with her familiar tender expression. "The *strange things* that you never wanted to talk about? I tried so many times to make you understand, but you always refused to face it. Deep down you knew you had special powers. It was just too hard for you to accept."

"Why didn't you tell me about Mum and Dad before?" I asked, determined not to cry. My voice wobbled a bit though.

"Because I had to protect you, darling. Your gift comes at a high price. When I realised your mother was special, I knew how hard her life was going to be. I didn't want the same for you." She looked sad. "You've led a normal life, with all the fun a child should have. I didn't want to take that away from you."

"All my life, I thought I was someone else. I haven't lived a normal life at all, Nana. I've lived a lie, and now I don't know how to change that." I leaned on the table and put my head in my hands.

"You don't have to change a thing. You're still Arianna Morelli. You didn't live a lie. You've been loved every day, and you were brought up with values like kindness and compassion." Her eyes were filled with pride. "It makes no difference if you're angel or human. You're still you, and nothing can change that."

"What about Mum? Did she know I was an angel?" I blinked away the tears.

"Of course she did. She loved you more than anything in the world. Rose always knew you were special, and she believed one day you would make an exceptional angel." She lowered her eyes. "I just wish she could have been here to tell you herself."

"I can't help feeling guilty. They died because of me." My bottom lip trembled as I spoke.

"No, Arianna, you mustn't think that way. An evil demon took their lives from you. But you'll bring them justice, I know you will." Nana seemed close to tears too. Why had we never talked like this before?

"Oh, Nana, I'm so scared."

I leaned over to reach for her. She held me tight, as I wept in her arms.

"It's all right, you cry, my darling, you cry." She cradled me like a baby.

"What do I do now, Nana?"

She dried my tears with a tissue she pulled from her pocket.

"Well, my dear. We do what we've always done. We look right ahead, we stay strong, and we do whatever is required of us." She patted my cheek gently. "I know you must feel lost, Arianna. But you'll find your way again. You always do. My Rose didn't die in vain, but only you can avenge her death."

"It sounds so surreal, Nana," I said.

"Oh, I know, darling. But you must take on your responsibilities with honour. You're a Morelli, and your father was a courageous angel of Rome. Make him proud, Arianna. Become the Angel of Light you were born to be. Don't be afraid of your gift." She held my hand tight, as silent tears rolled down my cheeks.

"I'll try, Nana. I swear I'll make you proud." I sniffed.

"I know you will. I have faith in you, Arianna." At least someone did. "Now, enough talking, how about a nice cup of tea for your old granny?"

I grinned. "Why don't you go and sit down on the sofa, Nana. I'll bring your tea in a minute." I helped her get up.

"Oh, it's at times like this I wish I had a gift too. I'd never get old and crippled." She sighed as she shuffled into the lounge.

She looked even frailer than the last time I saw her. I knew nobody lived forever, and Nana wasn't getting any younger. But the thought of losing her tore my heart apart. I couldn't bear it. Not now, not ever.

Stop it, right now. Don't think about that. I forced my

attention to the kettle boiling on the stove.

When I went into the lounge Nana was already asleep on the couch. I placed the cup on the coffee table and put the fire on.

"Oh, I'm sorry, dear. I was just resting my eyes for a minute." Nana yawned.

"It's OK. Do you want me to make you some dinner?"

Nana shook her head and turned serious. "You're not safe here. You must be with them, not me. I can't protect you the way they can."

"But what about you, Nana? You need protecting too." I sat on the floor at her feet.

"Nonsense, I'm just an old lady with no powers, my love. I'm no use to the Devil. Besides, I have Jill watching over me. She's a very loyal angel and she keeps a very close eye on me – too close for my liking, to be honest. But you have nothing to worry about."

"I do worry, you're my Nana." I put my head on her lap.

"And I love you, oh so very much, my darling. But right now the angels are the best ones to look after you. You have to trust them." She caressed my hair gently.

"I feel as if something really bad is about to happen," I whispered as I closed my eyes.

"Then you need to make sure you're ready, my child."

"I know, Nana, but right now I want to pretend I'm just Arianna, your grandchild. And you're consoling me after I've been hurt, like you've always done."

I found myself relaxing under her touch, when there was a knock on the door. I jumped up, assuming it was Keaghan coming back to collect me. Instead, it was Bruna.

"Where's Keaghan?" I said glumly.

"He's gone to London on business, didn't he tell you?"

"No, he didn't. Come in." I tried not to sound disappointed.

"Thank you, angel face." She looked around as she unfastened her leather jacket. She was wearing a black lace dress and red Dr

Martens. "Hello, Mrs Blight. It's so good to see you."

Nana didn't look pleased to see her. "You're always so loud, you people," she muttered under her breath.

"Nana, I have to go now."

She looked at me, her eyes filled with sadness. "Will I see you again before you go away?" That was an odd question.

"I'm not going far, Nana. I'm staying with the fallens tonight. Keaghan is in charge of my protection now. I'll see you soon, OK?" I hugged her tightly.

"You make sure she's safe, do you hear me?" Nana warned Bruna.

"I promise I'll guard her with my life."

Nana nodded, dismissive, before looking at me with a wistful smile. "Be careful, my darling. And remember, you can do this. Have faith." She kissed my cheek.

As soon as we walked outside I apologised to Bruna.

"Ah, she's OK. I've known your Nana a long time. She never liked us, which is quite understandable. Not many people like demons." She winked at me.

"I can't stand leaving her alone." I looked back. Nana was standing by the kitchen window, waving at me.

"She's not alone, Arianna. Angels are always around her." Bruna pointed at Jill, who was standing by the porch. She gave me a reassuring smile.

"What's this?" I looked at the huge motorbike by the pavement.

"It's my baby. A beauty, isn't she?" She caressed the leather seat, looking proud, and passed me a helmet.

"I'm not getting on that." I looked at her in panic.

"Oh, come on, angel face, don't be a chicken. You'll be safe with me. Trust me."

She put her helmet on, straddled the bike and roared the engine. I swallowed hard and then climbed on behind her. The control she had over the heavy bike was remarkable. She made it look effortless, as if she was riding a bicycle rather than a Ducati.

By the time we arrived at Keaghan's cottage, I was dizzy and my legs were shaking.

"Right, I'm on strict orders to keep you out of trouble," Bruna said. "No house parties or taking you out clubbing, or I'll be turned into a pile of ash when he comes back."

She sounded serious. Keaghan did give the impression that his orders were never disobeyed.

"Come on, angel face. You look like you're in desperate need of a party." She grabbed my hand and pulled me inside the house.

"B-but you just said Keaghan won't allow it." I looked at her baffled.

She threw me a mischievous grin. "Fallen rule number one: we don't necessarily do everything Keaghan says, we just make him believe we do."

14. ANOTHER GREAT FRIEND

Nana used to make a big point about how she expected composed and polite behaviour from a respectable young lady. I was always going to be a disappointment. My true nature was rebellious and stubborn, traits I'd been forced to suppress to keep her happy. I did my best, and most of the time I succeeded in behaving like a good girl. But keeping up that behaviour proved to be a real challenge once I met the fallens.

Within half an hour of our arrival, Keaghan's house was crammed with people I'd never seen before. Music was blasting from the stereo and alcohol was flowing freely.

"I thought you said it was going to be a small party," I said to Bruna, shouting to make myself heard.

"It is a small party," she said with a laugh. "Just concentrate on letting your hair down and have fun. I've heard you're a bit of a party animal. You gave those Feathers a run for their money all these years." She grinned at me. "I'm so glad you finally know. Now we can become friends and dedicate ourselves to having a hell of a good time together." She took a long look at my appearance, shaking her head. "We need to sort out your outfit. You look scruffy."

"I have no other clothes with me."

"Right, let's see what I can do." She pulled me up the stairs and into the bathroom.

On Bruna's instructions, I took off my hoodie. She tied my white vest top in a knot under my ribs, showing my flat belly and hip bones. Then took her silver hoop earrings and threaded them through my ears. After that, I had to stand still while she applied red lipstick and black eyeliner.

"Shake your hair upside down. There! Much better. Now get that down you." She passed me her glass, waiting for me to drink it there and then.

I downed it in one and started coughing.

"That's the spirit, angel face. Go mingle. And don't worry about these people. You're safe here, I promise."

It was true: a few hours spent dancing and drinking was exactly what I needed. I decided to stop worrying about what Keaghan would say if he ever found out. As we came down the stairs, I scanned the room to see if I knew anyone. Nope. And judging by the sharp pain in my chest – and the tinge of red in people's eyes – I doubted they were angels or human.

"It's full of fallens in here, right?" I asked Bruna.

"How did you guess?" She was being ironic.

"My heart has started doing the jungle dance in my chest. It really hurts." At least now I knew it wasn't caused by anxiety. Though I wasn't sure which was worse: that, or being caused by the presence of a load of partying demons.

"You'll be fine. Your aura will settle soon. You'll learn how to control it, trust me." Bruna passed me a beer.

Everything was going fine. The alcohol was loosening my inhibitions and I'd started dancing with Bruna. I was enjoying myself. Until Nero walked through the door.

"What the hell is she doing here?" He looked at me in disgust, as if I was covered in holy water.

"I'm the host, and if you don't like it, you know where the door is," I replied.

"You go, angel face!" Bruna laughed, putting her arm around my shoulders.

"If Keaghan finds out, he won't be pleased." Nero glared at me with loathing.

"Sometimes it's not just about pleasing him. This girl has

been through hell. She deserves a party. Right, guys?" Bruna shouted at the crowd, raising her beer bottle.

Everyone cheered and someone cranked up the volume on the music. Bruna was fun. Nero could go to hell. We were drinking and dancing, and I felt relaxed for the first time in ages. I was getting drunk. It felt great to forget about my troubles for a while.

"I think you're ace, Bruna." I shouted close to her ear as we danced. The alcohol was loosening my tongue.

"I think you're great too, Arianna."

"I feel like me again," I said.

"Good, just enjoy it and have fun. That's what life's all about." She passed me a shot glass. I downed it in one go.

I danced to another track and then stopped, swaying a bit. My head was spinning and I felt a bit queasy.

"Where are you going?" Bruna stopped dancing.

"Bathroom. Be right back." I realised I was slurring my words. Needed to ease off the alcohol.

"I'm coming with you," she said.

"Bruna." I stopped her mid-stride. "Can I at least pee on my own?"

She laughed. "All right. But be quick."

Climbing up the stairs proved quite a challenge. I was staggering from side to side, struggling to keep hold of the banisters. I hadn't realised how drunk I was till now.

"Here, let me help you."

I felt a warm hand under my elbow, and turned to look. I didn't recognise the guy. Tall, dark hair, black eyes. Buff. He smiled as he helped me up the stairs. I sensed heat coming from him, which could only mean one thing.

"Thanks," I mumbled.

He left me outside the bathroom. "Can you manage from here?"

"Sure can." I closed the door behind me but struggled with

the lock. After fiddling with it for a few seconds, I gave up.

I used the toilet and squinted at my reflection in the mirror as I washed my hands. I couldn't focus. There were two people staring back, and they both looked like me. No more alcohol tonight. I dried my hands and turned round to leave, only to find myself face to face with the guy who'd helped me up the stairs.

"What the hell are you doing in here?" I yelled.

"Thought you could use some more help," he said, licking his lips.

"No, thanks. I'm fine." A stinging throb in my chest helped me sober up. I tried to walk to the door, but he stood in front of me, blocking the way.

A surge of panic swept over me. "Get out of the way," I said. He didn't budge. "Move!"

I didn't feel drunk anymore. I took a deep breath, then another. The energy travelled from my chest to the top of my head like a fever.

"What's up, angel face? You don't want to have fun anymore?" His eyes turned red.

Did he know who I was? He pushed me backwards and I banged my hip against the sink, staggering sideways. Taking advantage of my momentary weakness, he pinned me against the wall, his arm locked around me. A hot gust spun towards me and I grew dizzy.

"You don't want to make me mad." I managed to say. "Let me go."

He laughed. "Ooh, I like it when girls play hard to get. It makes the chase much more interesting," he hissed against my ear. My heart was hammering in my chest.

I pulled my leg up and kneed him in the groin. He hardly flinched. Instead, he placed his forearm across my throat, pinning me to the wall. Damn. How did I always manage to get into trouble?

"You like to play hard, don't you, little Feather?" he said, gliding his tongue across my cheek. I shrieked, repulsed.

There was a thud, and the door flung open. Nero grabbed the guy from behind and held him by his arms as I flopped forward and gulped for air.

"I didn't know you had a death wish, Ty." Now Bruna stepped inside the bathroom, hands on hips. "I shall grant it to you immediately."

Two big men stepped forward and grabbed the guy by the throat, as Nero pushed him from behind.

"Take him out and dispose of him," Bruna instructed, her face like thunder.

They dragged him from the room, wriggling and protesting.

"Are you OK?" Bruna walked over to me, checking the burn on my neck.

"Yes, I'm fine. Thank you." I felt so embarrassed. "I'm sorry. I seem to be a magnet for trouble recently."

"Hey, that's all right." She gave me a reassuring smile. "You didn't know he was a jerk. But I did, so I followed him."

"Thank God you did," I said.

"Well, I wouldn't thank God, that's for sure. But you're welcome, angel face."

She wrapped her arm around my waist. "Come on, lightweight. I think it's time to call it a night. You're wasted."

Some time later, I woke up with a pounding headache. I couldn't even remember getting to bed. I forced my eyes open. The room was spinning and I felt sick. It was probably Keaghan's bedroom, judging by the smell of his aftershave lingering on the sheets.

The thought of him walking through the door and finding his house wrecked cured my hangover in an instant. I shot off the bed and ran downstairs. I needed to wake Bruna and start tidying up the house before Keaghan came back. At the bottom of the stairs I stopped in disbelief. The place was spotless. All the mess and all the guests had gone. It looked as if last night never happened.

I walked into the kitchen, where I found Bruna making coffee. "Did we have a party here last night, or did I dream it?" I said.

"Party? What party?" She winked. I sat on a stool, massaging my temples. She laughed, and passed me a glass of water and two aspirin.

"Too many Jagermeister shots, I think. Can't believe how much I drank." I felt sick at the thought.

"You keep forgetting, your brain still thinks you're human. You need to take it easier next time, angel face. Rumours were right, though, you truly are a party animal." She gently nudged my shoulder.

"I'm suffering for it now. If Nana saw me, I'd be in deep trouble." I held my head in my hands. "And thank you again for coming to my rescue. I owe you big time."

"Don't mention it – no, really, don't say a word about it. If Keaghan finds out, we're both dead." She looked serious. "Go and have a shower. I left some clothes for you in the bathroom. Thought you might want to freshen up before you go and see your Feather friends."

The clothes Bruna gave me weren't as bad as they could have been. Even so, the black jeans were hanging off me, my hip bones sticking out, and I wasn't too keen on the 'I HEART NY' T-shirt.

Bruna nodded in approval when I came back into the kitchen. "That's better. Don't ask me where I got them from, you wouldn't want to know. They're clean though."

I didn't feel comfortable in them anymore.

"Right, I need to get going. I'll drop you off." Bruna picked up the keys off the table.

"Where's Keaghan?"

"Don't worry, he'll be back shortly. He asked me to give you this." She passed me a black mobile phone.

"Right." I looked at it, puzzled.

"You're not allowed to give the number to anyone, unless

Keaghan agrees first. All the important numbers are on speed dial already. Mine's on top of the list." She grinned.

Ten minutes later, Bruna and I screeched to a halt outside Kayla's parents' house.

"See you soon, angel face."

I watched her ride off, happy to think that I had made another great friend.

15. MAIDSTONE

I had known Kayla, Megan and Julian since high school and had never noticed anything particularly odd about them. Not odd enough to think they might be *angels*. But now I knew why I was never hurt for more than five minutes when Kayla was around. She had always been there to heal me. I thought I knew my friends well, better than anyone. But I didn't at all. And I wondered how many more things they were hiding from me, and if I could ever trust them again.

The front door was open, and judging by the look on their faces, Kayla, Julian and Megan had been anxiously waiting for me.

"So, how did it go with the Order?" Kayla passed me a cup of coffee as soon as we were sitting around the kitchen table.

"Not as bad as I thought, I guess. I still can't believe you're all angels." I looked round at them all.

"*We're* all angels, Arianna. You need to start getting used to that." Julian smiled at me.

"Yeah, well, I can't get my head around it." I sipped my coffee, staring at Kayla's family portrait on the wall. "So, who are they really?"

"They're angels too." Kayla sighed. "They're not my parents. Just part of the cover."

"Shame. I really liked them." I shrugged, unimpressed.

Megan touched my shoulder. "I'm not an angel. But you most certainly are. How can we help you believe? What can we do?" she said.

"Wake me up and tell me that it was just a dream?" I placed my cup on the table.

"We can't do that, Arianna. But we'll be by your side every step of the way," Kayla said. "Once you start your training, everything will fall into place, you'll see."

"And when will that be?" I dreaded the answer.

"Tomorrow."

My jaw dropped wide open.

Kayla looked at me, puzzled. "Didn't you know?"

A deep voice spoke from by the door. "I was going to tell her, but you just beat me to it."

I turned round. Keaghan was standing there, hands in his pockets and an irresistible smile on his lips.

"I'd appreciate it if you knocked before coming into my house, if you don't mind," Kayla snapped.

He knocked on the kitchen door twice. "Is that better?"

I couldn't help but giggle. Kayla's face remained a cold mask.

"I'm here to pick you up," Keaghan said to me. "Are you ready?"

"She's only just got here, so, no, she's not ready," Kayla said, grabbing my hand.

"You're so boring, Kayla. When are you going to loosen up those feathers a bit?"

Julian stood tall in front of him. "Get out, now."

"Guys, please, calm down." Megan sprang up and stood between them.

"I'm ready to go." I stood and walked over to Keaghan. "I don't want you to fight because of me."

"This has nothing to do with you, Arianna. I've always despised him." Kayla's lip curled in contempt.

"Don't worry, the feeling's mutual." Keaghan gave her a wicked look, and then turned back to me. "Come on, Feather girl, we need to get going." He walked towards the front door without waiting for an answer.

"Arianna, be careful, OK? Don't trust him." Kayla held my hands tight.

I felt confused all over again. How could I not trust my protector?

Megan hugged me. "We'll see you soon. Good luck."

"See you soon, Einstein." Julian playfully messed up my hair.

"Don't worry, guys, I'll be fine. You know me." I had to swallow a lump in my throat as I followed Keaghan out.

"Are you all right?" he asked as soon as I sat in his car.

"Sure." I didn't look at him; it was hard to hide that I wasn't.

"When did you visit the Big Apple?" He nodded at my T-shirt.

I felt a rush of heat across my cheeks and looked away, embarrassed.

I remained silent as he drove fast through the countryside, heading towards the woods. The secluded road led to a tall building surrounded by a metal fence. It looked like a medieval fortress. Rain was bouncing against the windscreen and I couldn't see clearly.

Keaghan stopped and opened the car door for me. I ran through the rain towards the entrance, which stood open. As soon as I walked inside I was hit by the powerful scent of incense.

I stopped dead as I saw him. Marcus stood at the top of the staircase, gazing down at me. Next to him was Joya, a bright light shining behind them.

"Welcome to Maidstone Monastery, Angel of Light." Joya's voice echoed in the hall.

"Arianna. It's been so long. Too long." Marcus's smile was unchanged. His hair was much lighter and styled differently, but his brown eyes had the same spark. He was in great shape, as if he'd been working out, and he looked tanned.

"Marc," I whispered. I felt heat coming from Keaghan as he stood by my side.

"Look who it is: the son of Egan." Marcus came down the stairs slowly, looking directly at Keaghan.

"Look who it is: a son of a b –"

Keaghan was cut off by Joya. "Stop!" She hurried down the stairs and stood between them. "Stop it right now, both of you. This attitude is no use to anyone. Leave the past outside that door." Her voice shook with anger. "I won't tolerate this behaviour, do you understand?"

She looked at both of them, waiting for a reaction.

"I've no problem at all. I can handle his feathers," Keaghan replied with a sarcastic smile.

"Ooh, I'm shaking with fear, Blake." Marcus had the same irony in his tone.

"What did I just say? Are you both deaf? This is about Arianna and no one else, do you get that?" Joya glared at the two of them.

"As long as he stays out of my way," Keaghan replied coldly.

"Likewise."

What was going on? I couldn't understand the loathing between them.

Joya turned to look at me. "Hey, princess, are you all right?" She touched my cheek.

"I am, thanks, Joya."

Marcus cut in. "Are you going to talk to me at some point?" I looked up and met his eyes, but I couldn't say anything. I was happy to see him, yet I wanted to be angry at the same time. How could he just stand there, like nothing had happened?

I decided to ignore Marcus, and turned to Joya. "I met Lucius yesterday and you were right, he helped me understand things more."

"He's a true kind spirit. He'll guide you whenever you need him, and so will I from now on. That's what the Order is here for. I know we should have probably handled it differently –"

She was interrupted by a chuckle. "That's an understatement," I heard Keaghan mutter under his breath.

"But give us a chance to put it right." Joya ignored him and smiled at me tenderly.

Marcus came to stand in front of me, pleading with his eyes. "Arianna, come with me for a walk. All I ask is for you to hear me out. Please?"

I looked at Keaghan. I didn't know why, but I felt like I needed his approval.

"Do you want me to come?" Keaghan asked.

"I'm sure she'll be safe alone with me, Blake. I'm not the demon. I'm the good guy, remember?" They looked daggers at each other.

I spoke before Keaghan could answer. "It's OK, Keaghan. I'll be fine. You'll be waiting for me here, right?" I smiled as he hesitated, before nodding.

I followed Marcus in silence through the monastery, past huge bay windows which lined the corridor facing the garden. The rain had stopped. Marcus led the way as if he knew the place well. I didn't know what to feel. I wanted to hug him, scream at him, yell and hold him, all at the same time, but I did none of these things, just stared at his broad shoulders as he walked ahead of me. He stopped in the middle of a conservatory and stretched out his arms, looking at me, his eyes filled with remorse.

"Come on then. Punch me. I deserve it. Go ahead," he said.

I looked at him, and I did what came more naturally, something I had been dying to do ever since I saw him. I ran toward him and threw my arms around him, hugging him tight, hiding my face in his chest. He seemed surprised at first. He'd probably thought I was going to hit him. After a few seconds, he hugged me back, caressing my hair.

I realised how much I had missed him these past two years. I moved back so I could look at him.

"I didn't expect that. And I most certainly don't deserve it," he said.

"You're right, you don't." I pretended to look angry, though

I wasn't anymore.

"I'm so, so sorry, Arianna. When I heard that Aiden and Malyse had managed to get to you, I... I was so angry with myself for not being there to protect you. I couldn't get here any sooner. You have to believe me. I tried." He squeezed his eyes shut, then pulled me back into his arms and held me close again. "I would never have forgiven myself if anything happened to you." Drawing back, he stared into my eyes.

"Two years, Marcus. And not even a text or a phone call. Nothing. Did I mean so little to you?" I couldn't hold my resentment back too long.

"I know. I couldn't. I just couldn't, Arianna." He hung his head in shame. "But I wanted to, every day, I promise. I had to follow the Order's commands."

I moved away and sat down on a velvet sofa, feeling flustered. Marcus sat next to me.

"I'm an angel," I said. "And just saying it makes me sound crazy. I don't feel any different and I can't make sense of it all, Marc. It's too weird." I shook my head.

"I know it must seem illogical, but it's true. You're the most precious of all angels on earth, Arianna." He touched my cheek. "You're the Angel of Light. The powers you have are twice as strong as mine – and trust me, I'm pretty powerful."

"And how am I supposed to believe that?"

"I will train you to become who you are. I'll teach you everything I know. I promise, by the time I'm finished with you, you won't recognise yourself." He held my hand. "Just give yourself time to adjust to this new life, and when you know everything there is to know, Morfran won't stand a chance against you."

That name sent shivers down my spine.

"I was terrified, Marc. I've never seen anything like it before. Those horrible red eyes. They had flames in their hands and their faces were distorted. They looked like monsters." My voice trembled and he squeezed my hand tighter.

"I know. They're demons for a reason, Arianna. They're evil. Let me worry about them for now. It's my job to reap the life out of them and teach you to do the same." His tone was fierce.

"Keaghan's different though. If it wasn't for him and his fallens, I would be dead right now." As I mentioned Keaghan's name, Marcus's face hardened and his body tensed.

"Don't fall into his web, Arianna. Blake is dangerous. I don't trust him. I never have, and never will, and neither should you." He stood up, and looked through the window. The sun was peeping through the clouds, the auburn light glowing on his face.

"But he's here to protect me. He'd never hurt me. Joya and Lucius said he's here to keep Morfran away from me while I learn to become... an angel." It was still hard for me to believe that's what I was, and I wasn't sure if the *brainiac* in me ever would.

"He's evil beyond imagination, Arianna." His voice was cold.

"How do you know him? Why do you hate him so much?"

"We both started protecting you at the same time, as soon as your parents died." He looked at me with sad eyes. "I guess you know the truth about that now."

"Yes. And I know about Kayla, Julian and Megan too. Why do you all hate Keaghan so much? He saved my life."

He sneered. "It's his job, Arianna. That doesn't make him a good guy. Only a demon can understand how a demon's mind works." He sat back down next to me. "That's why the CO asked him to protect you."

"I already know that, and I'm not afraid of him. I trust him." I gazed into Marc's eyes with conviction.

"I'm glad you do." Keaghan's voice came from behind me and I spun round. "And I'm sure I can speak for myself should Arianna have any questions about me. I don't need you to fill her in, Feather boy. You concentrate on the training, and leave the rest to me. I presume you've been informed that I'm in charge now." Keaghan's voice was calm but harsh.

Marcus stood up to challenge him. Keaghan was considerably taller. I could feel heat waves coming from him, hurtling towards Marcus.

"Please, don't fight because of me. I thought we were all on the same side." I pushed myself between them, feeling the tension. "Keaghan, please?"

"It's nothing to do with you, Arianna. This feud goes way back before your time." Keaghan stared into Marcus's eyes intently.

"Oh come off it, Blake. It has everything to do with Arianna, isn't that right?"

"Enough, guys. What are you, eleven? I don't know where all this hatred comes from but I want it sorted, right now." They still looked tense. "Shake hands or I'm walking away from this, all right? I'm serious. Shake on it. Now."

Marcus nodded at me, before stretching his right hand out and addressing a cynical smile to Keaghan. "OK, boss, you call the shots," he said.

Keaghan shook his hand. I saw heat sizzling through their palms.

"OK, that's enough." I pulled them away quickly. "So, what's next?"

"Food," Keaghan said. "You haven't had anything to eat yet. Come on."

I followed him, Marcus walking behind me. I couldn't help but stare at the way Keaghan walked, his stride quick and effortless. The white T-shirt was tight on his shoulders, shaping the muscles on his back. His bronzed skin was glowing under the feeble sun rays coming from the windows. Marcus headed towards the dining room. I followed Keaghan outside the front door.

"Make sure you have something to eat, OK?" he said. "I have to go. Nero and Bruna need me." I didn't want him to leave. "I shouldn't be too long, a couple of days tops. You'll be safe here. You have the mobile on you, right?"

I checked my bag frantically and showed him the black phone.

"Keep it on you all the time, not in your bag. What if you forget it somewhere?" Like I did last time? Good point. "You'll be fine. I'll only be a couple of days."

It was as if he knew. His eyes looked worried even while he was trying to reassure me with his words.

"But I don't feel safe without you." I hated sounding so needy and childish. Pathetic, actually.

"Arianna, you couldn't be safer here. We're all on alert mode and we won't let our guards down ever again, I promise. You'll be busy with Walker for the next couple of months, anyway. I would only be in the way right now."

My eyes widened in shock. "I'm staying here for the next couple of months? Are you kidding me?" I fought a surge of panic.

"It's all been taken care of, don't worry. Keep the phone on you at all times. Anything happens, just call me. OK?"

He looked at me intensely and smiled, stroking my cheek with the tip of his finger. I was starting to get used to the burning sensation of his touch and the current of electricity running under my skin. It was a bearable pain. It was actually more painful having to watch him leave.

"I got to go. Good luck, Feather girl." He broke the trance by moving away from me, taking the warmth of his body with him.

I joined Marcus for dinner, and although he tried really hard to make conversation, I was in no mood to talk. I was still mad at him. Damn, he looked good though. Not hot in the way Keaghan was, but still handsome.

I wanted to stay angry at him. He left without saying goodbye, for crying out loud.

After we ate, Marcus showed me to my room, which was

buried in one of the corridors of the huge monastery. I wasn't sure I would be able to find it again on my own. The bedroom was old-fashioned, with dark furniture and bottle-green drapes from ceiling to floor. I noticed – to my surprise – that all my stuff had already been put away. My sweatshirts, my skinny jeans, my favourite knitted dress, sneakers, wellies… Wait.

"What are they?" I said, pointing at a pile of tracksuits and trainers in the wardrobe. "They're not mine."

"Ah, that'll become clear to you tomorrow." Marcus turned to leave the room.

"Hold on a minute. Is there any physical exercise involved in this training? I thought I was training to become an angel." I looked at him, alarmed.

"Yeah, you are. But you still think you're human - and a very unfit one, if I recall. I need to train your body as much as your mind… It's not as bad as it sounds." He grinned.

"You must remember how crap I am at sports, surely? I hate exercise." I shook my head in horror.

"Oh I remember all right. That's why we start nice and early tomorrow morning. See you in St George's Room at seven o'clock sharp. And wear your trainers."

He left the room before I could object, closing the door behind him.

16. TRAINING DAY ONE

The annoying buzz of the alarm clock woke me on my first day of training. As usual, I hadn't slept much. That was one thing that hadn't changed. I closed my eyes, reluctant to move. When the alarm went off for the third time, I forced myself out of bed. I pulled on a pair of black leggings, a black sweater and the dreaded trainers, as Marcus had instructed. A glance at the clock told me it was quarter past seven. My first day and, surprise, surprise, I was late.

I was supposed to meet Marcus in St George's Room, but I had no idea where that was. I rushed down the monastery's corridors, taking wrong turns and trying not to panic. They should have given me a map or a TomTom. It was gone half seven when I finally found the room. Classical music filtered through the door. I walked into the room, hoping Marcus wouldn't notice I was late. Fat chance. The curtains were drawn; the room was lit by candles. A table stood in the centre, and the music was coming from an old-fashioned gramophone against one wall. Marcus was leaning against it, his arms across his chest, wearing a tracksuit and trainers.

"Sorry I'm late, I couldn't find the room." I covered my ears with my hands. "What on earth is this noise?"

"*The Marriage of Figaro*." Opera. Just shoot me now. "Quite appropriate, since the subject of this piece is *lateness*. I don't expect you to know that. You're going to have to get used to the music. I like it, and we'll be using it during our training sessions." Great. He looked at his watch. "You're over thirty minutes late; but considering this is your first day, I'll let it go this time."

"Thank you," I said, feeling chastened.

"You only get one warning, Arianna. More late starts and I won't be as forgiving."

"That's fine." It wasn't really. "But considering I didn't find out about the training until yesterday, I guess I can be excused this once."

"Fair enough. But I expect you to take this seriously, and I won't tolerate any sarcasm or mockery in here, do you understand?"

"Yes, Marcus." I wasn't sure I liked his angelic vision.

"First thing first: this is your training schedule for the next ten weeks." *Ten weeks?* He passed me a sheet of A4 paper. "It includes a brief explanation of the activities you'll be undertaking, meals, break times and places where the training will be held. I want you to look at it carefully, so you know exactly what's expected of you every day. You have to follow it to the letter."

I stared at the sheet, realising how intense the programme was going to be. Every hour of every day was packed with physical activities, meditation and theory classes. Amongst other things, I would be studying the *Celestial Orders*, the *Bible*, the *Ancient Scrolls* and the *Book of Powers*, though I had no idea what most of them were. None of them sounded exciting.

"You've got to be kidding me. This is impossible. I can't learn all this in just ten weeks."

"Course you can. I have faith in you. Besides, you don't have a choice. It's part of your transition, Arianna." He shrugged.

"Cheers." I stared at the sheet again, overwhelmed.

"If you look at today's schedule, you're starting with a protein shake for breakfast, then there's a thirty-minute run followed by thirty minutes of stretching exercises, a quick shower break, an hour for lunch and two hours of meditation before a power walk and then dinner. I thought as it's the first day I'd go easy on you. Do you have any questions?" Dare I ask? He sounded like a sergeant barking orders at me.

"No." Every task sounded painful and unnecessary.

He passed me a glass containing a thick green liquid. Eugh. It looked vile.

"What's that?"

"Your breakfast."

My lip curled in disgust. "I can't, it looks horrible. Are you trying to kill me before we even start?" I sniffed at the gooey liquid; it smelled even worse. My stomach churned.

"It's full of energy, and trust me, you're going to need it. You must remember, Arianna, you're not a whole angel like me. You also have Lightworker blood flowing in your veins, and although it adds power to your angelic side, it also comes with human weaknesses that could be a problem. I need to train that side first, before we can move on to your angelic side. That's going to be the hardest part, because you're so unfit. Now drink." He pointed at the glass.

Oh God. I closed my eyes and gulped it down as quickly as I could. I was right. It tasted as vile as it looked.

"See? It wasn't that bad." He smirked.

I tried hard not to bring it all back up. "Not that bad? It tastes like strawberry milkshake mixed with vomit. I'm going to be sick." I held my hand over my mouth.

"No time for that, I'm afraid." He passed me a rain-jacket and pushed me out the door.

"I hate running," I moaned as I put the hood up.

"And I hate whining. You haven't changed one bit." He started running, laughing at me.

We ran through the nearby forest. It was pouring with rain, which made it even worse. After five minutes, I was already breathless, but Marcus wouldn't let me rest.

"You're so unfit, young lady, it's untrue. How do you keep so thin? It must be your angelic side, that's for sure. Come on, pick up those legs."

"And you call yourself an angel? You're a tyrant," I shouted between breaths.

"Keep up."

"Can we stop for one second, please?" I begged after fifteen minutes.

"Nope. The pain will soon go." He carried on running, without looking at me.

If only he could read my mind. When we finally returned to the monastery, I was exhausted. I collapsed on the front step to catch my breath.

"Well done. You did well to keep going, but you get a penalty for stopping once, I'm afraid." Marcus's breath sounded normal, as if he hadn't even exerted himself.

"What? It was just a second." I glared at him, gasping for air.

"Those are the rules. I said no stopping and you stopped. You'll do extra stomach crunches for punishment."

"No way. I'm not having that, Marc." I hauled myself up and glared in his eyes, challenging him.

"Keep complaining and you'll go without lunch as well. You choose." He walked inside the monastery, leaving me in the pouring rain.

"OK, OK, I'll do more crunches then." I followed him inside, my legs wobbling.

"Right, let's get on with some stretching and toning exercises. Then you have ten minutes for a shower and I'll get you some lunch before we go and meditate."

I didn't like the sound of any of that, apart from the food. I was starving.

An hour or so later, I was sitting cross-legged on the floor in St George's Room, trying to meditate. I was still ravenous. Lunch had been a bowl of chicken soup and a bread roll.

"Concentrate, Arianna. This is the part of the training where we prepare your human side to switch off and let your spiritual side take over. Once you can do that, you become untouchable, pretty much invincible."

I looked sideways at him. He was standing by the mirror. His blonde hair was falling around his forehead; the white vest was tight on his chest, enhancing the muscles around his shoulders and arms. He looked handsome – when he wasn't bossing me around.

"And how do I do that?" I asked.

"With practice and patience. And a lot of hard work."

"I'm a quick learner, remember?" I smirked.

"When it comes to solving equations, maybe. This is far from rational, which means you'll struggle with it – big time." He pointed at the full-length mirror. "What do you see, Arianna?"

My reflection. "I see... green eyes, a nose, a mouth, long dark hair that could do with a trim, actually. No wings, no halo." I couldn't help resorting to sarcasm.

"Arianna, you need to take this seriously. It isn't a joke." Marcus looked irritated.

"OK, OK, I'm sorry. I'll try again." I took a deep breath, focusing on my reflection. "It's not easy with this music. It's dreadful. Are we at a funeral or something? Can't we have something from the twenty-first century?"

Marcus shook his head. "I can't believe you don't appreciate *Adagio in G minor*. You bring shame to your heritage, Arianna." He stood and turned the music off, clearly disappointed. "I knew this would be hard, but you're not helping at all. It's not about the music. It's about learning to do things even when you don't want to, when you don't like them." He ran his hand through his hair, frustrated.

"You're right. I'm sorry. Just be patient with me, OK? I'm really going to try. Put the music back on, please?"

I tried to ignore the music and concentrated instead on the words Marcus was whispering.

"Try imagining what goes on beyond your superficial self. The inner you, Arianna." I heard him take a deep breath. "Listen to the sound of the violin. Let each note enter your being, and feel the vibrations tingling across your skin. Keep your eyes closed and picture who you really are."

I tried to keep a straight face, but a laugh burst from my throat. I couldn't help it.

"Oh, this is useless." Marcus shook his head, furious.

"Oh come on. You have to admit it sounds a bit weird. Picture who I really am? I know who I am." Or so I had thought. I stopped giggling. "Sorry."

"I'm going to leave you to it." He turned the music off again. "You figure out a way to stop messing around and concentrate, and then we can talk. I'm not wasting my time like this. If you're not in the mood for serious meditation by the time I'm back, you'll have no dinner tonight. I mean it, Arianna." He walked out, slamming the door behind him.

Oh for goodness' sake. I didn't ask for this to happen. Up to a few days ago, I thought I was a normal seventeen-year-old girl living a normal life – well, normalish. Now I was supposed to believe I was an angel, just like that. It was better when I'd believed I was mentally ill. It was easier to deal with.

In the mirror, I saw my mum's emerald eyes staring back at me. I took a deep breath, sat down again in front of the mirror, and this time I really looked. After ten minutes, nothing had happened. I still couldn't figure out what Marcus wanted me to see. I closed my eyes and tried to relax, breathing in and out and concentrating on the sound of my breaths. Still nothing. By the time Marcus was back, I was curled up on the floor, pulling split ends from my hair. I didn't even hear him come in. I shot to my feet. He looked at me, frowning in disappointment.

"I swear I've been trying for the past God knows how long," I said, feeling disheartened.

"We need to get your body tired, so your soul will become more cooperative. Get your trainers back on. We're going for a power walk."

I couldn't believe it. "More exercise? Oh, no, please, Marc," I moaned.

Without warning, I found myself blinded by the light shining above his head. I stepped backwards, gasping, hitting the table behind me.

"How did you do that?" I pointed at his head, aghast.

The light disappeared. "It's what I've been trying to get you to do all afternoon: engage your aura. But there's plenty of time, I guess. We can't expect miracles on day one."

The sight of Marcus's aura made everything seem a lot more real. I knew what that shining beam of light was. I'd seen it in my reflection before, but I had no idea how to make it happen.

After the exhausting power walk and another quick shower, we went in for dinner in St Antony's Room. I was starving and all I could think about was pizza, lasagne, garlic bread and KFC. Instead, the housekeeper placed a plate of asparagus, broccoli, sweet potatoes and grilled salmon in front of me.

"Eugh. What's this?" I groaned.

"Dinner. Take it or leave it, there's nothing else." Marcus looked at me from the corner of his eye, suppressing a smirk.

"I don't like you as an angel, I preferred you as my b... friend." I blushed, looking down at my plate. There was a brief silence.

Marcus sighed. "I'm sorry I left without saying goodbye. I always wanted to explain, but I couldn't at the time." He placed the fork on his plate, looking sad. "I was assigned a task in Sydney. I had to do what the Order told me to; but trust me, I didn't choose to leave you."

I nodded, moving the food on my plate. "It's OK. It's in the past. You had a duty to fulfil. You're an angel. That always has to come first. I get it." I didn't though.

"Still, I should have said goodbye properly."

Yeah. You should have. "Like I said, it's in the past. It doesn't matter now."

We spent the rest of the meal in silence. After dinner, Marcus left me at the top of the stairs.

"Night, angel. You did better than I expected today. Keep up the good work – but please, cut the whining. It really doesn't suit you. Bring out the fighter I know you are." He smiled.

I watched him walk down the corridor before I finally closed my bedroom door behind me for the day. Every muscle in my body ached, including places where I didn't think I had muscles. As I started running a bath, I heard the phone ringing. I rushed to pick it up.

"Keaghan, where are you?"

"I'm still in London. Why? Is everything OK?"

"If the definition of *OK* is being mentally and physically tortured by the Reaper Angel, then yes, I'm OK."

I heard him laughing on the other end of the line. "I take it the training has started then?"

I could picture his smile. "Oh yeah. It's hard work. I've been running, stretching, meditating and walking. I've hardly eaten anything all day. I had fish for dinner tonight. Fish! I hate fish. I want to die." I lay down on my bed, staring at the ceiling. "And if I'm late or I do something wrong, he punishes me by making me do more exercises. You should see my training schedule. Ten weeks of pure torture. It's hell." I knew I must sound like a wimp.

"Nothing is like hell, trust me." He obviously knew all about that. "Just do as he tells you, Arianna. I know he can be a pain in the backside, but he knows what he's doing. You'll get there in the end. Just keep working at it. I'll come and see you soon."

My heart leapt at the thought. "I hope so – and bring me some chocolate when you do, please? And pizza and chips." I heard him chuckling.

"Gosh, he is starving you. Don't give up. Show him you can do it. I know you can."

His optimism filled me with self-belief. "I'll do my best, I promise."

"Talk later, Feather girl."

And just like that, he was gone.

17. LIEUTENANT WALKER

My second day of training was as dreadful as the first, if not worse. The long run and stomach crunches I did the day before had knocked me out. Every muscle in my body had seized up and I could hardly move. Even so, Marcus had no pity and dragged me out for a morning run, after I'd endured another breakfast of vomit shake.

Even worse was when I saw what I had for lunch. "Is that it?" I stared at my plate of tuna salad.

I detested fish. Twice in one week was too much. I couldn't finish it.

"Stop sounding so ungrateful, Arianna," Marcus warned.

After a power walk in the afternoon, Marcus closed the day's session with another hour of meditation. He placed candles and incense sticks around the room. The scent was strong enough to kill a demon. I tried hard to breathe, concentrate and relax. I did everything he asked, but I still couldn't "engage my aura".

"I know you can do it," Marcus kept repeating.

"I know I can. I've seen it before. But I don't know how I did it. Maybe if I see you do it again, it might help," I said, frustrated.

"OK, let's try that." He sat in front of me on the floor. "Give me your hands. See if you can feel it."

We joined hands and Marcus closed his eyes. I watched closely as he projected light from his shoulders, rising to the top of his head. It was bright, but not blinding this time, its warmth expanding like sunshine. I closed my eyes and took a deep breath. A warm sensation spread from my chest, moving to my head. A beam of energy radiated out.

"That's it, Arianna. You're doing it. Don't break the concentration now."

Marcus's voice made me open my eyes. I sighed in frustration. "Why did you speak? I've lost it now."

"Sorry. Major progress there though. It wasn't a strong one, but there was definitely a start of an aura there. Great job. Again?" He took my hands in his once more.

After the third time I'd managed to get a small aura shining, I felt exhausted.

"It'll tire you out at first, but then it'll become second nature," he said. Maybe this was why I felt so worn-out all the time. "You've earned a rest. Go and lie down for a while. I'll see you at dinner. Kayla and Julian will be joining us." Marcus helped me stand up.

I felt light headed, and could barely walk. "I've missed them. Thank you, Marc." I placed a kiss on his cheek.

He jerked away, looking surprised. "What was that for? I'm torturing you, and you kiss me? Maybe I need to torture you more." He laughed, holding my arm to help me up the stairs.

"Oh, shut up. You torture me enough, thank you. I'm just grateful for all the time you're wasting on me, trying to make me something I'm still not sure I am."

He stopped outside my room and looked at me with his intense eyes.

"Now listen to me," he said, "no one is wasting anything here. You're worth all the effort and time that's going into this." He smiled, holding my face with both hands. "You're becoming the angel I know you are – and you'll see it very soon too, I promise."

"Even if it takes months?" I winced.

"Even if it takes years."

His face was close to mine. I could feel his breath on my

cheek. It would have been so natural just to lean forward and kiss him.

"See you at dinner, Arianna." He pulled away, looking uncomfortable.

"Yeah, see you later."

I closed my bedroom door, leaned against it and took a deep breath, feeling flustered and confused. I used to think I was in love with Marcus, till he left without an explanation and broke my heart. He was my first kiss – and my last. But first and foremost we'd been best friends from the start. We always had a special connection, and now I knew why. But something had changed. Or should I say, someone had changed me.

After a nap, I went down for dinner. As I walked into the dining room, Kayla came towards me for a hug.

"Kay, I feel like I haven't seen you in weeks." I was so happy to see her.

"It's only been two days. But I know what you mean. Two days' training can feel like two months in here. I hear you're working very hard, and you're actually *exercising*." She supressed a laugh.

"Yes, the torture has truly begun." I pulled a face at Marcus.

Julian smiled at me from across the table. "You have a session of Tai Chi with me tomorrow, so you better be ready."

"And Yoga with me, straight after." Kayla sat down by my side.

"Have I?" I grimaced.

"Haven't you got a timetable yet?" Kayla raised her eyebrows at Marcus.

"Oh yes, she has. She just hasn't read it properly." He glared at me.

After dinner, Kayla and I sat in the lounge, drinking coffee. "So how are you really coping?" she asked.

"Honestly? Like I'm in the army, getting ready to go to war." I sighed. "Although I'm sure soldiers get fed better than I do."

"Well, you're not far off. You are getting ready for battle. I don't want to scare you or anything, but facing Morfran and his demons is like going to war. This isn't going to be easy, but it's necessary. And you can do it." She squeezed my hand.

"I miss my Nana. I miss you and Megan. It's only been two days and I'm already finding it so hard. How am I going to cope for ten weeks?"

"What's this attitude, Arianna? You're better than this, come on. Show me some spirit. You can so do this."

I wished I could share her confidence.

Marcus walked into the lounge with Julian. "Is she whining again?" Marcus said.

"Me? Nah. I was just telling Kay how you've been piercing my eardrums with classical music and trying to intoxicate me with candles and incense. Oh, and let's not mention training for the London Marathon. I've blisters the size of potatoes on my feet."

"It'll get easier, I promise," Kayla said, and Julian nodded in agreement. "All new angels have to go through training. We did too."

But it didn't get easier. In fact, the next day was even harder.

After my vomit shake breakfast and the usual morning run, I joined Julian in the conservatory. He was sat on the floor with his legs crossed, wearing loose white trousers and a white vest. I had never noticed his toned body before. He was actually quite fit.

"Ready for your Tai Chi class?" he said.

"And what kind of torture is that?"

"Don't start moaning." He frowned. "I've never known you to be defeatist and negative."

"I was only asking." I rolled my eyes. "Come on, you've known me long enough to know I hate this kind of stuff."

"This stuff – as you call it – is going to help you connect with your aura, wherever you are, and in any situation. I'm the

Overseer Angel, which means I need to be able to orb from one place to another very quickly. Tai Chi helps me connect with my spirit and control the outside world so it doesn't affect my powers. It'll help you stay focused, regardless of noise, distractions – and in your case, tiredness."

I was determined to try really hard. "OK. Let's do this."

"That's the spirit. Let's start with some stretching."

I did everything Julian asked, but I couldn't help giggling at some of the exercises. He wanted me to create an *energy ball* between my hands and move it from side to side, very slowly. According to him, I should be feeling the connection of energy between my two hands. I felt something all right – I felt stupid.

Despite my giggles, Julian was very patient, but at the end of the class he sat me down, looking serious.

"Arianna, you need to start believing. This is the main barrier stopping you becoming who you are: you think all this is funny – it's not."

"I'm trying, Julian, I really am. But you have to understand that I've been 'Arianna the human' all my life, and now I'm supposed to believe I'm this angel with powers I don't even know how to switch on."

"I know you think you're trying hard, but until you start believing that you're the Angel of Light, you won't become it. And that's exactly what Morfran is hoping will happen, because that will make his job a lot easier." Hearing the name made me shiver as it always did. "He's right on your wings, but you can't see it because you don't believe it. I can't make you believe it. None of us can, but we can be here for you and support you with the best possible training. We'll never give up on you."

His words touched me. "I won't let you down, I promise." I hugged him.

"I know you won't." He pulled back and messed up my hair playfully.

I needed clarity and focus. It was time for me to seriously

commit. It was going to be tough but I needed to start believing, or I'd be wasting everyone's time and effort for nothing.

My next challenge was Yoga with Kayla.

"Arianna, Yoga is a discipline that, like Tai Chi, will help you stay relaxed in difficult situations. It will enable you to control physical perceptions like cold, heat and pain. That way you'll be able to shut out your human side and connect with your powers quicker."

We sat on a mat, candles flickering around us. Instead of music, Kayla was using sounds, like ocean waves, birds singing and the wind blowing. After an hour of deep breathing, trying to do different bends and twists and learning how to hold a "Revolved Triangle" pose, Kayla brought the class to an end by placing her hands on my head. I felt a beam of energy run through my body, and heat race to the tips of my toes. For a moment I thought I was about to levitate.

"Very good, Arianna. Not bad for a first-timer. You'll soon see the results, trust me." She put her arm around me.

"I wish I wasn't half human. It would make things so much easier." I looked through the bay window at the dark outside.

"Don't be silly. It can be an advantage, you know? You can feel things that I never can or will. I eat but I can't really taste – not like you do, anyway. I breathe but I don't know what it really feels like. I'm borrowing this body; I don't own it. I can't feel the waves of the sea caress my skin, or the wind blow in my face." I never realised how precious those little things were. "And you're not just any half human. You have Lightworker powers too. That's what makes you so unique. It takes a very special bond to create someone as wonderful as you."

I felt a wave of emotion, thinking of my parents. "Stop it. You're going to make me cry."

"I mean it. You're so special. We're lucky to have you on our side. You'll make an outstanding Angel of Light, Arianna Morelli." She nudged my shoulder. "Now, we best go get ready for dinner. I bet you're starving. See you shortly, angel." She walked back with me and left me by the staircase.

I checked my phone for the fourth time that day. No missed calls or text messages from Keaghan. How disappointing.

Kayla, Julian and Marcus were already sat at the table when I arrived for dinner, and all wearing white clothes again. I wondered if it was some sort of "angelic uniform".

"Hello, angel. Have you missed my tortures this afternoon?" Marcus said with a cheeky grin.

"Not one bit, thank you," I answered. "I'm starving. I could eat a horse."

I wolfed down my grilled chicken and veg. "Not that I'm whining or anything, but can I have something else? Surely you're not just going to feed me vegetables with every meal? Chips would be nice." I looked at my empty plate, still hungry.

"Nothing else, I'm afraid." Marcus said. "You've eaten enough proteins and carbs to give you the strength you need." Enough for a hamster, maybe.

"It's not like I'm fat. I don't need to be on a diet," I protested.

"You're not on a slimming diet, Arianna. You're on a balanced regime. I've replaced your junk-food diet with healthy meals. How many times must I repeat myself?" He shook his head.

"But I like junk food... I feel like I'm back in primary school. It's ridiculous," I snorted.

Julian looked at me. "He was a tyrant with us too, Arianna, so don't think it's just you. Isn't that right, Lieutenant Walker?"

"Enough now. Arianna needs her sleep. Come on, time for you to go," Marcus instructed.

"Hang in there. It will get easier." Kayla smiled, before closing the front door behind them.

After they'd gone, I saluted Marcus, army style. "Night then, Lieutenant Walker."

"Good night, Arianna. Seven o'clock sharp, yes? Remember,

no more late starts. And read the schedule this time, please," he shouted down the corridor before I closed my bedroom door.

I never thought meditation could be so exhausting. At least it was helping me sleep a bit better. But I was never free of nightmares for long. Before I went to bed, I picked up the phone to check for messages again. It started ringing in my hand.

"Is everything OK?" Keaghan didn't even say hi. He sounded anxious.

"Yeah, everything's good. Why?" I asked.

"I just... Nothing. Just making sure you're OK."

I heard a female voice in the background. Didn't sound like Bruna. I felt a stab of jealousy.

He hung up, leaving me holding the phone, gobsmacked.

That had to have been the most bizarre call ever. I couldn't figure him out. All I wanted was to hear his voice.

18. MENS SANA
IN CORPORE SANO

The timetable left no spare time in my daily routine. Marcus had arranged ten weeks of misery, in every single detail. True to his word, there was a lot more running, meditation, and agonising exercise routines. My knowledge of classical music was improving, but I still detested it. I endured a daily breakfast of vomit shakes, which weren't getting any tastier. My muscles were sore and I still wasn't seeing any sudden breakthroughs on my angelic side. The first thing I did when I walked into my bedroom each night was check my phone, but I'd had no more calls or text messages from Keaghan. I missed him.

At last, it was the end of my first week of training.

Marcus lit the last candle in St George's Room, ready for imparting another hour of mental torture. "Joya is planning a visit soon to see how you're progressing. Oh, and Keaghan is back in Featherstone."

"Right, sounds good."

I tried to sound casual, but I felt a pulse of excitement.

"Arianna, I want to try and trigger your aura again," Marcus said, before turning on the music.

I cringed as one of his favourite gloomy tunes filled the room. "I can't wait," I muttered.

No matter how hard I tried, I still couldn't control my aura. Yet again, I went to bed feeling defeated, upset and disappointed in myself. I didn't know what else to do. I was trying, but Marcus didn't seem to understand how difficult it was for me.

The phone rang, making me jump; my heart started pounding.

"Hello, Keaghan," I answered in a low voice, trying not to cry.

"Is everything OK?"

"Yep." I rushed out the answer.

"You don't sound OK. Has the Reaper upset you?"

His concerned tone made me feel even sorrier for myself. "No." I tried to hold back the tears, but they flowed regardless.

"Arianna? Talk to me. What's the matter?"

I sniffed. "I'm fine, really. I'm just tired." I dried my tears.

"Come on, tell me," he insisted.

"I just feel... helpless. I'm trying so hard and I don't feel any different apart from the fact that my body is aching like hell; I can't stand his vomit shakes in the morning, he's literally starving me and if I listen to more classical music I'll explode! He wants me to take meditation seriously when he expects me to hum like a cow. I'm useless. I really don't think I can do this, Keaghan." I was speaking so fast, I hadn't realised he was chuckling until I stopped for breath.

"Arianna Morelli, you make me laugh so much. I was hoping you'd give Walker a hard time. I bet he's well frustrated."

"He's doing his best. I'm just rubbish at everything," I moaned.

"Arianna, you need to be more patient. You can't give a bird wings and expect it to fly straightaway. It takes time. Don't be so hard on yourself, Feather girl. When you least expect it, you'll know exactly what to do. There'll be plenty of rewards, I promise." He was smiling, I could tell.

"Like chocolate brownies and blueberry muffins?" My stomach rumbled. I heard him laugh again.

"Whatever you want, Feather girl. Now take a deep breath, get under the covers and go to sleep. I'll see you tomorrow. OK?"

My heart bounced in my chest. I didn't want him to hang up. What I really wanted was to have his arms around me and have him tell me everything was going to be OK.

"Are you coming to see me?" I sounded too eager.

"Only briefly. Everything's going to be OK, Arianna. I promise."

I could swear there were times when I thought he could read my mind.

When I woke up the next day, I was shaking and short of breath after a bad dream. I wasn't as afraid as I used to be. At least I knew now who was chasing me in the dark. The thought still petrified me, but I could control my fears better.

Marcus had planned another day of suffering, starting off with the usual gruelling run. Today, the road that led to the woods was mucky and wet. The run was going to be even harder and more unpleasant than usual.

"I was hoping you'd start enjoying this at some point." Marcus shook his head at me as I struggled to run up a hill.

"Are you mental? I'll never enjoy this."

The rain lashed my face, and I cursed. Marcus grabbed my hand and pulled me until we came off the muddy path. We reached the main road and Marcus kept on prompting me to run faster, until at last I could see the monastery in the distance.

I increased my speed, aiming for a final sprint, but I was still well behind Marcus until he slipped and fell. With a surge of adrenaline, I ran faster than I had ever done before and reached the main gate a split second before him. I knew he had let me win. We were both still laughing when I realised we weren't alone.

"Keaghan?" My voice squeaked as I gazed at him standing by the metal gate.

"Oh, look who's here." Marcus scowled at him.

Keaghan sneered. "Sounds like you're enjoying your training after all."

"H-hi. It's good to see you." I smiled, blinking at him through the rain.

"Can you tell your *dogs* to let me in?" Keaghan said.

Huh? What dogs? As I looked up, I realised angels were standing on the roof, guarding the monastery from above. They were too high up for me to take a proper look at them. I could just about see the light gleaming from their auras. Marcus nodded at them, and the gates opened. Keaghan strode in and I walked next to him. Marcus was instantly at my other side.

"How's everything? Any news?" I struggled to keep up with Keaghan's long stride.

"All is fine. Have you made any progress?" Keaghan asked, his voice cold.

"Did you want anything, Blake?" Marc interrupted me before I could reply.

"Not from you, Walker."

"Well, Arianna's busy at the moment. She's on a very tight schedule." Marcus put his arm around my shoulders.

"She's entitled to a break. I'm her prime guardian and you can't stop me seeing my protectee. Check with the Order, if you like." Keaghan had a hint of a victorious smile on his lips.

Marcus didn't look pleased, but it seemed he had no choice. He placed a kiss on my cheek and threw an icy look at Keaghan as he left. What was that for? I was thrown by his sudden display of affection.

I tried to hide how happy I was to be alone with Keaghan, but I stumbled on the steps. I would have fallen if he hadn't been quick enough to catch me. I breathed in his scent, feeling the familiar sweltering breeze from his body.

"W-would you like a coffee?" I mumbled, staring into his eyes.

"Sure," he said.

His proximity still made me feel nervous and uncomfortable like the first time. He finally released me, but my heart was still hammering and my skin was burning where he'd touched me.

Keaghan lit the fire in St Helen's Room with a flick of his

finger. Even so, I still found it difficult to believe he was a demon. I sat by the flames, trying to dry my wet hair and muddy clothes.

"I hate the rain dripping down my back."

I was trying to make conversation – shame it was the dumbest conversation ever. His eyes were glued to me, making me feel nervous.

The housekeeper walked in with a tray of fresh coffee, breaking his spellbinding gaze. As Keaghan handed me a cup, my fingers brushed against his hand. Feeling a current running down my arm, I jerked away, spilling some coffee. Argh. Stop acting like a complete idiot.

"Have you brought me any chocolate?" I asked to cover my confusion.

He pulled an irresistibly sexy smile. "Not this time. But keep up the good work and we'll see." I had a feeling he was a bit anxious too.

There was a brief, awkward silence. I hoped the sound of the crackling fire covered the thumping of my heart.

"What's happening in London, Keaghan?"

His jaw tightened and he ran a hand though his raven hair.

"I have a feeling this isn't just a social visit." I frowned.

He looked at me and sighed. "You always were smart. We've been tracking down demons around the area, and we've found a few. But you don't need to worry. My best fallens are on their tracks." His face relaxed into a smile. "As long as you're here, I'm not worried: you're in the safest place you could possibly be right now. I'm going back to Featherstone tonight to check on your Nana. She's safe too, Arianna, there's nothing for you to worry about." His eyes sparkled in the glow of the fire. "Apart from my wrath, if you ever host another party in my house behind my back." He looked serious for a second, before smiling again.

"H-how did you find out?" Mortified, I covered my face with my hands.

"I know everything, Arianna." He winked. "I just make Bruna believe I don't."

"I'm so sorry. It wasn't Bruna's fault, honest. I hope you weren't cross with her," I said.

"I'm used to her behaviour. Don't worry, she's fine. By the way, she says she can't wait to test your powers." He looked at me, his eyebrows raised in challenge.

"Well, she'll have to wait a while. It won't be anytime soon," I said glumly.

"Don't be too hard on yourself, Feather girl. If you carry on working hard you'll be in full possession of your powers well before your birthday." He gazed at me as he stood up slowly. "I've got to go now, but I'll be back soon. I need to keep an eye on Walker, make sure he doesn't use his whip too much."

He walked over to me and brushed my cheek with his finger, smiling at me in his sensual way. I wished he would hold me. Kiss me. Kiss me, now. I beg you.

"Make sure you do." I said shyly.

We looked in each other's eyes, frozen for a few seconds. I didn't want him to leave, and I had a feeling he didn't want to go.

"Be safe, OK?" He tapped my nose, sending shivers along my spine.

I watched him walk to the front door and shut it behind him. I felt alone and cold.

At least I had my first Combat class to distract me. I watched Marcus as he showed me the basic technique. It looked like martial arts, and there was a lot of body contact, throwing and kicking. I didn't know much about Jiu-Jitsu but I didn't think it was meant to be so aggressive. Marcus kept yelling at me, expecting me to get it right first time. What was up with him?

"You're fighting with your body and not your mind. That's why you're getting so tired."

His tone was unsympathetic and frustrated. "You're an

angel, Arianna, and you need to fight like an angel. That means you forget about your body and you engage your spirit. Once you do that, you'll be able to punch forever and never get tired."

"And how the hell do I do that?" I replied, drying my sweat with a towel.

"I can't tell you. Only you know how to switch your powers on. I'm giving you the tools but it's up to you to work out how to use them. You need to concentrate, Arianna." His harsh tone hurt me.

"That's unfair, Marc. I am concentrating. I've never done this before. You make it sound so easy but it isn't. I can't do this anymore. I want to stop." I threw the towel on the floor.

"I never said it would be easy. But you'll do as I say, Arianna. You have no choice. You stop when I say you can."

"Why are you being so cruel? I don't know what I've done to make you angry, but I don't deserve this. I'm working my butt off, and you don't seem to even notice." I was close to tears.

"Don't start whining, Arianna. I'm really losing my patience. Go for a shower and cool down that head of yours before you even think about coming down for dinner." He strode out of the room, looking furious.

Marcus didn't speak to me when I walked in and sat down at the table. There was no reason for him to be so nasty. I was trying my best but it wasn't good enough for him.

I stared at my plate: sliced turkey breast with a mountain of veg – again.

"Are you planning to starve me? No, really, I'm being serious now. I'm not whining or anything, but seriously?"

"I'm feeding your spirit more than your body. *Mens sana in corpore sano*."

"Do I really want to know what that means?"

"Healthy mind in a healthy body. They're both equally important, Arianna. One cannot live without the other, especially in a half angel." He still didn't look at me.

"Whatever. At this rate it's more like healthy mind in a starved body." I snorted, eating the food in silence. I would have given anything for a burger and fries.

"See you in the morning." Marcus stood up and left the room before I'd even finished.

It had been another tough day, and I was glad it was finally over. As I opened the door and walked in my bedroom, I had a feeling I wasn't alone in the room. The pain in my chest warned me that something wasn't right. Fire was burning through my core. I closed the door, switching the light on. As I turned round, I jumped and screamed.

"You scared me to death!" I yelled.

Keaghan was sitting in the armchair by the side of the bed.

"Sorry, I didn't mean to frighten you." Yet somehow he always managed to do just that.

"How come you're back so soon?" I looked at the window. "And how did you get in?"

"Sit down, Arianna."

His face was serious. I felt a shiver of apprehension in his manner as I sat on the edge of the bed, waiting for him to talk. His face told me that this wasn't good news.

"I went back to Featherstone to check on your Nana, but someone beat me to it."

I brought my hand to my mouth. "Nana!" I felt a stab of panic.

"She's OK. Jill and Father Chris are with her at Milton Abbey. She's safe, don't worry." He touched my hand; his heat passed through my skin like a flame.

"What happened?" I murmured.

"They set the place on fire."

I gasped. "Oh no. Who?"

"We don't know yet. Bruna is trying to salvage whatever she can. I'm sorry, Arianna. We didn't see it coming."

I sprang up. "You said there were people protecting my

house, my family and the people I love. I'm here, locked in this hell-hole, working my butt off trying to become this *angel* you all want me to be, and all you can say is *I'm sorry?*" I threw the words in his face.

"Arianna, I was in London, I didn't –"

I interrupted him. "You didn't what, Keaghan? Give a damn? What was so urgent in London? Oh, I forgot, I'm not allowed to know. But it's OK for you to come here and tell me my house has been burned down and you didn't see it coming!" I was desperate not to cry, but tears were falling down my cheeks. "What am I supposed to do with that?"

I turned away from him as I started to sob. I felt his hand on my arm. He pulled me towards him and held me close to his chest. He was so tall and strong, I felt lost in his embrace. One of his arms curled around my waist, his other hand resting on my head. Sparks ran under my skin and across my body.

"I know. I'm sorry. I've let you down – again. Shush, it's OK. It'll be OK, Arianna. I'll sort it, I promise," he whispered in my ear.

Keaghan held me tight in his strong arms. After a while, he loosened his grasp, dried my eyes with his hands and smiled tenderly.

"I'm sorry," I said. "You must think I'm such a wimp. All I seem to do these days is cry."

I walked to the bathroom to wash my face. Back in the bedroom, I crawled onto the bed, hugging my knees to my chest.

"You're not a wimp. I'm so sorry, Arianna. Bruna and Nero are doing everything they can to save as much as possible. Your Nana is safe. I promise this won't happen again. I swear to you." He sat on the bed, hanging his head in shame.

"It wasn't your fault... I know he's getting closer." I swallowed. "My dreams are getting clearer. The shadow has red eyes, and I can make out the other features a bit more now. He has a scaly skin, red-coloured and shiny. But the black hood stops me from seeing the rest. " I closed my eyes to shut down the image in my head.

"I'm going to be honest with you, Arianna. Morfran knows who you are. His followers know where you live and who is protecting you." He levelled his eyes with mine. "But I've got my best fallens on it, day and night. I swear no one will find you here. From now on, I'm not going to leave your side."

He touched my cheek. I jerked as my skin was singed. A hot blast of air encircled me like a tropical breeze.

A thought occurred to me. "We'd better wake Marcus up. We should tell him what's happened."

As I stood up, Keaghan grabbed my arm. "He knows."

My jaw dropped. "Why didn't he say anything to me at dinner?" I couldn't believe he'd hidden such a thing from me. That must be why he'd been in such a foul temper before.

"The CO has probably ordered him not to." Keaghan sounded cynical. "They'll want Joya to break the news."

"But you came here to tell me immediately. Why?" I gazed at him, searching him.

"Because I promised never to lie to you again. I hated having to hide from you all these years."

His expression was so intense, it took my breath away. He cares for me?

"Can I ask you a favour?" I whispered.

"Depends on the favour, but yeah, go ahead."

"Will you stay here and keep me company? I don't think I'm going to be able to sleep. I don't want to be alone. Please? I know I must sound pathetic. It's just... I – I'm being silly, I'm sorry. Forget I asked," I mumbled, looking away to hide my embarrassment.

"Of course I will." His quick answer surprised me. He took off his leather jacket and put it on the chair by the dressing table. "I said I'm never going to leave you from now on, and I meant it. Can I get you anything? Water? Tea?"

"I – I'm OK." I cleared my throat; my mouth was dry.

"I'll go and get you some water. I won't be long." He took one look at me, then closed the door behind him.

I was shaking. My heart was thrashing with excitement and panic. Oh my God. I couldn't believe Keaghan was going to stay with me tonight – and every night from now on. I pulled on my pyjamas and buried myself under the duvet.

"Wow, in bed already?" he said when he came back a minute later.

I took the glass from his hand and gulped the water down.

"Try and get some sleep, Arianna. I'll be here."

He took the empty glass from my hand and sat in the armchair. I lay down, turning my back to him. I was certain I could feel him watching me.

"Night, Keaghan," I whispered.

"Good night, Feather girl."

"If I fall asleep, don't go. Please stay," I mumbled.

"I'm not going anywhere."

The grass was soft under me. I heard a dragging noise from a distance, creeping up slowly. Something was on my leg. A slimy, slippery creature was crawling on me. The scarlet snake was smooth, gripping my skin as it crawled to my chest. The hissing turned into a cracking sound, like bones snapping. Red and gold eyes stared into mine as the snake twisted its head, allowing its jaw to dislocate. As it opened its mouth wide, the forked tongue swirled. I screamed.

I woke to find myself in Keaghan's arms, dripping with sweat. He tried to hold me still, but I was kicking and screaming.

"Hey, hey, it's OK. Arianna, it's me, Keaghan. Wake up!"

I opened my eyes. I was in my bedroom. I threw my arms around his neck, shivering.

"It's all right, I'm here." He caressed my hair. I clung to his chest as if my life depended on it. I kept my eyes shut, breathing in the intense scent of his aftershave. "I've been trying to wake you for ages. You were in a trance. What was it?" He pulled back, drying the sweat off my forehead with his hand.

"It was him. I'm sure of it. It was him."

"Tell me what you saw," he said, intensity in his eyes.

"A red snake. Crawling on my body. Its eyes were staring at me. It was him, Keaghan, it was Morfran. He's coming to get me. I know he is." I couldn't stop shaking.

"It's OK. Calm down." He cupped my face in his hands. "He might burn down your house, slither into your dreams, but he won't get to you unless it's through me."

Those blue eyes bored into mine. The sparks firing from them made me think of a lightning strike. His hands stroked my cheeks and his warm touch ignited a blaze inside me. God, if I was under a spell, don't break it.

"Why a snake?" My teeth were chattering.

"He's a demon, Arianna. He's trying to scare you. Your subconscious perception of what a demon looks like is heightened in your dreams. Once you can control it, he won't be able to frighten you anymore." He moved my hair away from my face; his smile made me feel warm and fuzzy. "Try and get back to sleep." He laid me down gently, tucking me under the covers, and sat back down in the chair.

But I was too terrified to close my eyes and risk seeing *him* again.

"I don't want to fall asleep," I whispered. "I can't."

He stood up. I heard him walk over to the bed. "Budge up a bit," he said.

I felt his body next to mine, warming the bed within seconds. He pulled me towards him, turning me around and placing his arm round me over the covers. I gasped as I curled up against his chest, his heat passing through my pyjamas. My heart was in my throat.

I heard him breathing in deeply. "Your hair smells like strawberries," he whispered close to my ear.

Stop shaking. Keep breathing.

I closed my eyes, feeling safe in his arms. There was nowhere else I'd rather be. I didn't want him to ever leave me. If only this night could last forever.

19. EASILY PLEASED

The day after Keaghan arrived, I had my first theory lesson. Joya was going to teach me the *Sacred Scriptures*. I'd made sure I'd read the schedule this time.

"Morning, Arianna." Her warm smile and shining aura lit up the room. "You look different, my child. You've blossomed since the last time I saw you."

"I don't feel any different, just more tired and hungry."

The fact is I felt disappointed – furious even. Partly because Keaghan had left my room in the morning without saying goodbye, but mainly because neither Marcus nor Joya had mentioned what had happened to my home yet.

"I'm sorry about what happened last night. I'm sure Keaghan has filled you in already."

She must have read my mind. I sat in the chair by the desk. "He has." I didn't change my expression.

"I'm sure you understand the gravity of the situation now. That should make you more determined to progress with your training and get ready to fight."

I nodded.

"Today you have a lot of reading to do. You can ask me or Marcus all the questions you want. This evening you'll be tested on what you've learned." Joya placed a pile of books in front of me.

"OK." I swallowed hard, stunned at the size of the books.

"There's a vast selection of books in the library here that you can consult. You can have a break at lunchtime and resume just before four o' clock. Is everything clear?"

"Yes, Joya."

I was a fast reader, and I thought I would have no problem with this part of the training. But the books were challenging, to say the least. Almost impossible to understand. Much was written in Middle English, some was in Latin, and some was in a language I didn't know at all. Even so, by lunchtime I had managed to get through the first two books. I was so absorbed that I ignored my rumbling stomach. I ate my lunch in the library, reluctant to leave my studies. The history of the Celestial Order was fascinating, expounding on the existence of the various Angelic Ranks, each with a different gift and power. It spoke of the origin of angels and their duty to assist mankind against evil forces. I couldn't put it down.

It was afternoon when Marcus came in.

"Arianna, you've been reading all day. Take a break." He stood by the door in the dark; the only light in the room was the lamp on my desk.

"Five more minutes." I carried on jotting down notes.

"OK, but then take a break. You look exhausted."

I glanced up, and he smiled at me for the first time since we'd had that last argument.

"Marc?"

"What is it?" He walked over to me.

"Have you ever read this book before?"

"Of course. It's *The Ancient Scrolls*. Why?"

"I can't make sense of it. I don't know the language it's written in."

"It's Aramaic." He looked at me as if I should have known that. "I see: you've been reading with your brain." He shook his head.

"Huh? Is there any other way?" I frowned.

"You're an angel, Arianna. Don't read with your head. If you switch to your angelic side, you can read and understand any language you want."

What?

"You need to start believing, Arianna. Lose your shrewdness, Einstein; only then will you truly embrace who you are." He turned and left the room.

That was easier said than done. I was a quick learner and an avid reader - in English, not in *gobbledygook*. I had thought I'd been starting to get my head around all this stuff. Now this. I stared at the page, but the words still made no sense.

I carried on reading, although it was a struggle, when my attention was drawn to a particular passage. It was in Latin. It took a while to fully translate the section, but when I finally did, I felt like I had been punched in the gut. I gasped out loud. According to one of the Angelic Laws, a demon and an angel could never be together: such a union was strictly forbidden. While this wasn't really a surprise to me, it was a shock to see it written down. I felt a knot growing in my stomach. Oh God. I was so angry and upset with myself. Angry because I'd always known my infatuation with Keaghan was absurd. Upset because my heart just didn't seem to care about the law, although I knew I should.

Stop it. Forget the damn law. I pushed the thought to the back of my head and went on with the rest of the book.

Joya returned later and I settled down to take my first theory test of the week. For the first time in my life I was nervous about sitting a test.

"You have one hour to complete the ninety questions. Good luck." Joya turned over the silver hourglass on her desk.

Only one hour? Just fail me now. The test seemed difficult at first; but then, all of a sudden, the answers started popping into my head as if I'd always known them. I finished the last questions after forty-seven minutes.

"Well done. I'm impressed. I'll check the answers and then we can discuss the results."

I waited, tapping my pen on the desk nervously as she marked the paper.

"So?" I asked when she looked up ten minutes later.

She handed me the results. "You did very well, Arianna. You got all the answers right. But I had no doubt you would. You've always been very intelligent and mature for your age."

I read the paper, feeling proud of myself for the first time in weeks. "Thank you, Joya." I ran out of the room and climbed the stairs to my bedroom two at a time.

True to his word, Keaghan was waiting for me.

"Wow. It's official. You're still a geek," he said as he read my test result.

"Hey, I like studying. Books never let me down." I snatched the paper from his hand.

"I know. It's physical exercise that's never been your forte," he chortled.

"Actually, for your information, I've developed muscles I didn't even think I had. Look, I even have a six-pack." I lifted my top, realising too late what I was doing.

"I'm very impressed." Keaghan grinned as he stared at my abs.

I tugged my top down again, embarrassed.

"Let's not start comparing muscles, Feather girl."

He pulled off his T-shirt, showing his bare chest. Oh my God. My cheeks were blazing so much it felt like my face was throbbing. I wanted to look away, but couldn't.

"Do you mind if I take a shower? I came here straight from patrolling the area."

"Y-yeah, sure, g-go ahead," I managed to stutter at last.

By the time he walked back into the room, I was in bed, the covers pulled over my head, pretending to be asleep.

"Budge up," he said. His voice was low and terribly sexy.

I was shaking, my heart bouncing in my chest like a frog. I moved right to the edge of the bed, leaving plenty of room between us. We lay there in silence for a while.

"Keaghan?" I turned to face him. "Can I ask you something?"

"Here we go." He pulled one of his disarming smiles.

"Today I read about Morfran in *The Ancient Scrolls*. I couldn't understand much, it was written in a weird language I can't even remember the name of, but one part was in Latin. It talked about Morfran's followers, called them *Obscurum*. Who are they?"

"You were reading with your brain." He smirked.

"I wish people would stop saying that. If I knew how to switch sides, I would – trust me." I glared at him before turning onto my back and crossing my arms.

"*Darksiders*. They're Morfran's demons."

I turned onto my side to look at him again. "Are they different from other demons?"

He moved closer and placed his head on the pillow next to me. "Oh yeah. They're merciless and possess much stronger powers. But the Angel of Light can turn them into dust with just one blast."

Hmph. I suppose that'll be me, then.

His heat waves were making me sweat. I had to pull down the covers slightly.

"Now try and get some sleep, OK? Night, Feather girl."

I didn't mind being called that. It was actually quite sweet. I was his Feather girl. You're getting way beyond pathetic, Arianna. "Night, Keaghan."

For the next few days, I worked harder than ever before. I was doing my best, but the more I tried, the tougher Marcus was on me. At least I was getting better at running, and I tried not to moan or argue with him all the time. I was even starting to get used to his agonising classical music, though the vomit shake still tasted as vile as on the first day. The Jiu-Jitsu class became my favourite: I got to kick his butt.

"Remember, Arianna, Darksiders are big. Some are twice

your height," Marcus told me. "Jiu-Jitsu will teach you that strength isn't just about the size of your muscles or how tall you are. It teaches you to defeat even the largest opponents."

One of Marcus's Warrior Angels was teaching the class with him that day. Although Keera was much smaller, she grabbed him and threw him across the room as if he weighed nothing. I particularly enjoyed that part.

"Keera will teach you how to use your attackers' energy against them, applying very little force. Enjoy," Marcus said as he left the room.

As the physical training got easier, the spiritual training got tougher. Every time I engaged my aura, I felt even more tired, drained of all strength. My human body just couldn't take the energy my aura could produce. The best part of the week was theory class with Joya. For our next session, she taught me about the order of the Angelic Hierarchy. I read twelve books in two days – all in English this time - and passed my test with flying colours, again. The *brainiac* in me never failed.

Keaghan sat on my bed, smiling at my paper.

"All correct again? If you carry on like this, I might have to treat you to some chocolate."

"Really?"

"Just kidding. Time for bed, young lady. You've had another tough week. Well done." He smiled, his eyes sparkling at me.

Lying next to him was my favourite part of the day. He'd listen to me go on and on about how tough my day had been and never judge me, or dish out useless words of wisdom, like Marcus and Joya so often did. I felt like he was always on my side. I liked having him staying in my room. In my life.

"I know I'm good with books, but I'm not making any progress on controlling my aura and switching off my stupid human side," I sighed, sitting cross-legged on the bed.

"It's just a matter of time, Arianna. The point will come when you know just what to do and how to do it." He went back to texting on his phone.

"That thing never stopped beeping last night." I knew I sounded jealous and pathetic.

"Yeah, something important has come up. I've got to go to London for a couple of days." He stood up and put his leather jacket on.

"What do you mean? You said you'd never leave. Who's going to protect me?" I looked at him in panic.

A hiss came from my window. "Me." Bruna appeared from behind the curtain, bringing in a swirl of heat.

"I don't understand. What's going on?" I could sense something bad; my chest burned with pain.

"Nothing at all, angel face." She took her leather coat off and sat on my bed. "You just relax. You and I are going to have some fun."

"Bruna, the rules are still the same: no alcohol, no parties and no misbehaving. Understood?" Keaghan's eyes briefly turned to red.

"Crystal clear, boss."

"I'll be back soon. And Bruna? No sneaking her chocolate behind my back either." He pinned her with a glare.

I didn't want him to leave. "B-but how long will you be?" I couldn't have sounded more pathetic if I'd tried.

"Not too long. I promise." Keaghan glanced at me briefly, then he climbed onto the window sill, crouched forward, and jumped out. I felt my heart sink.

"About that chocolate rule..." Bruna waved a box of Maltesers at me.

"Oh-my-goodness." I leaped off the bed and hugged her, bouncing around the room, ecstatic.

"Gosh, you're easily pleased." She laughed.

"Thank you, thank you, thank you." Chocolate! Exactly what I needed to cheer me up.

"Calm down before the Reaper finds out and walks in here

and turns me to dust."

Bruna sat on my bed and watched me eat the entire box.

20. OUT OF THIS WORLD

The following week, I had to deal with four of my tutors at the same time. It was Marcus who took control.

"This week's training is going to be significant for you, Arianna," he said. "You've learned about your powers, now you need to know how to use them."

We were in St Andrew's, the biggest room in the monastery. Kayla and Julian stood on Marcus's right; Megan was on his left. I was surprised to see Bruna. She wasn't scheduled to be here today.

Apart from Bruna, who was wearing her usual Goth clothes, Megan was the only one not dressed in white. "I'll help you focus and channel your aura with my energy. Use your mind to control what goes on around you. That's what Lightworkers do best." Megan gave me the thumbs up. "Hopefully today's the day, Arianna."

"I hope so," I whispered. I needed more than hope to get through this session unscathed.

Marcus pinned me with his gaze. "You need to engage your aura without any help from us first. Remember to control it with your breathing," he said.

Kayla's aura began to shine above her head. "We'll show you our powers first," she said.

A beam of light shimmered around them. Megan stretched her arms out in front of her, her eyes shut. Heat radiated from Bruna, creating a pattern of wavy lines around her.

Julian's body started to levitate, becoming a blur. "Arianna, as the Overseer Angel I have the power of pathfinding and orbing," he said.

And with those words, he disappeared into thin air, leaving behind bubbles of light.

"Boo."

I jumped and spun round. Julian was standing behind me, chortling away.

"Did you just fly?" I gasped.

"No, I orbed. It's like flying, but I use orbs to tele-transport wherever I want." Like it was a normal option for travel.

Kayla spoke and I turned back to her. "Arianna, as a Healing Angel I can heal other angels. I've healed you many times before without you knowing. I also have the power of astral projection and omni-powers." She lifted her hands and threw a beam of light across the room, creating a translucent shield. "Bruna, try and cross the astral projection." Kayla looked at Bruna, challenging her.

"You know I can't." Bruna crossed her arms.

"I know. But I want Arianna to see what happens if a demon tries to cross."

Bruna puffed and scowled, before running towards the shield. As soon as she made contact with the shimmering field, she was thrown across the room by a tremendous force.

"Brue, are you OK?" I ran to where she lay.

"'Course I am, it's only a little sting." She clambered to her feet, looking at Kayla with loathing. "Let me show you what I can do." She took her leather coat off and put it on the floor.

Bruna held her hand high, towards the ceiling light. The energy drained from it, the light switched off and Bruna threw something towards Kayla. A bolt of lightning?

"Ouch! That hurt," Kayla shouted. She rubbed her arm as if she'd had an electric shock, as the light came back on.

"Don't be so dramatic, Kay. It was only a small one." Bruna grinned and turned to me to explain. "As a Fallen Angel I can use energy sourcing to create electricity, fire, and heat. I have omni-powers too, and I can create fire blasts." She looked smug, as she put her coat back on.

It was Marcus's turn. "I'm a Reaper Angel, and I train warriors and new angels – like you. I have the power to create energy blasts that can immobilise the enemy temporarily. I have superhuman senses, and omni-powers like strength, vision and speed." His mouth twisted in a superior smirk. "Bruna? Catch."

He threw a beam of light in her direction. Before she had a chance to dodge, it blasted into her chest, knocking her off her feet.

"What is it? Let's Get Bruna Killed Day?" She shook her body as she stood up.

"Don't be so dramatic, Brue," Marcus said. "*It was only a small one.*"

They all laughed – except Bruna.

Megan spoke next. "I don't have any of these super-powers, Arianna. I'm a Lightworker. I see things, like spirits. I sense evil and I can possess a demon's mind. I can cast spells and use telepathy to communicate with angels."

She lifted her hands and her eyes flickered. When she opened them again her pupils were white. I shuddered as a wind rose from the floor and swirled around her, creating a storm.

"*Ventus adducere pluvia.*" Her hollow voice made her sound as if she was possessed.

I felt a drip fall on my shoulder. Torrential rain started to pour down from the ceiling. She wasn't kidding – wind brings rain all right.

"Why always that spell, Meg?" Kayla moaned as she shook the water from her face and hands.

"It's OK. I'll dry you now." Megan joined her hands together above her head.

"*Lucem et Sol.*" She called for the light of the sun.

I was blinded by a bright light. A hot gust swirled around us.

Within seconds we were dry.

"Wow. How have I never noticed your powers?" I shook my head, amazed.

It was Marcus who answered. "We weren't allowed to show them to you, Arianna. Not until you were ready to face the truth. Now it's your turn, Angel of Light. What are your powers?" He waited for an answer.

"Well, apparently I should be able to make *things happen* with the power of my mind, use telepathy to communicate with other angels. Oh – and this is a good one – I should be able to create an energy blast so strong it can kill a demon instantly."

I shook my head. Really. How could I take any of this seriously?

They all stared at me; no one was laughing.

"Go on then, time to show us what you can do." Marcus and the others walked closer, forming a circle around me.

I raised my eyebrows, dubious. They were joking, right?

"Come on guys," Marcus said. "Let's give her a little nudge."

"I'll start." Bruna threw a spark at my feet.

"Are you kidding me?" I shouted at her, shocked.

"How about this then?" Julian threw a cluster of bubbly orbs in my face, making me sneeze and cough convulsively.

"Come on, Arianna, react," Kayla cried. "Use your powers." She threw an energy blast at my feet. The light shone so bright it blinded me, throwing me off balance.

"Engage your aura. Come on, angel face." Bruna threw a fire blast and Megan picked it up in the air and swirled it around me, creating a hot breeze.

"Stop it. What are you doing!" I yelled, covering my head with my hands. My hair would catch on fire!

"Switch off your brain, Einstein." Julian threw an energy blast against the fire, turning it into an explosion.

I screamed again. A rush of anger swept through me. I slowed down my breathing by taking several deep breaths with my eyes shut. As I lifted my hands, I felt a tingling move from my chest to my head. I'd done it! My aura was engaged. I opened my eyes, and as Kayla threw a blast at my feet I lifted my hand towards her. I channelled my rage through the energy that was expanding all around me like a burning light.

I intended to push Kayla, but as I stretched my arm forward, she flew across the room as a beam of light left my body and smacked her in the chest. There was a horrible crack as she crashed against the wall.

Julian and Marcus ran towards her. Kayla was lying on the floor motionless.

"Kay, oh please God, no." I froze in shock, staring at my friend.

Blood was trickling from the corner of her mouth. What had I done?

Julian took her in his arms. "Kay? Come on, baby."

Bruna stood by my side, placing her arm round my shoulders, protective. "Well, we did provoke you."

Marcus placed his hand on Kayla's chest. "Kay? Can you hear me?"

A bright light expanded around Kayla, and she opened her eyes. "That was incredible." She stared up at me, mesmerised.

"I'm so sorry. I didn't mean to hurt you, Kay." I knelt at her side, holding back my tears.

She took my hand in hers. "Are you kidding? You were amazing, Arianna. You should have seen yourself: the light coming from your aura; the energy around you. It was out of this world." She stood up and wiped the blood from her mouth, seemingly unhurt.

"What do you mean? I nearly killed you, and I don't even know how."

"My human shell may bleed, but don't worry. I'm fine." She didn't look fine.

"That was too dangerous." Marcus agreed with me for once.

"We shouldn't have done it like this. We need to wait till she's ready. One of us could end up getting killed if we're not careful." He looked disappointed.

"It was worth a try," Kayla said. She turned to me. "When you were getting angry, your aura was supported by the energy overloaded by your core. Your aura created the blast. It was so powerful. I've never felt that level of energy before. Not from a new angel." She gazed at me in awe.

"That was your first energy blast, Arianna," Marcus explained.

"Actually it was her second." Bruna nudged me on the shoulder. "She's knocked me off my feet before." I recalled her body flying across the church and smashing one of the pillars on the night I was attacked. I'd forgotten about that.

Marcus sneered. "I don't mind it being used on a fallen, but we're not to try this again in training. It's too dangerous." His voice made it clear. The decision was final.

"But can't you see? It worked," Kayla insisted.

"It didn't work at all, actually," Marcus said. "We made it happen, not her. It needs to come from Arianna spontaneously. She has to be in control." He flicked a hand at me. "If I asked her to do it again now, she wouldn't be able to. And what if she'd projected a stronger blast? You could have been vaporised."

I agreed with him – which was a first. I stared at Kayla, appalled. "I can't believe you made me hurt you."

Megan touched my arm. "It was part of the training," she said. "We thought it would help you. Don't feel bad, Arianna."

I pulled away. This was all wrong. I couldn't do this. "What if I had killed her?" I said. "I don't know who you are anymore. I don't even know if I can still call you friends. All you're bothered about is that I turn into this freak you need so badly. I'm not a person to you, I'm a weapon. You've lied to me all the time we've known each other. I don't even know if you actually care for me." A lump lodged in my throat. I was drained of energy.

"Arianna, don't be silly. Of course we care," Kayla said.

"I don't believe you, Kay. I don't believe any of you anymore."

I stormed out of the room, ran upstairs and slammed the bedroom door behind me. I jumped. Bruna was sitting on my bed.

"How the hell did you get in before me?" I grimaced, feeling angry and confused.

"Chocolate?" Bruna waved a bar of Dairy Milk at me. The anger ebbed away and I couldn't help but grin.

"Sit down, angel face." She patted the bed. I curled up next to her.

"I know this is tough, and I know what we did was a bit unfair. But it worked. Do you believe you have powers now?"

21. SATURDAY NIGHT FEVER

Another week spent in my prison. It was Saturday evening and I hadn't seen or heard from Keaghan for the last five days. How depressing. At least I was allowed one phone call from my Nana today. It was so good to hear her voice.

Bruna sat down on my bed. "Right, so what do you normally do in this crap-hole on a Saturday night?" she asked.

"Nothing. I'm not allowed out, even at weekends. I'm going crazy in here." I lay down, staring at the ceiling.

"Not surprised. I'd be suicidal by now. The life of an angel is way too boring – hence why I'm not one anymore." She grinned.

"I haven't got much choice. Apparently, I'm the one who has to save the universe."

Bruna laughed. "So, what shall we do?"

Good question. I knew what I wanted to do, but being able to do it was a different matter. I'd just had a brilliant idea. A stupid one, more like. No way. I couldn't. But why not? Come on. I just needed to convince Bruna to go along with it.

"Listen," I said. "Why don't we sneak out and go clubbing?"

A laugh burst from her throat. "Yeah, right."

"I'm not kidding. Please Brue, I beg you. You've got to get me out of here." I was actually on my knees, begging.

"No way, Arianna. We can't." She was shaking her head, profusely. "Keaghan would kill me if he ever found out."

"Please Bruna. I'm begging you here. Keaghan is still in London, right? He never has to know. Just a couple of hours. What do you say?"

"I say no."

"You're my only hope, Bruna. I need to get out of here. I'm going crazy. Please?" I looked at her with puppy eyes.

I recognised that look on her face. She was planning something. Say yes, say yes, say yes!

She let out a big sigh. "To hell with it. Let's do it."

I climbed to my feet and hugged her. "You're the best."

"If Marcus finds out, we're screwed," she muttered as she started rooting through my wardrobe.

She was right. Marcus would be furious. The Order would probably banish me forever. Still, a thrill of excitement ran through me.

"Bloody hell," Bruna groaned. She grimaced at the pile of tracksuits. "Who's your stylist? Dora the Explorer? Have you got anything in here that doesn't scream *hiking* or *running*?"

"Not really." I looked at her, glum. "I'm not supposed to leave the monastery during training, remember?"

"We'll soon see about that. Wait here." Bruna opened the window and jumped out.

I was still staring at the window, aghast, when she climbed back up. In less than a minute, she'd managed to change into a black jumpsuit and picked up an outfit for me too.

"Did you just pop to Oxford Street?" I said.

She threw me a short black dress with purple sequins on the neckline; in the other hand she held a pair of sky-high purple shoes with red soles.

"You don't want to know. They should fit you though. Come on, get changed." She hurried me into the bathroom.

At least the dress wasn't pink. I emerged a couple of minutes later.

"Wow, you look stunning, angel face."

Bruna nodded at me with approval. She styled my hair in soft waves and applied some make-up, giving me a sultry look. The dress was too short for my liking, but I reckoned I looked OK.

But then I caught myself on. Should I be doing this? If Marc did find out, he'd have my guts for garters.

"No time to change your mind, Feather girl. Come on, let's go." Bruna stood by the window, waiting for me.

"Are you kidding me? I'm not jumping out of a window." I gazed at her, horrified.

"Oh yes you are. Come on." She grabbed me by the waist, holding me tight. "We don't want to alert the Guardians, so don't scream."

I squeezed my eyes shut as Bruna plunged into the dark night, hiding my face in the fold of her neck, petrified. I only realised we'd hit the ground when I felt the earth shudder under me.

"That wasn't too bad, now, was it?"

I looked up at my window and swallowed. I couldn't believe I'd just jumped from that height and wasn't hurt.

Bruna steered her motorbike fast down the country roads, but I couldn't feel the cold breeze of the night. Heat encircled me like a blanket.

A few minutes later, we stopped. A neon sign told me we'd arrived at the *Alley Cat* nightclub.

"Whoa. It's busy tonight," Bruna said. "There's going to be a few fallens in here, but don't worry, they're harmless. Still, stay close and never leave my sight. You're with me, so you've nothing to fear. Let's inject some fun into those feathers."

She grabbed my hand and we walked towards the long queue. Bruna sauntered past everyone and went straight to the front.

"Freddy, darling, how the hell are you?" She shook hands with the big guy standing by the door.

He let us in, staring at me with red eyes as I passed him. I swallowed hard, feeling suddenly vulnerable. Did I really want to do this?

"You'll never need to wait for anything when you're with me," Bruna said as we walked in, oblivious to my anxiety.

I couldn't back out now. This was my idea in the first place.

Come on. Stop fretting.

I had been in clubs before, but never one this big. The club had three levels and each one was packed. Bruna took my hand again. I jerked as I felt a current passing through my skin. It made me think of Keaghan. God, how I missed him. I could feel everyone's eyes on me. My aura was throbbing in my chest. Bruna greeted everyone she met on our way to the bar. I was certain most of them weren't human.

Bruna handed me a glass. I drank it in one. The alcohol hit the back of my throat, making me cough. The effect of the whisky was almost immediate. My muscles relaxed and I felt giddy.

I began to move to the music, holding Bruna's hand as we walked onto the dance floor. I'd lost count of how many drinks I'd had by the time we went to the upper floor. Psychedelic trance music pounded out and the flashing lights were blinding.

"Are you OK?" Bruna shouted in my ear.

"Yeah, yeah. Time for another drink, I think." I smiled, trying to ignore my burning aura.

Nero appeared from behind us. He looked at me with disgust. "What the hell is she doing here? Are you out of your mind, Brue?"

"Shut up, you idiot. She's with me. She needed a night off." Bruna glared at him. "And calm down. Your eyes are red. You don't want to draw attention to us, do you?"

"Oh yeah, because bringing her in here isn't drawing enough attention already? If Keaghan finds out, we're both dust in the morning."

"Oh, chill out, Nero. You're starting to sound like a Feather," she said. "Keaghan's out of town, remember? As long as you keep your trap shut, he'll never find out." Bruna squeezed my hand.

"Your call, your responsibility. I want nothing to do with it." He stalked off, spitting by my feet as he walked past.

"Ignore him, he's a miserable git. Let's dance." She pulled me back onto the dance floor.

Over her shoulder I noticed a couple sat on a sofa in a corner. They were all over each other. There was something familiar about them, especially the redhead girl. Circles of heat fluttered around them.

As the girl moved her head, I saw the guy and felt a stab of jealousy and panic. What the hell? No way. I stood paralysed in the middle of the dance floor, my jaw dropping open. The girl was the one I'd seen at the Annual Exhibition Show. But it was the guy she was kissing who held my attention.

Bruna stopped dancing and followed my eyes. Her jaw snapped open. "Shit!"

"I couldn't have put it better myself." I swallowed, hard.

"W-what the hell is he doing here?" Bruna's voice was filled with terror.

Between snogs, Keaghan caught my glance among the crowd. His pupils turned crimson. With one movement, he threw the redhead out of the way, before striding towards us.

Bruna gasped, holding my hand tighter. "Keaghan…" He dragged us both off the dance floor as if we were weightless.

"Explain now, before I tear you to pieces. What's she doing here?" His face was inches from Bruna's.

"Leave her alone." I pushed my way between them and stood in front of Keaghan. I found it hard to keep my balance, battling with the dizziness. "It was my fault. I came here on my own. Bruna found me – she was about to take me back."

Keaghan glared at me. "Do you honestly think I believe that? You stink of booze. It's full of demons in here. Are you insane?"

Insane? This whole situation was insane.

"I'm allowed some fun, you know. Who do you think you are, speaking to me like that?" I wasn't sure where that came from, but held my ground, trembling.

"Leave it, Arianna. He's right," Bruna said. "I'll take her back to the monastery now. I'm sorry."

Tension was radiating from him but I refused to be intimidated.

"No. I want another drink and a dance and there's nothing you can do to stop me." What the hell was I doing? Was I just challenging him? The image of him kissing the redhead was still painfully impressed upon my mind.

"Arianna, please, let's go." Bruna tugged at my arm, but I wasn't listening.

"You're coming with me now," Keaghan growled.

"No. I've had enough of people telling me what to do. I'm having fun, why should I go just because you're here? You seemed to be enjoying yourself."

"You little –"

He stopped himself, then tried to drag me away by my arm. I freed myself with just one movement. Whoa. It was true. I was stronger than I thought.

"I said no. Don't you dare touch me again. I'm not afraid of you," I snarled.

I managed to hold Keaghan's glance longer than I ever had before. He was livid. His heat was choking me and his eyes were burning red.

A sensual figure appeared behind him. The redhead looked at me with a wicked smile. She placed her hand on Keaghan's shoulder. "Oh, come on, baby. Give the poor girl a break. What's the worst that could happen? We're all here, you're here. Let her shake her feathers for a bit."

"It's none of your business, Donna," he hissed, shaking her hand off his arm.

I could see I wasn't going to win this fight, but I carried on. "Please, Keaghan. Let me stay. I know you'll protect me," I begged, making my voice sound calmer. "You're here. Nothing bad can happen." His jaw relaxed a little.

A white flash burst across the room. It wasn't the club's lights. The alarming sound of an explosion shook the ground under me. I wasn't sure whether my knees had buckled or if the blast had taken me off my feet. What the hell was that? A ball of fire was travelling towards us.

"Get down!" Keaghan's voice rang in my ears as he shielded me with his body and pushed me to the ground.

I didn't feel a thing. Keaghan took the full brunt of the blast. Giant flames were dancing around him before they burned out. He looked unhurt.

"We'll take care of it, Keaghan," Bruna shouted, flames resting in the palm of her hands. "You go! Get her out of here." She threw a fire blast in the opposite direction. Another loud bang echoed in the room. More flames and smoke rose around us. Panic set in.

"Nothing bad can happen. Right, Arianna?" Keaghan yelled.

He took my arm and dragged me towards the stairs. Bruna, Nero and Donna must have stayed behind, as I couldn't see them anymore. People were screaming and running in every direction. I managed to stumble down the stairs – what was left of them. Keaghan's hand gripped my wrist as he hurried us out to the back of the building. Dozens of car alarms were going off.

"Ouch, you're hurting me," I moaned. He let go of my wrist.

He stopped and looked at me as if he wanted to say something. His eyes were scarlet. I stumbled backwards. Bruna and Nero arrived.

"Sorted," Nero said. "Donna is making sure there's no trace of the demons we vanquished."

"I'm sorry, Keaghan." Bruna hung her head in shame. "It's my fault."

"No it isn't." I couldn't let her take the blame. This one was all on me.

Keaghan lifted his hand to silence us both. "This is the last time something like this happens. Understood?" He turned to look at Bruna and Nero. "One more mistake from you two and I'll make sure your ashes aren't good enough for cat litter. Is that clear?"

"Hey, I had nothing to do with it," Nero protested.

"I don't want to hear it." Keaghan looked angry and cold.

I felt queasy, unsteady on my feet. The fresh air hit me, making me feel the full effect of the alcohol. The world started spinning and I grabbed Keaghan's arm.

"Look at her. She's wasted," Keaghan hissed. "She's underage, for crying out loud. She almost got blown up in there. How could you let this happen?" He was trying to keep his voice down. Police cars, a fire truck and an ambulance pulled up outside the club. "Don't answer, Bruna. I'll talk to you two in the morning. Clean up this mess now."

Keaghan rushed me across the street. He held my hand tight at first but his grip gradually loosened. His stride was faster and longer than mine and I struggled to keep up. At least I was warm again.

"I'm sorry," I muttered. "Please don't be mad."

He stopped in the middle of the road and looked at me, furious, shaking his head. Though he said nothing, when we set off again, he walked a little slower.

I kept quiet, clamping my hand in his to absorb his warmth. How did I always manage to mess everything up? He opened the door of his sports car for me.

"Don't you dare be sick," he warned, before slamming the door shut.

As soon as we were on the road, he began lecturing me again.

"What the hell were you thinking, Arianna? Have you forgotten who you are?"

"I'm Arianna Morelli. I used to be a normal seventeen-year-old *brainiac*, but I don't know who the hell I am anymore." I burst out laughing.

"It's not funny. Look at the state of you. Drunk and dancing with demons. Is that even a dress?" I looked down. The fabric was barely covering the top of my thighs.

"I feel sick. Stop the car!"

He slammed on the brakes so hard I thought I was going to fly through the windscreen. I staggered out of the car and was sick by the side of the road. When I'd finished, I sat down on the grass, breathing slowly, my head spinning.

"What are you doing? We're in the middle of nowhere. The monastery isn't far. Come on, get up." He held out his hand. I didn't move. "Get up," he cursed, shaking his head. "Do you know what will happen when you go back? Do you honestly think the Order won't find out? You're still in training. You're my responsibility. It's my job."

His icy tone hit me. My life wasn't my own. It was too much.

"All I've heard from everyone these past few weeks is that I'm a job, a task to fulfil. I'm no longer a person. No one has shown me any understanding, apart from Bruna. Who cares what Arianna feels, right?" A tear slid down my cheek. I wasn't putting it on. I had never felt so miserable. "Don't worry, Keaghan. I know you have a job to do. Come on, let's go. We can't have you getting into trouble with the CO, can we?" I didn't mean to sound so cynical and bitter, but the words carried on spilling out. "I know you don't give a shit about me, none of you do. You need me. That's all I am to you: a weapon." I fought the urge to break down and sob.

"That sort of language really doesn't suit you, Feather girl." Keaghan puffed before sitting down, shaking his head. He pulled a tissue out of his pocket and passed it over to me. "You forget, while you're having your Saturday Night Fever, that Marcus is seriously going to kill you tomorrow." He gently nudged my shoulder. He didn't sound angry anymore. Though he had every reason to be.

I stared at him closely. "Do you know you have really beautiful eyes?" I regretted the words the moment they were out.

"You're pissed." He laughed, trying to hold me up as I leaned against him.

"I know, isn't that great?" My slurred speech was accompanied by an obnoxious leer. "I really am sorry, Keaghan. Please don't blame Bruna. I begged her to take me out. She felt sorry for me. You have no idea how hard it's been for me. Marc is worse than ten Sergeant Majors put together. I'm so tired, all the time – you know?"

I was talking in slow motion. Keaghan picked me up in his arms and placed me gently back in the car.

I carried on talking. "I needed a night off, you know what I mean? I'm not allowed junk food. I'm not allowed chocolate, never mind alcohol. And I like alcohol. It helps me forget how tragic my life is." I could see Keaghan suppress a smile as he fastened my seatbelt for me and drove off.

"You're not allowed alcohol 'cause you're underage, Arianna."

So that was it. I felt hurt. He obviously saw me as just a kid. It wasn't fair.

"I've never worked so hard in my life, yet no one has noticed how unhappy I am. I miss my Nana. My old life. I miss school. But no one truly cares. Isn't that great?" Somehow I was laughing, on the edge of hysteria.

"Of course people care. Don't be silly."

He said *people*. Of course. Why would he care for a pathetic girl like me?

"I used to have a brilliant life. Now I've turned into a Tibetan monk who spends her days breathing in and out to the sound of violins." I closed my eyes.

Keaghan took a deep breath. "I guess you needed to wind down a bit. Walker can be pretty boring. I get it."

"I know he's doing it for me. It's his job. But... I'm still human in my head. You know what I mean?" I said.

"You acted more like a fallen tonight than either a human or an angel, Arianna. It was appalling behaviour, Ms Morelli." Was he being serious?

"I know. It was fun though, wasn't it?" I chuckled.

"You nearly got blown up, Arianna. It won't be funny when the Reaper finds that out."

"That I do believe." I nodded, turning serious. There was a short silence.

"You OK?" he asked.

I forced a feeble smile. "I'll worry about the consequences tomorrow."

"Don't worry. I'll talk to Walker in the morning. Try and do some damage control." Was he sticking up for me? I sure didn't deserve it.

He parked the car outside the monastery's fence. "Right, I better help you to your room. Try not to wake Walker up. We don't want the Guardians to see you either."

He lifted me in his arms. I gasped as I inhaled his scent. He climbed over the metal fence, still holding me – made it look effortless. He jumped through my bedroom window in a fraction of a second.

"Did you think I looked nice tonight?" I asked him as he lowered me onto the bed. "I'm sorry, Keaghan. I really am."

"Shush, it's OK, be quiet," he whispered, placing his finger on my lips.

His touch sent shivers down my spine. Through the blur of alcohol I felt the tingling touch of his fingers as he eased my shoes off.

"I ruined your romantic night with the red octopus girl." Oh God. Was I slurring? I heard him laugh under his breath.

"What are you on about?"

He lifted my legs to pull the covers over me. I opened my eyes. His face was inches away from mine.

"Donna Brooks." I faked an American accent. "She had her tentacles wrapped around you good and proper. I saw you kissing her."

He turned the light off but I could sense him looking at me

in the dark.

"You're going to have such a bad head in the morning. I've left some aspirin on the side. Take one as soon as you wake up."

"You go back to her. She's waiting for you in her hot pink dress, with her tentacles stretched out." I knew I sounded pathetic, but I was obviously too drunk to care.

Keaghan sat on the edge of the bed. The woody scent of his aftershave wafted over me.

"If it wasn't for the fact that you're drunk, I'd say you were jealous, Feather girl."

His sensual voice made me shiver. He moved a curl off my face. I could just about make out his face in the darkness.

"Me? Nah. I just, I'm just drunk. Ignore me." I blinked twice, trying to look sober.

"I have to go, but I'll stay if you want me to."

I felt his breath on my cheek. My heart was beating against my chest like I was running for my life.

"No, it's fine. You go. I'll be fine. I've caused enough problems for one night. Go." That wasn't what I wanted to say.

But he didn't go. Instead, he gently pushed his way onto my bed, lay next to me, and put his arm round my shoulders so I could rest my head on his chest.

"What am I going to do with you, Feather girl?" he said softly. "I hope you realise the danger you put yourself in tonight." It certainly made everything seem more real.

Just as I was about to fall asleep, I heard Keaghan's voice whisper close to my ear.

"And for the record, you looked gorgeous."

Oh my God. Did I hear him right? I might have been drunk, but I was sure I hadn't misheard his words. He did care. After tonight, I was sure of it.

22. I KNOW WHO I AM

I opened my eyes and blinked several times. Keaghan was gone.
My head was throbbing and the room was spinning. I managed
to stagger to the toilet just in time before I was sick. As I walked
back to my bed, I glanced at the clock. Oh God. Twenty past ten.
How much did Marcus already know about last night? He must
have noticed I hadn't turn up for training.

A sticky note on the mirror caught my eye.

When you finally wake up, get yourself sorted and come down to
St George's Room. We need to talk

My stomach churned. Memories of Keaghan, the club, and
me acting like a complete idiot flooded back. I swallowed an
aspirin with some water, needing to lie down. As I lurched to the
bed, I stumbled and fell over. My dress stank of booze. I pulled it
off and crawled under the covers. Had I really been sick in front
of Keaghan? No way could I face Marcus in this state. I was late
anyway; another hour wouldn't make a difference.

My phone vibrated. I managed to pick it up without falling
out of bed. Two text messages and six missed calls. The missed
calls were all from Marcus; both text messages were from
Bruna, asking if I was OK. How embarrassing. The thought of
last night made me cringe. What would the consequences be?
Probably a nasty punishment inflicted by the CO. I closed my
eyes and had a flashback of Keaghan kissing Donna. I had no
right to feel jealous. I'd behaved like an immature teenager. And

I almost got us all killed.

I slept till lunchtime, but I was still feeling rough when I forced myself out of bed. A shower helped to wash off the hangover. I'd delayed facing Marcus long enough. As I looked in the mirror to tie my damp hair in a plait, I could see how dreadful I looked. No way could I hide those dark circles under my eyes. I sent Marcus a text to pre-warn him that I was on my way down.

The monastery felt cold today; I could see my breath. I walked into the dining room. Marcus wasn't there.

"Are you ready for some food?" the housekeeper asked. "You must be starving after skipping breakfast."

"Has Marcus had his lunch already?" The words came out in a croak.

"He has. He said he'll see you in St George's Room, after you've eaten."

I had the impression she knew why I was late.

"I'm not hungry, but thank you. I'll eat later."

I thought about every possible excuse to defend myself, but there was nothing I could say that could justify my behaviour, apart from insanity.

I crept into St George's Room, my eyes lowered. The music was playing, but as soon as I walked in Marcus turned it off. That was something to be grateful for at least.

"Hi," I muttered.

Marcus was sitting on the edge of the table, his arms crossed. His face was a cold mask.

"So, come on. I'm waiting to hear your excuses. Let's see what you come up with."

His arrogant tone griped me, like I was a naughty schoolgirl being told off by the Headmaster. Who did he think he was?

Suddenly I didn't feel like I had to apologise at all. My guard came back up. "Nothing too bad happened. I went out, I got drunk, and I overslept this morning. I know I shouldn't have, but there's nothing I can do about it now. Just tell me what my punishment is. I accept it." Instead of all the apologetic, grovelling speeches I had prepared, I picked confrontation. Great job, Arianna.

Marcus's jaw tensed. He looked furious. "Nothing too bad happened? You were out with fallens till the early hours in the morning, got drunk, and were attacked by demons in a public place. Innocent people could have died. Did you think of that? Not to mention that you could have been killed. You broke all the rules, and you call that nothing?" It sounded like he despised me.

"I'm not twelve, Marc. I can look after myself. " I was shaking.

"Oh, so you're a grown-up only when it suits you? Your behaviour was disgusting. You made a fool of yourself, but most importantly you brought the rank you belong to into disrepute." He jumped off the table and stood up straight. "But that doesn't matter for Arianna. This is just a game to you, no big deal, right?"

"This is ridiculous. I haven't done anything wrong. I'm free to do as I please, Marc. This isn't the first time I've been clubbing and got drunk. And I'm sure it won't be the last. I'm almost eighteen. It's what people my age do. Not that you would know anything about fun." I knew I was handling this all wrong, but I just couldn't stop myself.

"You're right. That's what most normal teenagers do. But you're not a normal seventeen-year-old, are you? Have you forgotten that there are demons out there waiting for the opportunity to kill you?" A shiver rolled down my spine. "Last night you were surrounded by the worst demons in the whole area; you were attacked and you still don't know how to defend yourself properly. Do you have any idea what could have happened if Keaghan wasn't there?"

I'd never seen him so angry. I wanted to apologise, but the

words wouldn't come out.

Marcus took a deep breath and sighed. "But that's no longer my concern. You do as you please, Arianna. You're obviously not bothered about any of this. You don't care that we're all putting ourselves in danger for you – another minor detail that you don't seem to give a damn about."

I couldn't look at him. "Am I not being punished?"

"What's the point? It wouldn't make the slightest difference. You do what you want anyway. Your father would be ashamed of you right now. You're no Angel of Light. Maybe the Order made a terrible mistake." He looked at me, his face twisted with disappointment, and left the room.

As he shut the door, I burst out crying. I should have apologised to him; instead, I'd made things worse. Me and my big stupid mouth! Why couldn't I just say sorry? I ran out of the room, through the front door and down the steps. The Guardians opened the gate and I lurched into the forest, not looking where I was going. The tears in my eyes obscured the muddy path. The rain was drenching my clothes and hair but I carried on running till I was breathless, and collapsed on the ground under a tree. The echoes of my sobs filled the air.

I wasn't sure how long I lay on the wet grass, shivering, until I fell asleep, exhausted. When I opened my eyes, I was pressed against a warm chest. I recognised the scent of his aftershave instantly.

"Are you OK, Feather girl?"

Keaghan's voice was deep and low. I looked up. The warmth in his eyes took me by surprise. I shook my head as my bottom lip started to tremble. I started sobbing uncontrollably again. He took me into his arms and held me close. It was still raining, but the tree sheltered us, and his heat kept us dry.

"Shush, it's OK. It's all right, Arianna." He stroked my hair gently.

"I'm so sorry, Keaghan. I don't know where to start. I'm

sorry." I couldn't stop weeping.

"We all make mistakes," he murmured.

"But my behaviour was despicable. You were right, I forgot who I was and I can't do that. I can't forget my responsibilities. I'm the Angel of Light." I still wasn't sure what that meant.

"It was worth it to see Walker's face this morning, though."

He flashed me a cheeky grin, trying to cheer me up. I was surprised he was still talking to me after the way I'd behaved.

"I'm so sorry for getting Bruna into trouble. She felt bad for me. I practically begged her. It wasn't her fault, I swear."

He dried my tears with his hand. I jolted at his touch, but didn't back away this time.

"It's OK, don't worry. I'm fully aware that Bruna has a soft spot for you. She knows the consequences of breaking my rules. I wasn't too harsh though." There was something so incredibly sexy about his wink.

"Good, because she's my friend now. And I knew nothing bad would happen to me, 'cause I always feel safe around you. You saved my life, again, and I'll never forget that."

I swallowed the lump in my throat. He moved his face closer, my heart racing like a sprinter's.

"Stop beating yourself up. No one was hurt – apart from the demons – and that's all that matters. You were lucky they were rubbish. But you need to make a choice, Arianna. Which side are you on?" He gazed into my eyes. "You have to decide if you want to be a human or an angel. You can't be both. Morfran is getting closer to you, and you're making his job easier by exposing yourself like this."

"But I am human, and I always have been. I don't know how to be an angel." I eased away from his hold. The emanations coming from him were overpowering me.

"That's fine. You just made your choice, Arianna. The Order will understand. You want to live as a human – that's fine." He stood up, gently pulling me to my feet. "You have a right to choose. No one will force you into doing what you don't want to do."

"I – I..." I mumbled, confused.

"It's fine, Arianna. You just need to tell the Order you decline your right to become an angel, and they'll place you somewhere safe. Angels will guard you as you carry on leading a normal life as a human. Don't worry about Morfran. We'll find a way to sort him out without you."

His voice sounded calm but I wasn't sure I liked what he was saying. Somehow it didn't feel right.

"But, I never said... I didn't mean..."

He didn't let me finish. "Relax, Arianna, it's OK. You don't have to do this. You never have to see us again. We'll go our separate ways and forget this ever happened. You can forget about being the Angel of Light. You don't have to go through with it if you don't believe in it."

He backed away, standing in the rain, while I was still sheltered under the tree. I hated the way he was looking at me, as if he was saying goodbye. If I chose to live as a human, I would never see him again. I couldn't do that. Just the thought of it was agony.

"You're wrong." I stood tall, stepping towards him. "I can't and won't forget who I am. I won't turn my back on the people who've been protecting me my entire life. I'm the Angel of Light and I'll fulfil my duty to the Order, my duty to my father." I looked straight into his eyes. Rain was dripping from my face and hair. "I can't be just human, because I'm not. I'm an angel, I know that now. I wish I'd started believing sooner. But I do now."

He arched his eyebrows, dubious. "Is this what you really want, Arianna? Are you sure you can do this?" The rain bounced off him.

"Yes. I know what I have to do. I know who I am. I do believe I'm the Angel of Light, and I'll prove that to anyone who says I'm not."

For the first time I turned on my aura by myself, effortlessly. It shone brightly around me, before I slowly disengaged the energy, making it disappear.

Keaghan grinned at me. "That's the spirit, Feather girl. I knew you'd come round. Now let's get you back indoors before you catch pneumonia."

We walked back to the monastery side by side, his fingers entwining mine, neither of us speaking. There was no need. I was perfectly happy just feeling the warm touch of his hand. When I stepped inside the monastery, everyone was waiting for me, looking concerned.

"Arianna, where have you been? We were so worried." Kayla ran over to me.

I lifted my hand to stop her. "First of all, I want to apologise to all of you for my appalling behaviour these past few weeks. It took me longer than it should have, but I know what I have to do now." I looked at Marcus. He was sitting on the bottom stair, watching me.

"I promise I'll regain your trust, Marc. I'm so sorry for the way I spoke to you before, and for being so difficult during my training. I'll work harder than I've ever done in my life, I swear. Can you forgive me?" I felt a lump in my throat. "Please, give me one last chance to prove to you that I'm worthy of becoming the Angel of Light."

Julian stepped forward. "What do you say, Marc? Should we?"

"I'm not too sure, Julian." Marcus stood up, shaking his head.

I couldn't hold back the tears. "Please? I promise I believe now. I know who I am. I'll prove to you I can do it. Please give me another chance."

Marcus walked up to me, his eyes level with mine. "No more spoilt-brat behaviour?"

"I swear, hand on my heart."

He smiled at last, pulling me into his arms and holding me tightly to his chest.

23. THE FIRST SNOW

Finally, there was just one week left of training. I lay in bed feeling both happy and petrified. My phone beeped on the bedside table. I already knew who it was.

Look outside your window

I jumped out of bed. Oh my God, it was freezing. As I pulled the curtains open I gasped. Snow!

I got dressed and ran downstairs. Today was my big test. I wasn't as nervous as I thought I would be. If anything, I was looking forward to showing off my knowledge – the fruits of my long hours spent buried in the library.

Joya stood in the middle of the empty room. I sat down at my desk. In front of me were four sheets of A4 paper turned upside down.

"Are you ready, Arianna?"

"Yes." I think.

"You have one hour to complete the test, starting now."

She turned the hourglass around.

Forty-eight minutes later, I put my pen down, stood up, and approached Joya's desk.

"I'll give Marcus the results later," she said. "You can have the rest of the day off."

Huh? "What do you mean? Doing what? I'd rather train, to be honest. Can I go and practise my powers?"

"Arianna, you've earned a break. Besides, Keaghan wants to

see you. He has some news for you."

I looked down at my jogging pants and slouchy sweater. "Oh, right. OK. I'll go get changed then."

Joya stopped me. "Arianna, just be careful, all right?" The worry in her tone was evident.

"I will."

Careful about what? I didn't understand. I ran upstairs, feeling excited. Keaghan wanted to see me.

He stood by the front door, waiting for me as I came back down the stairs.

"Wow, you look cosy." He ran his eyes along my figure, wrapped in a white knitted dress and tights.

"Well, it's winter, you know? Not that you can feel the cold, of course." I smiled as I wrapped my red scarf around my neck and slipped into my red wellies.

"First snow of the year on the first of December, it's a good sign." He opened the front door for me.

"So? What have you got to tell me?" I asked as I followed him outside.

"We've caught the demons that set fire to your cottage."

"What? Who were they?"

"Darksiders." He helped me cross an icy stretch of the road.

"Morfran's followers," I said glumly. His name always made everything sound more real.

"Don't worry about them, Arianna. They've been dealt with. You just concentrate on finishing your training."

Dealt with? I wondered what that consisted of, but decided not to ask.

"But Keaghan, I need to be prepared. How can I defend myself if I don't know what's going on?"

I trotted to keep up with his fast pace. The snow was so thick you couldn't distinguish the road from the fields.

"What do you want to know?" he asked.

"Why do you want Morfran dead? I mean, you were his

pupil, right?"

Keaghan hesitated before replying. "Morfran's evil beyond imagination. He wouldn't spare a child if he could. Then again, your God doesn't either, when you think about it." He climbed over a low wall and held his hand out to help me.

"I don't think the comparison is fair. My God is merciful." Why was I being defensive about something I've never believed in?

"Not the one I know. Maybe yours is a different one." He smiled cynically.

Keaghan stopped and brushed the snow off a wooden bench. The snow melted under his touch. He hovered his hand over my side of the seat. Warm energy radiated out of his palm, drying the spot.

"There you are." He invited me to sit down.

"Wow, that's seriously cool."

I settled myself on the bench and wrapped my scarf tighter around my neck.

"You used to be an angel before you fell, right?" I wanted to know who he was, his history – everything about him. I realised I knew nothing of his past, really.

Keaghan twisted his head to look at me, his brow furrowed. "Where did you hear that?"

"Erm... I... I just presumed..."

"You presumed wrong. I was never an angel, or a fallen, Arianna. A long, long time ago, I used to be human."

I was shocked. I wasn't sure why I'd thought he was an angel before. I assumed that since he led the fallen angels, he must be one too. I didn't expect that answer.

"A human? B-but how? How did you... I mean... what happened?"

He sighed. "It's a long story, Arianna."

"Well, it's your lucky day. I have plenty of time. Joya has given me the rest of the day off."

He gazed into the distance at the snowy hills, but said nothing.

"Please tell me, Keaghan. What happened to you?"

I waited for him to speak. It was the longest few seconds of my life.

"I was born in Ancient Rome. I was a Pretorian of the Roman Empire. A loyal and trusted friend of the Emperor's son. Then it all went wrong." His jaw clenched. "I was accused of something I didn't do and sentenced to death for it. I wanted revenge, more than anything in the world." I could hear the resentment in his words.

"Is that when you found Morfran?" My voice shuddered when I said his name.

"He found me. The night before my execution, he came to my cell and offered me a way out. If I joined him and his legion of demons, I could carry out my revenge and live under my rules and mine only. In exchange for one tiny recompense, of course: my soul." The snow melted on the ground around him.

"I accepted without hesitation, and I became the most merciless demon on earth. I was making my own justice by killing evil people, tormenting murderers and sucking the life out of criminals." He sounded passionate, his words sending shivers down my spine.

"That's not so bad, I suppose. You were killing evil people." So now I was defending a murderous demon.

He tutted. "You're so naive, Arianna. You of all people should never condone killing of any kind."

"So why did you rebel against Morfran?"

I couldn't catch his eyes. "Morfran is the father of all lies. He twisted the truth to get me to do his dirty work. He's a clever demon. He always finds a way to make people do what he wants. I still felt like I was human back then – even without a soul – and he had to manipulate the truth to get me to do his will." He glanced at me. "One day, I realised he was getting me to kill innocent angels and fallens. He'd persuaded me they were evil people who had escaped justice. In truth they were all innocent. Morfran was framing fallen angels for his treacherous crimes and his demons were getting away with murder – literally." His eyes were filled with rage.

"Wait, I'm confused. Aren't fallen angels the same as demons?"

"Not exactly. Fallens are angels who rebel against God, but they're still angels. They don't have it in them to kill without a reason. Demons are evil through and through. They kill for the sake of killing, and enjoy it. But once I got to know the fallens, I grew fond of them, and I didn't enjoy what I was doing anymore. I hated Morfran for what he'd turned me into."

"Is that why you want him dead?" I asked.

"It's one of the reasons. When I rebelled against him, I created an army of fallens that hated him as much as I did. He still has my soul, and I kind of want it back."

"Hang on –" I was lost "– if he has your soul, what's he doing with it?"

"He keeps it to use as leverage: if we stop doing his will, he can cash our souls in and send us to hell."

"So why hasn't he done that already? Surely if you're now against him, he would want to get rid of you?"

Keaghan shrugged. "I've been asking myself the same thing. I haven't got a clue."

Although I still had many questions left unanswered, some things had become a lot clearer. Now I knew why Keaghan was protecting me. If I killed Morfran, he could have his soul back. I had one more reason for wanting to fulfil my mission. There was no doubt in my mind. I would kill Morfran. And I was going to do it for the both of us.

"Keaghan Blake. The Roman soldier who sold his soul to the devil to save innocent people. You're quite a character." I looked at him, feeling admiration, in spite of the chilling nature of his revelations.

"It's not as fascinating as you make it sound, Arianna."

"I always knew you weren't evil." I touched his arm gently.

He turned his head to look at me. For a split second his eyes flickered like burning embers.

"I never said I wasn't evil." His words sent shivers down my spine. "I'm still a cold-blooded killer, Arianna. I take lives and souls, and I have no mercy for people who don't deserve it. Maybe now I use my wickedness to protect the innocents, where the justice of your God has failed them. But I'm still a soulless creature." He stood up, looking away from me.

I didn't know how to answer that. I was still in shock. Yet, no matter what he'd said, I couldn't change the way I felt about him. Even if he tried *really* hard, he'd never be able to scare me away.

"Come on, there's a village at the bottom of the hill. Let's grab some food. You must be starving after all this nonsense." He flashed me one of his drop-dead gorgeous smiles.

I got up and walked at his side in silence. What he'd just told me should have frightened the life out of me. Instead, I was drawn to him even more. We stopped at a little country pub, arriving just in time to avoid a blistering storm.

I watched Keaghan as he ate, flirting with the waitress to make me jealous. I was convinced he was doing it on purpose. When he took my hands in his to warm them up, I flinched. The fire was glowing on his face; his olive skin shimmered under the light and his eyes sparkled as he talked to me. How could he possibly be a demonic creature when his eyes reminded me of a heavenly sky? I was staring at him so intently that I wasn't listening to what he was saying.

"Hello? *Earth calling Arianna...*" Keaghan's voice brought me back from my thoughts. "Where have you been for the past ten minutes?"

"Sorry, I was just thinking."

"Ouch, you haven't done that in a while, have you? Did it

hurt?"

"Hey! Stop it." I threw a napkin at him. He laughed.

"I was asking how you're feeling now that your training is almost over."

I thought for a moment. "Pleased, 'cause I can finally leave my prison. But petrified, because I haven't got a clue what happens next." I put my cup on the table, staring at it.

"How are you controlling your powers now?" he asked in a whisper.

"I can engage my aura and control it better. You were right, it happened when I was ready. Using my powers is a bit more complicated. I'm struggling still." A total disaster, more like.

"Which is your favourite power?"

"Probably telekinesis. I love doing that."

I concentrated on the spoon in front of me, engaging my aura. The spoon moved from my cup and dropped into Keaghan's.

"Whoa, Arianna. Not here. Turn off your lightbulb before anyone sees it." Keaghan looked apprehensive as I disengaged my aura.

"No one saw. Chill out, you're turning into a Feather," I said.

"You're a wicked child, do you know that?" He shook his head, flashing his trademark grin.

The breath caught in my chest. "I'm not a child, Keaghan. I wish you'd notice."

"Oh, I've noticed. Trust me." The sensuality in his tone made me blush. "Time to head off, it's getting late." He stood up, helping me wrap my scarf around my neck.

There was a raging snowstorm outside. But it turned out I wasn't going to have to walk in it. Instead, Keaghan lifted me off the ground, I tucked my head against his chest, and we were back at the monastery in less than a minute. The snow was falling thick and fast. Maidstone looked like a shadow in the storm. He dropped me off outside the front door – under the inquisitive eyes of the Guardians.

"I had a really nice time," I said. "Thank you for telling me more about... stuff. Sometimes I think you know me better than I do."

Please don't leave. Don't go. I was desperate to stay with him longer.

"I know there're a lot of things you still can't make sense of, Arianna. But you will, I promise." He suddenly leaned in, and his fingers brushed my cheek. Warmth flooded my skin. "Hang in there, it's almost over."

He vanished under the storm before I had a chance to reply.

24. DARK AND EVIL

The next day, Marcus told me he was going to question me on my final test answers. He wouldn't tell me my score until we'd done this additional oral check.

"But I haven't cheated, I swear. Ask Joya," I protested.

"I know you haven't. It's protocol. I have to make sure these things are in your head and not only on here." He was pointing at the exam paper.

"Fine, whatever. Ask away." I sat back, crossing my arms in frustration.

"Less attitude, young lady." He raised his eyebrows. "Start by talking to me about the different ranks in the Celestial Order."

"Seraphim are the highest rank in the Order. They ensure that all the other Orders are clear about God's message." My voice was clear and confident. "The second Order belongs to the Cherubim. They make sure His will is delivered according to His plan."

Heat was coming from my chest. My aura was shining, I could sense it.

"The third Order belongs to the Thrones. They send a message of harmony and kindness to humanity through the angels of God."

Hard to believe I remembered it all so easily. I was calm and focused, and in total control of my aura.

"The fourth Order belongs to the Dominions. They're in charge of regulating the duties of all angels, making known to them the commands of the Order."

Marcus's aura was radiating around him too. I continued my exposition.

"The fifth Order belongs to the Virtues. They have control over nature, the seasons, planets, and they're in charge of miracles on earth."

I stopped for a few seconds to draw breath. Why was I feeling tired all of the sudden?

"The sixth Order belongs to the Powers. They're in charge of the Warrior Angels. Their task is to defend humans and angels against evil forces."

I closed my eyes for a moment, taking another deep breath.

"The seventh Order belongs to the Archangels. They're the messengers of God and deliver holy messages on earth." I took another quick pause. "Last but not least, there's the Order of the Angels. We are the closest to humans and we deliver God's will on behalf of the Celestial Order. Our task is to assist those assigned to us for protection. We're in charge of making sure the Divine Design is accomplished." As I stopped talking, I felt weary. My mouth was dry.

"Are you all right, Arianna?" Marcus looked concerned. "You look pale. Here." He passed me a bottle of water. "I expect you're tired. Your aura was shining all along."

"I'm really dehydrated." I gulped down the water.

"It's quite normal. Your human side still isn't used to carrying your spiritual force. That's why I've been training you so hard physically. To help you handle the pressure."

"Shall we carry on?" I said as I placed the bottle on the table. I felt better now.

"If you're sure?" he frowned.

"Yes, I am."

"Let's move on to the Angelic Powers." My favourite part. "Which class of angels can orb?"

That was easy. "Only the Overseer Angels. They're in charge of supervising and tracking angels' locations anywhere on earth.

They can orb from any place apart from a demon's den, where their power to orb doesn't work," I answered with confidence.

"Well done. That's Julian, of course. What other powers does he have?"

"The power of pathfinding, which allows him to find angels or track individuals with the help of omni-powers."

He nodded. "And what are omni-powers?"

"All angels have omni-powers, which include heightened superhuman senses, strength, durability, telekinesis, ultra-vision and super-intelligence."

"Correct, Einstein. Now tell me about Kayla's powers."

"Healing Angels have the power to cure other angels. They can't heal humans and they only have a limited time to heal half angels. They have the power of invulnerability, which means they're immune to physical damage. They can perform astral projections to protect a specific area or place from evil forces, and can perform energy blasts to immobilise demons."

Marcus looked pleased with my answers. "That's right. Only a demonic blast can actually kill an angel. Kayla can't bring angels back to life once their spirit has gone, and her healing powers work differently with half angels. You're stronger because of your Lightworker heritage, but you're still vulnerable."

"Tell me something I don't know."

"Kayla would only have a limited time to save you. In other words, if your human body dies, she only has a short time to save you before your spiritual soul dies too. Do you understand what that means?"

"Yes. I'd better stay alive."

"What about you, Arianna? As the Angel of Light, what are your powers?"

"Telekinesis allows me to manipulate and control objects with the power of my mind. Like this." I focused and lifted the bottle of water, unscrewed the cap and hovered it above Marcus's head. All without touching it.

"Don't even think about it, Arianna. Put it down."

I chuckled, placing the bottle back on the table. "I can create an energy blast too, but I won't try that now, I promise."

"What about a psionic blast?"

"That's the ability to transform energy into physical strength. Only I can create a psionic blast that could kill a demon as strong as a Darksider. Though I haven't been able to create one so far." I pouted.

"It's OK, you will. What about telepathy?"

"All angels have telepathic powers, but can only communicate among themselves. We can only use telepathy if there are no demons to block the passage of thought. We have to choose to listen, or we won't be able to connect." I hoped he was impressed by how well I was remembering everything.

"What about me?"

I looked at him and smiled. "Marcus, the Reaper Angel. You also possess energy-blast and pathfinding powers. Your role is to train and prepare all new angels to defend themselves and embrace their destiny. One of your omni-powers is speed."

"Correct, and I also train Warrior Angels for battle. Well done. You've done great. Look at your aura. You've certainly learned to keep it under control. I told you that would happen." He touched the top of my head, stopping the light from shining.

"You made me suffer for it though." I stuck my tongue out.

"Right, do you want to know your final score?" He held my paper out.

"Too right." I snatched it from his hand.

"One hundred per cent?" I punched the air in triumph.

"Yep. You're my best pupil so far, *brainiac*." He smiled. "I'm so proud of you, Arianna. You look ready."

"I am ready." There was no hesitation in my response.

"I'm sorry if I've had to be so tough on you these past few weeks. You understand I had no choice?"

"I do. I've not made things easy for you either. I'm sorry

too." I stretched my hand out. "Friends?"

He grabbed my hand and pulled me into his arms, hugging me tightly. "Always."

Kayla and Julian burst into the room. "Marc? We need to speak with you."

"What is it?" Marc spun round.

"Joya has just sent in the last report. Can we talk in private?" Kayla looked at me.

"Hey, I have a right to know. It's about time you made me part of this. I need to be prepared. Marc?" I looked at him, defiant.

"OK, go ahead. What does it say?"

"There's been another murder in London." Kayla's voice was trembling.

"Who?" Marcus asked.

"Aryssa."

Marcus's jaw dropped. "Oh no."

"Who was she?" I looked at him puzzled.

"She was one of the Overseer Angels. She's been watching the City with Julian for months." Marcus's shoulders slumped. "Anyone else?"

"Two fallens." Julian's words made me shudder.

"Oh my God." I looked at Julian, my heart thudding with panic. "Who?"

"You don't know them, Arianna," he said. I let out a sigh of relief.

Marcus turned accusing eyes on me. "You seem more bothered about losing a fallen than one of our angels."

"I'm worried about anyone who loses their life because of me, Marc," I snapped.

He rubbed his forehead. "Of course, I'm sorry. I'm just upset."

"We're all upset," Julian interjected. "A dark force is stalking the streets of London, and it won't stop killing until it gets what it wants." That would be me.

Marcus sighed. "Now that Arianna's birthday is close, fear is spreading among the Darksiders. These killings are linked, I'm sure," he said hoarsely.

I felt guilt eating at my stomach. Innocent people were dying because of me.

"By killing our angels, Morfran must think Arianna will expose herself, giving his Darksiders a chance to get to her," Julian said.

Kayla put her arm round my shoulder. "Arianna, you don't have to worry about this. We'll sort it out. You need to concentrate on reaching your peak as an angel. We promise to get you to your eighteenth birthday in one piece."

25. HAPPY BIRTHDAY

On the day of my birthday, I woke up, opened my eyes and stretched. I thought I would feel different, but I didn't. Leaping out of bed, I stood in front of the mirror, examining my face and body, then twisted round, half expecting to see feathers poking out of my shoulder blades. Nothing. Today I turned eighteen and I was going to become a fully-fledged angel; yet I felt exactly the same as I always had.

The monastery was icy and dark as I made my way down the stairs. Even though I was wearing a thick black jumper, wool leggings and sheepskin boots, I was still cold.

"I've been instructed to serve you a special breakfast today." The housekeeper smiled warmly at me.

I was surprised not to see any banners or balloons hanging around the place. It was the least I expected from the girls.

Marcus walked in just as I finished eating my full English breakfast, down to the very last baked bean. Never thought I could miss bacon so much.

"Happy birthday, Arianna." He sounded more excited than I was.

He handed me a small pink box and a card, before kissing the top of my head.

"Thank you, Marc." I opened the box. "Oh, it's beautiful."

I held up the silver necklace with a pendant in the shape of a feather, and then threw my arms around him.

"You can look at it and remember who you are." He fastened the clasp at the back of my neck.

"A Feather girl, you mean?"

"An angel," he corrected.

Megan and Kayla walked in with balloons, presents, flowers and a cloud of pink feathers. They screamed "Happy Birthday!" as they entered the room. I nearly choked on my coffee. I jumped up and ran towards them. They hadn't disappointed me after all.

"My baby is eighteen at last." Kayla looked at me proudly, as if it was the event of the century.

We sat in St Helen's Room while I opened my presents and cards, screaming with each one I unwrapped. Megan placed a pink feather boa around my neck and a tiara on my head. Her gift was a silver key ring in the shape of a pair of wings. Kayla put a bracelet around my wrist, with one charm dangling, in the shape of a heart. Julian's present was brilliant.

"Wow. *The Quantum Universe: Everything That Can Happen Does Happen.* I've wanted this book for ages. Thank you, Ju." I gave him a kiss on the cheek.

"You must be the only girl in this century who still reads paper books." Julian shook his head.

"Thank you, guys." We shared a group hug.

"Today is special, Arianna. You don't get to become an angel every day," Kayla said.

"So, this is the beginning of my... evolution?" Was that the right word?

Marcus looked at me, proud. "Today marks the end of your life as a human and the beginning of your life as an angel. There's nothing and no one that can stop you now."

"So, am I capable of fighting Morfran now?" My voice shook.

"Well, this is definitely the age Morfran wished you'd never reach," Megan said. "From this day on, you'll keep on getting stronger and stronger and your powers will make you almost invincible. Trust me, he's not a happy demon today, I can guarantee it." She gave a happy laugh. "We're going to celebrate in style. Just wait and see what we've got in store for you." Her red curls bounced as she jumped with excitement.

"That sounds like heaven. I can finally get out of this monastery," I said.

Marcus shot me a serious look. "Almost. But first you need to go and meet the Order. They'll be waiting for you at ten o'clock in Milton Abbey."

"Do I need to go through some kind of ritual to turn into an angel?" I was anxious at the thought.

Marcus gave me a reassuring smile. "You don't turn into an angel, Arianna. You were born one. You'll meet some of the highest angelic ranks in the CO today. They'll welcome you, and explain what your duties are and what's required of you." He placed a hand on my shoulder. "You'll be asked to become an angel, Arianna."

"Asked? Do you mean I can still say no?" That was a surprise.

"You still have a choice. But no one has ever turned away from their destiny before, and I doubt you will, Arianna." Marcus nodded, confident.

Kayla held my hand. "It's a very intense experience, a little overwhelming, but it's an amazing sensation. You'll see. Don't be afraid of what's happening around you."

I sensed energy coming from her skin unlike anything I'd ever quite felt from her before. It had to be a sign of a new connection between us.

"Did you feel that?" I asked, looking down at my tingling hand.

"Oh yeah. Welcome to the angelic world, Arianna." She grinned at me.

Marcus checked his phone. "Come on, we need to get going. Keaghan and his fallens have just sent an update. There's masses of demon activity around the world. They know exactly what day it is today, and they're all petrified."

"But you're safe, sweetheart," Kayla said. "You're surrounded by an astral projection that will keep you protected." Both our auras were shining.

"The astral projection is only temporary, right?" I asked.

Kayla nodded. "The energy I created will protect you from any evil forces, but just for a few hours. Megan's spell should keep away any Darksiders. They don't like her very much."

"I'll make sure of that, sweetie," Megan said.

"Yeah. Darksiders hate witches." A laugh burst from Julian's throat.

"If you call me a witch one more time I'll put a spell on you and turn you into a statue," Megan warned.

"See what I mean?" Julian carried on sniggering.

Leaving the monastery with Marcus was a relief, but I also felt nervous. I'd been safe within these walls. Now I was vulnerable, exposed to danger, and I didn't feel a hundred per cent ready. I still hadn't mastered some of my powers to their maximum potential. But I didn't have any choice. Morfran wasn't going to wait for me to be ready.

Marc drove us to the abbey. I shuddered as I looked at the imposing façade.

"This is where I leave you. I need to meet the others for an update on patrolling. We want this day to be perfect for you. You'll be OK, trust me. Today you get to know all the truths you've been waiting for."

So this was it. And suddenly I wasn't so sure I wanted to go ahead. Marc held me close, and I hugged him tightly. He kissed my forehead and I watched him walk away before taking a deep breath and turning towards the main entrance, shaking like a leaf.

A sudden pain stabbed in my chest; my aura started to burn without warning. There was a sound like a hiss. I turned round and there he was, standing tall in his black jeans and leather jacket. He was leaning against a lamp-post, with his arms crossed, and a wicked smile on his face.

"Keaghan." I smiled too as he walked towards me. My legs were wobbling and my heart raced.

"So the angel finally gets her feathers?" He flashed a cheeky grin.

"I guess so."

He looked down and picked up the chain round my neck with his fingers. My breathing accelerated. I could barely move.

"Another Feather girl. Hell help us."

"But I'm not just a Feather girl, am I? I can kill Morfran now," I said proudly, even though I had trouble believing it.

Keaghan burst out laughing. "I wouldn't say that too loud around here, Arianna. Not today, of all days."

He leaned forward, his eyes inches from mine. "The Devils are very upset, Arianna."

Did he sound sexy or scary? His blue eyes turned to red for a brief moment. I could feel his warm breath on my cheek.

"I would be too, if it wasn't for the fact that you're so cute," he murmured.

He gently pressed his finger on my frozen nose. I shuddered.

"You best get going. You don't want to keep the Order waiting." His voice changed, breaking the spell.

I managed to tear my gaze away from his eyes and stepped back a few paces, flustered. "Yeah, I – I better go."

As I walked away, a gust of hot air spun around me, breaking my stride. Keaghan was standing in front of me, leaning towards me, his lips millimetres from mine. I could hardly catch my breath.

"Happy birthday, Feather girl," he whispered. I closed my eyes and I felt his lips pressing against my neckline. Fire ignited inside me. I gasped, feeling as if my heart was about to burst in my chest. He disappeared in an instant, leaving a trail of heat behind him. What just happened? Breathe, Arianna. Start breathing again.

The noise of the church bells ringing brought me back to

reality.

I looked around for Keaghan, but he was gone. I forced my feet to walk through the door and across the nave, passing the transepts and the quire, before reaching the secret area, where no one could enter but my kind. This was it.

I went through a wooden door that led on to a dark, narrow corridor. At the end was another door, this time leading to a long staircase. I was heading towards the pinnacle of the tower. At the top, I went through at least another two doors, before finally stopping in front of yet another wooden door.

The room wasn't what I expected. Whatever that was. It was a normal-looking living room. There was a small couch, a window with red curtains, and a little table with a vase of white roses on top. I walked in, puzzled. I sensed a bright light behind me and spun round. As the light disappeared, Joya was standing in front of me.

"Happy birthday, Angel of Light." She placed her arms around me.

"Oh Joya, I'm so glad you're here. I'm scared."

She held me tightly. "Don't be afraid, child. You're going to be just fine. Actually, you're going to be brilliant. I have a surprise for you."

She moved away from me and closed her eyes. A huge beam of light appeared above her head. She opened her eyes again, smiling.

"Look behind you, Arianna."

I turned to see a beautiful white dress hanging by the window; it was silky and flawless, like a cloud. The corset was embellished with sequins and pearls and the sleeves were made of soft chiffon with white ribbons around the wrists; a floating layer of skirts flowed from the waist.

"Wow. Is this for me?" I gasped.

"You didn't think I was going to let you go to the ball without a dress, did you? What kind of a godmother would I be?" She smiled warmly.

"I do feel like Cinderella right now."

There was a beautiful pair of white shoes on the floor, with a silk flower on the sides. I picked them up and gazed at them.

"Come on, you need to get changed. Raphael is waiting outside to escort you. I'll see you shortly, my darling." She threw me a reassuring look, then left the room.

I slipped on the dress and shoes and looked at my reflection in the mirror. I hardly recognised myself. I looked like a princess. Wow.

I had always felt uncomfortable with my looks. That's why I preferred to hide my long dark hair under a hood and kept my emerald eyes pointing down at the floor. It was easier that way. I didn't want to draw attention. Gazing at my reflection now, I smiled, proud, no longer afraid of the way I looked or who I was.

As I walked outside the room, I found an angel waiting to escort me. Raphael looked about my age, maybe a few years older, and was dressed in white clothes. A million questions went bouncing round my head as we walked. What was going to happen? No one had prepared me for this day.

"Arianna?" Raphael brought me back from my thoughts as we stopped in the highest part of the tower. I could see the forest from the arched window.

He pointed to a small door in front of us. It looked as if it was made of solid gold. Raphael placed a white cloak over my shoulders and I tied it around my neck with trembling hands. I felt afraid of the unknown, and yet incredibly curious to find out what was hidden behind that golden door.

26. DESTINY

I had always believed in facts. There had to be a reasonable explanation for everything. I found the logic in every apparently irrational concept. Before all this began, I'd even found a justification for the beam of light I'd sometimes seen radiating above my head, the floating objects, the shooting pain across my chest. Those *strange things* of mine. But there was no way to rationalise the past ten weeks, nor what I was about to witness next.

"Don't take your hood down until they do," Raphael instructed.

The golden door opened by itself. I swallowed hard as I stepped inside. The room was huge and empty. There were no paintings on the white walls, no ornaments, no furniture. My heels clicked on the marble floor as I walked.

I stopped in the centre of the room and looked around. What was I supposed to do now? Ten seconds went by, then fifteen, twenty, twenty-five.

All of a sudden, a bright light shone in front of me, almost blinding me. It faded away. Six people were standing in a line opposite me. They all wore long cloaks with hoods covering their heads. My heart raced, my knees were knocking together. They looked so... tall.

Then, as I looked more closely, I realised their smiles were friendly and reassuring. A sense of wellbeing spread around me. I felt my spirit connecting with theirs, and knew I belonged there, with them. I wasn't afraid anymore.

"Welcome, Arianna. We've been waiting for this moment for a long time."

The gentle voice came from a woman in the middle of the line. She was wearing a purple cloak, her brown hair and beautiful face peeping from under the hood. The lady on her left was wearing a bronze cloak. Joya! A familiar face, at least. They divided into two groups, leaving a gap through which I saw a light coming towards me. They all bowed their heads as the white light made its way through.

The light solidified and took the form of a man in a silver cloak. He pulled his hood down. His features were distinguished. He had short white hair and thick stubble. His aura was shining bright above his head, in the shape of a circle. It looked different from the auras I had seen before. More like a basketball hoop. But without the net.

"She has her father's sense of humour, don't you think?" Joya said to the others. The elderly man smiled, nodding.

They could hear what I was thinking? Oh God. I was going to have to be more careful from now on. Not easy when faced by a bunch of people wearing cloaks. Just a few weeks ago, I would have thought they looked ridiculous. Who were they?

The other members of the Order took their hoods down to allow their auras to shine above their heads. Their light was different from mine: a more intense golden colour.

I remembered what Raphael told me, and lowered my own hood.

"Don't be afraid, Arianna. Today is a very special day for you." The elderly man's voice was soft and calm, a voice I could never get tired of listening to. "You've been wondering who these people in ridiculous cloaks are. Right?" I had to smile. He'd voiced my thoughts, word for word.

"Let me introduce you to the people who will be your guide and strength throughout this journey, Arianna. And trust me, we're not as serious as we look. My name is Argenteus. I'm a member of the Seraphim, the highest rank in the Celestial Order. I'm the guardian of God's Throne." With every word he spoke, I had to keep telling myself I wasn't dreaming.

The woman in the purple cloak spoke next. Her dark skin contrasted with her blue eyes, and her smile looked warm and gentle. "My name is Viola. I'm a member of the Cherubim. I'm the guardian of God's Glory." I understood now why I had needed to read all those books.

The lady in the azure cloak also had beautiful blue eyes, but her skin was very pale against her dark hair. "My name is Zaffyra. I'm a member of the Thrones. I'm the guardian of Peace and Humility."

Joya was next to speak. "Arianna, we already know each other of course, but what you didn't know until now is that I'm your godmother. I belong to the Order of the Dominion. I'm in charge of regulating the duties of angels on earth, making them aware of the commands of God. That includes you too now." Amid this surreal scene, I was relieved to see Joya's familiar face smiling at me.

The woman in the green cloak had brown eyes and a very young-looking face; her curly blonde hair was glowing under the light of her aura. "My name is Virydia. I am a member of the Virtues. I have control over nature, the seasons, the stars, the moon, the sun and all the planets. I will support you with courage, grace and valour." I gazed in awe at her enchanting smile.

The red-cloaked man was wearing a military uniform under his cloak and held a sword by his side. "My name is Ruben. I'm a member of the Powers, a Warrior Angel in charge of defending humans and angels against evil and demonic spirits." He pierced me with his brown eyes.

The last man in line was wearing a gold cloak and had brown eyes and blonde hair. "My name is Aureus and I'm an Archangel, a messenger of God. I offer support during critical times and I deliver important messages on earth."

I felt overwhelmed by the presence of people who looked normal, but were in fact Divinities. The *brainiac* in me still struggled to believe what I was seeing. But there was no way I could deny the evidence of my eyes. They were real, standing in front of me – glowing.

"And now we come to you, Arianna." Argenteus spoke again. "You belong to the Order of the Angels, the closest to humans, the deliverers of God's prayers. Each angel has a power, a task and a destiny. You are the daughter of the Archangel Moriel – the Superior Angel of Judgment."

I listened to the sound of his voice, captivated by every word. That was my dad he was talking about.

"He brought to justice those accused of infamous sins. But he was also a kind and gentle soul," he continued. "Your mother was Rose Morelli, a powerful Lightworker. A pacifist and a merciful soul capable of melting the hardest of hearts. Their union was part of a Divine Design, destined to bring you to us, Arianna. You are the Angel of Light. You have many powers, all unique to your rank." I was rooted to the spot as his words washed over me. "Angel of Light, you have the power to destroy the most evil and ferocious demons, those which inflict pain and misery and death all around us. We cannot control their evil without your help. We've engaged all the angels to protect mankind. We've joined forces with Fallen Angels to help us in our task. But we've reached a point we can't go beyond. Only you can, Arianna. So we call upon you today, on this day of your Angelic Birth, to fulfil your duty. The time has come for you to take your place in the Order."

I swallowed hard as his solemn voice echoed in the room.

"Arianna, are you prepared to embrace your angelic life?"

Everyone's eyes were on me. Although I felt intimidated, I didn't hesitate.

"I am."

"My task is to make you aware of the risks and dangers you'll be facing. You're part of the Angels of the Firmament, the most powerful angel so far – but you're not immortal." I suppressed a shudder. "Arianna, only you can defeat Morfran. Only you have the power to vanquish him. Are you prepared to sacrifice your life for the needs of mankind?"

Was I? I hesitated this time. Could I really do this? I needed to give him an answer, but I couldn't form words when I tried to speak. Speak, Arianna. Say something. Anything.

"I'll do whatever it takes. Just tell me what I need to do."

I wasn't sure where those words came from, but I was sure I meant them.

"I admire your courage, and I had no doubts about your bravery. Your parents would be so proud of you today." Argenteus's words brought a lump to my throat. "You won't be alone in this battle. You'll have the support and the guidance of the entire Celestial Order. Angels and fallens will fight with you and will protect you with their lives. It's your duty as the Angel of Light to annihilate Morfran and every other demon obstructing your path."

The members of the Orders stood together, their auras shining even brighter than before.

"Arianna Morelli, are you ready to take your place in the Celestial Order?" Argenteus asked, his powerful voice ringing out.

"I'm ready." My voice resounded in the empty room. No indecision this time.

Heat spread from my chest to my head. My aura was engaged, shining bright around me.

"Welcome to the Celestial Order, Angel of Light."

That was it. I was in. No going back now.

Argenteus spoke again. "But let's not forget that today is your birthday, and I can therefore grant you a wish. Before you embark on this journey, have you any requests, my child?"

Huh? I didn't see that question coming. What should I ask for? I had no idea. Think. Then it hit me, and I knew what I wanted right now, more than anything else.

"I'd like to go back to Rome to visit the places where my father was the Angel of Judgement." I took a deep breath and looked up at him. "Rome has always reminded me of my parents' death, so I chose to hate it. But now I'd like to shed some light on my past and speak to the people who knew my mother and father best." I swallowed hard, waiting for a response.

"Are you sure this is all you wish for?" Argenteus sounded surprised.

"Yes."

"Very well. Your wish is granted. Your destiny was always going to take you back to Rome. It's where you belong, where it all started. You'll be accompanied by your protectors. This could be an opportunity for you to become stronger still."

There was a buzz of agreement from the others.

"These are dangerous times, Arianna. You'll be safer within the walls of the Eternal City. You'll be in the presence of the highest entities ever assigned to an angel. Keaghan Blake will accompany you. Angels and fallen angels will be by your side on this journey, have no fear, my child."

I shook as I heard Keaghan's name. "Thank you."

The members of the Order replaced their hoods and the room lost its light.

"Go, child. We'll see you again very soon. I bless thee, Angel of Light." Argenteus raised his hands and shone a bright light at me, forcing me to close my eyes.

When I opened them again, they'd all disappeared and I was alone in the room. I couldn't find words to describe how I felt. I couldn't cling on to science anymore. These beings were totally and utterly real – and I was one of them. As I looked down at the floor, near where my mentors had been standing, I noticed something. A long white feather. I smiled, making my way towards the golden door and out of the secret passage.

I could hardly contain my excitement, feeling empowered and astounded at the same time. As I walked through the abbey, I saw no one. None of my friends were waiting for me. It didn't matter. My thoughts belonged to someone else: Keaghan.

27. BEST BUDDIES

I had never felt this way before. I thought I knew what being in love meant. But even though the feelings I once had for Marcus were strong, they didn't come close to the way my heart thumped every time I saw Keaghan. No matter how hard I tried, I couldn't stop feeling drawn to him like a magnet.

As I stepped from the abbey, a text came through. I looked up from the phone. Keaghan was waiting for me, standing in the middle of the churchyard – sexy as ever.

"Gosh, you smell *holy*." He scrunched up his face as if he was in pain. "So, Rome, hey? Of all the wishes you could have asked for, you choose to go into the snake-pit."

"How do you know about that?" I asked.

"I'm your protector, Arianna. I know everything there is to know about you." He turned away and suppressed a retch.

"What's wrong?" I touched his arm.

He pulled away abruptly. "It's you. Your scent. I can smell the Order on you. It stings my eyes. Give me a minute to adjust." He shook his head; his eyes flickered from blue to red. "So, what do you think of the good old CO?" he asked, still keeping some distance between us.

"Great, I guess. I can't remember all their names, but I already knew most of what they told me. All the books I've had to read these past few weeks were useful in the end, just like you said."

I smiled at him, trying to catch his eye. But he was still *adjusting* – whatever that meant. After a few more seconds, he finally looked up at me.

"Come on, let's go." He seemed to have recovered, and led me to his car parked nearby.

"You look gorgeous, by the way." His eyes flickered furtively towards me, moving up and down my body, making me blush.

"I had to dress up for the occasion, didn't I?" I looked away to hide my red cheeks.

"You should dress up more often," he said, opening the door for me.

He closed the door after I got in, and in an instant he was by my side in the driver's seat, giving me no time to catch my breath.

"So you want to go to Italy. Why now? Why not wait till you're more used to your powers?" He still seemed tense.

"Because I want to go to the place where everything started. My dad was an Angel of Rome. I want to go and search the Vatican's library. I need to see the proof with my own eyes, Keaghan."

"Here we go, Einstein's back. I knew it wouldn't take long. Can't you just accept that some things can't be explained?"

The car sped along the country roads, going so fast I felt queasy.

"No, I can't. Besides, once I'm there, I might be able to remember more about my life before everything changed. The fire I survived that my parents didn't." I shuddered at the thought.

"What do you remember of it?"

He was looking at the road, occasionally glancing at me from the corner of his eye.

"Nothing," I said glumly. "Not one clear memory of my life in Rome. Just blurred, scattered glimpses of the night of the fire." I closed my eyes for a moment. "I hated Rome because of that. But now I realise it's the only place where I can find the truth."

I looked out of the window to find that we were heading towards the forest. "Where are we going?"

"I need to take you somewhere." His answer was cold and distant.

"Where?"

"You'll see. Stop asking questions."

Ouch. What had changed his mood? I kept quiet for a while and he didn't look at me again.

"If you don't want to come to Italy with me, I can go by myself, you know." The disappointment was clear in my voice.

"Don't be silly, of course I'm coming with you." He finally looked at me.

"Then why are you angry with me?"

"I'm not angry with you. I'm all right, Feather girl. I'd be delighted to accompany you." He smiled, but I sensed that it was forced.

He parked the car outside a small cottage. Jill and Megan were standing by the gate.

"Hello, gorgeous." Megan placed a kiss on my cheek.

"Why are we here?" I asked.

"This is your new home, Arianna."

What? "Where's my Nana?"

"She's OK. She's inside, waiting for you." Jill gave me a reassuring smile.

"Keaghan," Megan said, giving him a lukewarm reception. He nodded at her.

I walked to the wooden porch, where I turned to look at Keaghan. He smiled as if to reassure me. I walked inside the house and down a short corridor to the front room, where a cosy fire was burning.

Nana sat in a rocking chair with a white blanket on her lap. Her eyes were shut and her breathing seemed short and irregular.

"Nana?" I whispered. I sat on the floor, by her feet.

"Arianna, my darling." She opened her eyes and gazed at me. "Look at you. My little angel is ready to fly." She patted my cheek with shaky fingers.

"Are you all right, Nana?" She looked so pale and gaunt.

"I'm fine. I'm just old, Arianna. Happy birthday, darling." She smiled tenderly, and pointed towards the fireplace. "There's a box on the mantelpiece. Will you get it for me, please?"

I picked up the little white box and passed it to her, sitting back down at her feet.

"This was your mother's. She wanted you to have it today, on the day you became the Angel of Light. Your parents sacrificed their own lives so that this day could arrive."

She gave me the box. I opened it with trembling fingers.

"Oh, my goodness, Nana. It's beautiful." I gasped as I looked at the ring with its deep blue stone dazzling in the centre.

"It was chosen for you by my dear Rose. The blue star sapphire is the stone of destiny. It means hope, a hope that is placed upon you, my child." She took the ring and placed it on the third finger of my right hand.

"I'll make her proud, Nana, I promise. I just wish I could have had more time with them. I have so little memory of my childhood, of what happened before the fire. It's as if my brain has erased my life before I was eight."

She lifted my chin and smiled at me. "I know, and I'm sorry I can't change what happened. It was written before you were born. But you know now, and you're able to change the future."

"Why could we never talk about this before?" I held her hand in mine and rested my head on her lap.

"Because you were too scared. You've always been an angel, you just didn't want to see it."

"I knew I was different, but I always found explanations for the *strange things*. I suppose you're right. I was scared to see." I took a shuddering breath. "I still am."

She touched my head. "I wanted you to have a normal childhood, enjoy the things normal children do. Your mother had such a hard time coming to terms with her powers when she was a child. It's not easy to feel different, an outcast."

I groaned. "I thought I was mad, a nut case."

"Well, you're no picnic, Arianna, you never were. But you're not a nut case. You're simply more special than you thought."

"I've missed you, Nana." I kissed her wrinkly hand.

"Aw, darling, you never have to miss me. I'll always be by your side, even when you can't see me."

I looked up, staring into her eyes; they were sparkling. "Why does this feel like goodbye?" A tear fell from the corner of my eye.

"Nonsense, child. I'm not going anywhere. I'm not even allowed to go to the back garden alone. Jill never lets me out of her sight. The perks of having a Guardian Angel, I suppose." She giggled, but broke off into a cough.

"I heard you asked to go to Rome," she said when she had caught her breath. "I have to say I was surprised. I knew you'd change your mind, but not this quickly."

"Who told you that?" I looked at her, surprised myself.

The answer came from behind me. "Me. I hope you don't mind."

I turned to see Keaghan standing in the doorway with a cup in his hands.

"Keaghan, come in, boy."

What? Nana spoke to him with affection, as if she knew him well.

"I hope I'm not intruding, Mrs Blight." The room filled with heat as he walked in.

"Of course not, my dear. Aw, thank you. You're always so kind."

Keaghan placed the cup on the coffee table by her side. What on earth was going on here?

"Make sure you look after my girl, won't you?" Nana said. She seemed to trust him.

"Of course I will. Haven't I always?"

He was speaking in such a gentle, caring tone. I'd never heard him talk that way to anyone before.

"You have indeed. Arianna, you make sure not to cause Keaghan any trouble. I know what you're like. Be sure to behave."

I couldn't believe my ears. My Nana was telling the angel to be good for the demon.

"She's all right, Mrs Blight. Arianna's no trouble at all."

Nana struggled to pick up the cup with her shaky hands. Keaghan moved faster than me. He held it for her as she sipped. I watched them, gobsmacked, as they chatted. They looked at ease in each other's company, as if they'd known each other for ages. I thought Nana couldn't stand demons. Didn't apply to this one, obviously.

"Are you OK, Arianna?" Keaghan asked. His eyes moved from my face to my hand.

"Look, this was my mum's ring. Isn't it beautiful?"

I stretched my hand out to show him. He twitched at first, but then surprised me by gently stroking my finger. A spark travelled along my arm.

"It is indeed," he said.

Nana's eyes were closed and I assumed she had fallen asleep. "Since when have you and my Nana been best buddies?" I whispered.

"Is that a problem?" he whispered back.

"No, it's just weird. You seem to know each other so well."

"Your Nana certainly knows me, better than anyone else, probably." He gave me one of his disarming smiles, setting my cheeks on fire.

"You knew my parents too, right?" I dared ask again. The last time I asked he'd avoided the question.

He sighed. "I did. They were good people, the best you could ever meet. They didn't deserve what happened to them." He lowered his eyes to the floor; his expression became hard.

"They didn't, you're right, and I'll make sure Morfran pays

for it." I pressed my lips together with conviction.

"I know you will. And I'll be right by your side to give you a hand." He stared at me. It was an intense moment, and I could hardly catch my breath.

We were interrupted by Megan. "Your Nana needs her rest now, Arianna." Her words were directed at me but her cold eyes were trained on Keaghan.

I adjusted the blanket on Nana's knees, placed a kiss on her cheek, and we made our way to the front door.

"Kayla and Julian are waiting for you at the house." Megan smiled at me, before turning cold again as she spoke to Keaghan. "Make sure she doesn't get there late." She faked a grin, and so did he.

"Of course, Ms Granger." Keaghan's sarcasm didn't go down well.

"I'm not a witch. But I'd love to use my powers against you." Her eyes looked furious. "I'll see you there, Arianna." She climbed into her car and sped off down the road.

Keaghan placed his hand on my shoulder, making me jump. "Are you OK to go?" I nodded. He gently guided me towards the car.

Before he could open the door, a text message came through on his phone.

"I need to pick up some stuff in London," he said, staring at the screen.

"Can I come?" I didn't want to sound too eager, but the high-pitched tone of my voice must have given my feelings away.

"It's too dangerous. I'll drop you off. Can't take you with me this time." He held the car door open.

"Please? I promise to be good and do everything you tell me to do. I swear I'll be no trouble," I begged.

He thought for a while before replying. "All right, but you promise to do as I say?"

"I promise," I smiled, victorious.

Half an hour later, we were driving through the streets of London.

The City centre was busy, but Keaghan managed to avoid the traffic, driving at his usual speed. He parked the car down an alley in an area I'd never been to before. Derelict buildings loomed on both sides of the alley, which didn't appear to have an end.

"Right, I need to go and talk to some people. I won't be long. Stay in the car till I'm back."

"Are you insane? You're not leaving me here on my own. I'm coming with you." I opened the door and stepped out of the car.

He looked me up and down, shaking his head. "Not in that dress, you're not. Stay in the car. I'll lock the doors. Don't worry, it's bulletproof." Was that supposed to make me feel safer?

"I'm not waiting alone in the car in this neighbourhood." I stood firm.

"I told you not to come," he said with an impatient flick of his hand. "Fine. But you stay right beside me, don't say a word, don't look directly in their eyes, and don't touch anything."

I nodded obediently.

We walked together towards the shutter of a warehouse. Keaghan knocked on the door twice. The aluminium door slid open. I peered in. The place was full of dismantled cars. It looked dodgy to me. We walked past some rough-looking guys. They stared at me as if I was fresh meat on a market stall. Keaghan grabbed my hand and held it tightly. It felt like I was holding flames between my fingers.

"Blake, what an honour." A chubby, dark-haired man walked towards us.

He showed us into a small room, staring unashamedly at every inch of my body as I walked past. Keaghan kept hold of my hand, pulling me even closer.

"Eddy, you 'right?" he said to the man.

"Yeah, not bad at all, mate. Business is thriving. How about you?"

The guy had a deep scar on his neck. He caught me staring at it. I looked away, squeezing Keaghan's hand until my knuckles turned white.

"I'm good. You got my stuff?" Keaghan asked.

"Yeah, easy. Is it for her? Your flavour of the month, is she?" he sneered.

The man brought something from his coat pocket, still looking at me with greedy eyes. I didn't like his remark, or his dirty looks.

"I'm nobody's flavour," I snapped.

I immediately regretted speaking, as Keaghan squeezed my hand so tight it hurt.

"Sharp tongue. Definitely your type. Here you go." He gave Keaghan two passports.

"And for the other thing, let's go in there." Eddy turned to the door. I went to follow with Keaghan, but Eddy stopped our stride. "She doesn't need to follow you everywhere, does she? I need to talk to you alone."

Keaghan let go of my hand. I shook my head at him. Don't you dare leave me.

"I'll be right back," he said. He leaned over as if to kiss me, and whispered, "Don't touch anything." He placed a kiss on my jaw before leaving me alone in the room, closing the door behind him.

I was still shaking from the unpredicted kiss. I looked around. The office was dirty and smelly. There was a calendar with photos of naked girls on the wall and empty takeaway boxes scattered all over the place. A huge cockroach scuttled across the floor. My attention was caught by a picture on the desk. I walked round and moved some of the mess away so I could have a good look. The photo showed a scene covered in ashes and debris. Underneath there was another photograph: a burnt body. The date of the picture was stamped in the top corner: three days ago. I shuddered, rifling through more photos of corpses.

I didn't notice the two men walk into the room until I heard the door slam shut. I jumped, dropping the pictures on the floor.

"What the hell are you doing?"

They glared at me with scarlet eyes, hissing like angry snakes.

Oh crap.

28. A BLAST TO REMEMBER

I always did have a talent for getting into trouble. I never counted to ten before speaking my mind; I never listened; and I regularly caused problems by not doing as I was told. One of these days it would land me in danger. Today was possibly the day.

The thug was glaring at me with his red eyes. "I said, what are you doing, little girl?"

I stepped away from the desk, staggering backwards as my legs trembled. "Nothing."

"Doesn't seem like nothing to me," he said.

A sinister smile pulled at the lips of the other guy. "She was snooping around," he snarled.

Where was Keaghan? Why hadn't I listened for once?

"I wasn't doing anything wrong." I tried to keep my voice even, but my fear betrayed me.

The first guy walked over to me. "Oh, I think sticking your pretty little nose in our business is classed as wrong."

My heart was in my throat. He stopped just a few inches away, lifted his hand, and brushed his finger across my face. Heat travelled along my skin like raging flames. I suppressed a yelp of pain and stepped back.

"You're beautiful." He grabbed my wrist and held it in a tight grip.

"Don't touch me," I yelled.

I felt my aura shining above my head. I hoped it would scare him off, but it didn't.

"Let her go, Kyle," the other man said. He seemed nervous,

darting glances at the door and then back at me. "This isn't a good idea."

The skinhead pulled me closer. "I've always wanted to know what it feels like to kiss an angel," he said. "They say it's mind-blowing."

"I wouldn't dare if I were you," I snarled, tugging at his hold.

My skin was burning under his grip, my chest rising and falling fast. I felt a surge of energy in my core. My aura was fully engaged. I was ready to release an energy blast. I hoped.

The door flung open, and Eddy and Keaghan walked in.

"What's going on?" Eddy said, his eyes darting about.

The skinhead let go of me and stepped away. "I caught her snooping in your things, Ed."

Keaghan's eyes were bright red. I rushed over to him; he put a protective arm around my waist. His hold was tight enough to take my breath away.

"Blake, tell your girl to keep her fingers out of my business. Or she won't have any fingers left," Eddy growled.

I swallowed hard, grabbing Keaghan's hand. "I was only looking. No harm done," I said. "And tell your ugly men to stay away from me, or I'll blow their heads off."

What was wrong with me? My mouth was always saying the wrong thing at the wrong time.

"You need to teach her to keep her gob shut, Blake." Eddy glared at me, his red eyes flickering.

"Trust me, I intend to." Keaghan squeezed my hand, forcing me to suppress a yelp of pain.

As we walked out, I felt all eyes glued on me. I was relieved when we finally made it outside.

"Ouch! Keaghan, you're pulling my arm out of its socket," I yelled.

He finally let go of me. "I want to pull more than just your arm right now, Arianna. Your neck will be next if you don't shut up and get in the car."

I sat in the passenger seat without saying a word. Keaghan sped off.

"All I asked was for you to be quiet and not touch anything. Was that so hard?" His eyes were still red; he looked furious. The car was getting so hot, I started to sweat.

"Sorry," I said, though I wasn't sure if I was. "Who were those people? And what's with the passports? And those pictures, did you see the pictures?"

"Will you shut up for a second?" he snapped. "I need to calm down."

His skin-prickling voice echoed in the car. His face was dark and his eyes still weren't back to normal. His expression was enough to silence me. I looked away, frightened.

Keaghan drove out of the city like a maniac. I kept my eyes shut most of the time, trying to ignore the transformation I'd witnessed: evidence of the demon he was, a fact that I kept blocking out.

It was scorching in the car so I opened the window a crack to catch my breath. Keaghan turned to look at me a couple of times, but I still couldn't bring myself to look back. As I recognised the hills around Featherstone, I started to relax. He stopped the car by a field, turned the engine off, and spoke without looking at me.

"I'm sorry, Arianna. I didn't mean to scare you. It's my fault. I shouldn't have taken you there. I get worked up, and when I get mad I *change*. I can be scary, I know. I'm sorry."

I wasn't looking back at him yet, but I could feel his piercing gaze from the side. "I'm sorry. I should have listened to you. I put us both in danger unnecessarily – as usual." I turned to look at him and he couldn't have looked more gorgeous if he tried.

"You don't need to apologise."

"I wasn't scared of you, Keaghan. OK, maybe for a second. I'm upset because I always manage to disappoint you somehow. But I'm not frightened of you."

He took my hand, entwining his fingers with mine. I flinched but didn't pull away.

"You could never disappoint me. You've embraced this weird truth that has been thrown at you with grace and honour. I'm so proud of you, Arianna." He gazed into my eyes. "But you don't have to lie. I know you were scared of me, I saw it in your eyes. I am who I am, and I can't change that, so please, from now on just do what I tell you and think before you act." His voice was mellow, not angry. Somehow, he could never stay mad at me too long. "I don't want you to see me like that again, not unless it's to rip someone's head off to defend you, OK?"

I squeezed his hand tight, even though it burnt more. "OK – but truly? I'm not scared of who you are, Keaghan." I held his eyes for as long as my beating heart would allow before I looked down, embarrassed.

We were interrupted by the sound of his mobile coming from the glove box. He let go of my hand. As he leaned over to open the compartment, he brushed my leg with his arm, sending shivers across my body. Why did he have such an unnerving effect on me?

"Sorry." He looked at me with a cheeky grin. "What do you want, Walker?"

Marcus.

"Yeah... Yeah, she's with me. I'm dropping her off now, don't worry." He hung up and turned to look at me with a frown. "Time for the Birthday Angel to join the rest of the Feathers." He switched on the engine.

"What did Marc say?"

"Nothing. Time to head back." He drove off.

There was silence for a while, but I couldn't repress my burning questions any longer.

"Who were those passports for?" I looked at him but he carried on staring at the road. "I saw pictures of burned bodies back in there, Keaghan. Were they who I think they are?"

"The pictures you saw were of Darksiders who had been instructed to find you. Eddy works for me, but he's twisted and I don't trust him around you. I don't trust anyone." His protective instincts flattered me, but I was sure he didn't mean it to sound that way.

"What about the passports?"

He reached for the inside pocket of his leather jacket and lobbed two British passports onto my lap. "They're for us."

I picked them up. "Elizabeth Bennett?" I looked at the other passport. "Mark Darcy? Come on. Is this a joke?" I asked, confused – and also embarrassed.

"Those are the passports we're going to use to go to Italy. We can't use our real names. I'm sure you understand why."

"OK, I do understand. But who the hell picked those names?" I dropped the passports back on my lap.

"I don't get to choose the names, Arianna." He flashed me an innocent-looking grin. I didn't buy it.

His phone distracted me as it beeped on the dashboard. Keaghan ignored it.

"Is it Marc again? What does he want? What's going on, Keaghan?" I asked.

"Ah, now that would be telling." I recognised that cheeky smile. He was hiding something.

"Oh come on. I know something's going on. Tell me?" I threw him a cheeky grin.

"I can't. Your Feather friends would nail me to a post if I told you."

"It's a surprise, isn't it? Is it a party?" I looked at him, excitement building.

"I'm not saying a word."

"Tell me. Where? Who's going? Are you coming?" I was feeling giddy at the thought. "Oh my goodness, that's so cool. I can legally drink alcohol now, no more sneaking around required." I jiggled on my seat with anticipation.

"What are you like? Are you sure you're eighteen and not eight?" He carried on smiling, shaking his head.

"Will you be there? I promise I'll act surprised." I gave him an angelic look.

He lifted his eyebrows. "Don't know what you're talking about."

I sat back, pretending to be upset. Keaghan parked the car outside Kayla's house.

"Bye," I said, slamming the door shut.

"Arianna, wait."

I smiled, victorious, before turning round and walking back over to the car. "Yes?" I couldn't keep a straight face much longer.

"Happy birthday, Miss Bennett." He winked at me before speeding off down the road.

I walked to the porch, cursing him the whole way, and rang the bell, shivering in my silk dress. It was cold now Keaghan wasn't around radiating heat to keep me warm.

Kayla opened the door. "You're here at last. Where have you been?"

We hugged. I smiled as I walked in, and looked around, but there was no one there waiting for me: no balloons, no banners, no surprise party. Maybe Keaghan wasn't hiding any secrets after all. I'd got it wrong.

"Where are Julian and Megan?" I asked, trying to hide my disappointment as Kayla led me towards the lounge.

"Gone to pick up your cake." She flung the lounge doors open, screaming, "Surprise!"

The room was full of people yelling and pulling party poppers. Banners and balloons screaming '18 Today!' festooned the walls.

"Let's get the music going..." Kayla shouted, and then waited for me to finish the sentence. "And the drinks flowing!" we yelled in unison, before knocking back a glass of champagne.

Some of our friends from St Nick's were here. I recognised a couple of my neighbours too, but I had a feeling most of the guests were angels, including Kayla's "fake" parents.

Marcus stepped forward, looking handsome in a blue shirt and dark jeans. "Happy birthday, angel." He held me tight.

"Thank you, Marc." I looked up at him. "For everything."

I wandered round the room, mingling and catching up with friends I hadn't seen in almost three months. They all thought I'd been finishing my studies abroad, which wasn't entirely incorrect.

An hour or so later, I looked up and saw that Bruna, Keaghan and Nero were standing by the patio doors. Oh my God. I managed to contain my happiness, though I wanted to scream. He was the one person I really wanted here.

"I'm so glad you've come." I hugged Bruna, soaking up the warmth of her body.

"Have you stopped sulking now?" Keaghan looked at me with his trademark cheeky grin.

We stared at each other, entranced.

Nero looked around, his lip curling with disgust. "My nose is itching. There are too many Feathers under one roof. I'm starting to develop an allergy."

"You don't have to be here if you don't want to," Bruna snapped. She turned back to me. "How are you feeling?" she asked, draining a glass of champagne in one gulp.

"Like this has been the weirdest birthday of my life." I smiled, still glancing sideways at Keaghan.

"One that will never be forgotten," Keaghan said, his voice husky and sensuous.

He kept his eyes fixed on mine. My legs were wobbling and my heart was hammering in my chest like a pneumatic drill. I could feel the flush on my cheeks.

Nero sniffed. "I might as well get drunk. The holy smell in this place is killing me." He drank two glasses of champagne, one after another, glancing around as if surrounded by lepers. "I feel like I'm paying for all my sins in one night."

"Oh, shut up, Nero. For God's sake! You're giving me a headache," I said. Keaghan and Bruna burst out laughing.

For the next hour or so, I couldn't help noticing Keaghan constantly gazing at me as I mingled. No matter where I was in the room, his eyes were glued to me. I found myself searching for him all the time as I was chatting to other people. Were we flirting with each other from a distance?

After a while, he came over and interrupted me. "Are you having a nice time?"

He had asked me that question ten times already.

"I am. Are you?"

I didn't feel shy or embarrassed anymore. The urge to look away, flustered, had gone. Instead, I wanted to put my arms around him and feel his breath on my neck, his hands on my waist, and his lips pressed against mine. Oh, if only.

"Keaghan, can I speak to you for one second?" Bruna's voice brought me back to earth, breaking the spell.

Keaghan looked irritated. "Sure, Bruna. What's up?" He forced a smile.

"In private?" She was looking straight in his eyes.

"Is everything OK?" I asked.

Her face relaxed as she smiled at me. "Oh yeah, Arianna. Nothing for you to worry about."

She disappeared into the back garden with Keaghan and Nero. I didn't buy it. They were up to something.

Julian came over. "Just going to get some more ice from the garage. We're running out fast."

"I'll go," I said, snatching the bucket from his hands.

I crept across the garden, flattened myself against the garage wall, and listened.

"I don't like the tone of your voice, Bruna. What the hell are you trying to say?" I heard Keaghan hiss.

"I know what I saw, Keaghan. You're getting too close to her. I can see the way you look at her."

"I look at her the way I look at every hot female on this planet. It's my nature, and you know it." His words hit me like a bullet.

"That's different," she said. "We've noticed how much time you spend with her when you don't need to. Come on, Keaghan. We're not stupid. You're getting too involved and that could jeopardise everything." I heard Nero's voice agreeing.

"Are you both out of your minds? Did you drink holy water or something?"

I couldn't see Keaghan's face but he sounded furious.

"So why are you spending so much time with her without telling us?" Bruna demanded. "Like today, why was she in London with you?"

"Because the Feathers asked me to keep her away until the party was ready. I can't believe we're having this conversation," Keaghan replied.

"Then why did you ask the CO if you could go with her to Rome, without telling us?"

What? How did he know that that would be my wish before I'd even asked?

"Because it's the only way I can keep her safe. The fewer people who know, the better. I don't trust anyone, not even her. She's so hasty and clumsy – always getting herself into trouble." My heart was pounding as I tried to control my ragged breathing. "I need to make sure I know where she is and what she's doing. I have to be with her all the time. Why am I even explaining my actions to you, anyway? I'm your Master, remember? You answer to me, not the other way round."

"So you're not developing feelings for her?" Bruna persisted.

"Listen to me, Bruna, and I'll only tell you once. I don't feel anything for that girl. I don't feel – full stop. Have you forgotten who I am? Arianna Morelli is just a job." I felt a stab of pain in my chest. "Sure, she's stunning. I'm a demon, and you know what tickles my fancy. It's who I am, and that's the best part of being a demon, right? She has a crush on me. Big deal. I can't help it. My nature is to attract, seduce and keep people under my power." I felt sick. His cold, hurtful words cut me like a thousand knives. "It's what we do. We tempt. We're demons."

Bruna seemed convinced. "I'm sorry. I thought I saw a different light in your eyes tonight. I don't doubt you at all, but I think she's falling for you big time. And the way you act around her doesn't help. But that's just you being you, I know. She has an incredible personality. It's contagious, even with me. I like the girl a lot. It's hard not to."

Keaghan snorted. "I can't believe you thought I had *feelings* for her – or any feelings for that matter. She's a nice girl, for a Feather, but that's it, Bruna."

Nero cut in. "It's the *saviour* thing, isn't it? They always fall in love with their knight in shining armour. Pathetic."

Nero's mocking tone didn't hurt me nearly as much as Keaghan's words. I could feel my eyes filling with tears.

"I'll deal with it, don't worry," Keaghan said. "We're close to the end now. We'll soon be able to move on and leave." He sounded like he couldn't give a damn one way or the other.

"She's a sweet girl, Keaghan. I don't want to see her hurt. Let her down gently." Bruna's concern made me cry more.

"She's not a problem, Bruna. Morfran is, and he's closer to her than ever before. We need to stay focused and not dwell on stupid things like this. She means nothing to me and never will."

He sounded utterly convincing. I had not a shred of doubt that he meant every word. A sob burst from my throat. Tears were streaming down my face. I dropped the ice bucket on the ground.

"There's someone there!" I heard Nero say.

I ran as fast as I could, away from the crowd, away from the party, away from him. I was sobbing as I surged through the back gate, desperate to disappear.

As I ran down the street, pain tore through my chest. The streetlights were few and far between, the road almost in darkness. I kept slipping on the melted snow, but I carried on running until I had no breath left in my lungs.

How could I have been so stupid? I should have listened to my brain instead of my foolish heart. I felt humiliated. I'd known who Keaghan was all along, yet I'd refused to see his true nature and how cruel he could be. How naïve was I? Pathetic. Nero was right. After all, how could a demon feel love when he was the incarnation of evil?

Doubled over, I gasped for breath and then looked around. My old cottage loomed in the distance – what was left of it after the fire.

The silence was shattered by the roar of a car speeding down the street; its headlights shone behind me. I knew who it was, and my tears turned to fury as I dried my eyes. The red sports car slowed down by my side.

"Arianna, stop right now."

His voice was like a knife digging in my wounds. I started walking, trying to control the sobs rising from my chest.

"Arianna, please, get in the car. We have to talk."

Why did he bother to put concern in his voice? We both knew it was forced. I stopped, spun towards the car, and looked at him with loathing.

"What makes you think I'd want to talk to you? Get lost." I spat out the bitter words. They tasted like bile.

Keaghan got out of the car and stood in front of me, stopping me as I was about to stalk off again.

"Arianna, please let me explain." He'd never sounded so agitated and desperate, but I didn't give a damn.

"Get out of my way, Keaghan." I looked him straight in the eye, and saw my hate reflected there. My aura was stinging between my ribs.

"I'm sorry about what you heard, but you shouldn't have been eavesdropping, Arianna." His jaw tensed as he ground his teeth in frustration.

So that was his problem. Not what I'd heard, but the fact that I'd heard it.

"I won't ask you again. Move, Keaghan." I stepped to the side, but he grabbed my arm.

"Arianna, I hate to see you like this. You're freezing, let me warm you up. Please, get in the car so we can talk."

I clenched my fists, feeling my control leak away. I was enraged and heartbroken at the same time and my aura was fully engaged.

"I warned you," I said, my voice icy.

I looked straight at him, took a deep breath, and then pushed my hand forward, sending a beam of energy hurtling towards his chest.

He flew across the street. The snow melted around him, and chunks of tarmac lifted off the ground as his body crashed to the pavement. I continued walking towards my cottage.

He shook his head and cricked his neck back in place, before staggering across the road. "Whoa, Arianna, that was impressive," he said. "You're stronger than I thought."

I carried on walking, ignoring him. But once again he stood in front of me and I was forced to stop, directly outside my old home.

"I'm sorry. Please, will you hear me out?"

He reached out and took my face in his hands. I shuddered as his face moved closer to mine. My judgment was impaired. Heat waves encircled me; they felt so soothing. A current of electricity was warming up my shaking body. Damn. It was hard to think straight. He's lying! Nothing about him is real. He was trying to tempt me, just like he said. Like a slimy, demonic snake.

"Get your hands off me, Keaghan. This is your last warning."

He moved his hands away. "Do what you have to, as long as

you hear me out."

He opened his arms wide, inviting me to hit him. I hated him for being so arrogant and gorgeous at the same time. But I wasn't going to let him fool me.

"Fine, have it your way." I tilted my head and took a deep breath.

Heat rose above my head. I closed my eyes and engaged my aura. As my eyelids snapped open, I blasted a blow across his chest, so powerful that he crashed against the wall. He fell to the ground, bringing a cascade of bricks down with him.

He limped towards me, brushing off the grit and snow from his clothes. "I deserved that. That was a blast to remember, for sure. Now will you listen?"

No. I was far from done. "Why are you challenging me like this? Haven't you hurt me enough?" I screamed.

I stretched both my arms in front of me. A huge blast of energy hit him with such violence that he crashed through the window of my wrecked cottage. The blow was so intense that he flew through every wall, all the way to the back of the house. My breathing became laboured, and I wilted under a wave of exhaustion.

There was no sound from the cottage. What if I had killed him? Could he actually die? I remembered who I was. The Angel of Light can kill powerful demons – like Keaghan.

I peered through the window but I couldn't see him. Moving closer, I spotted him on the floor, lying motionless. A wave of panic swept over me.

Oh my God. I had killed the demon I loved.

29. SCARY DIFFERENT

I've always hated fire. Could never stand the flickering flames, the charcoal-coloured smoke, the sharp-tasting smell. The whiff of scorched wood rose from the wreckage of my old home, sending shivers along my spine and bringing back memories of my mother screaming through the flames as I was dragged away. For ten years I'd managed to shut out those dreadful moments. But there was no hiding from them now. They began flooding back.

The cold wind blew the trees, rustling the branches, but all I was aware of was my thumping heartbeat and the fire burning in my chest.

"Hello, Arianna."

I didn't recognise the voice coming from across the street. Spinning round, I saw a dark man in a black suit standing in the middle of the road, a hundred yards or so away.

"I don't suppose you remember me. You were barely eight the last time we met." Heat waves were radiating from his body. His eyes were red. My blood turned to ice.

"Who are you?" I said, my voice shaky. He was taller and larger than the other demons I had met.

"Allow me to introduce myself. My name is Set," he said. "I'm here to accompany you to Morfran. He wants to give you a birthday present."

I felt a chill roll down my spine. "I'm not going anywhere."

I stood firm. For one moment I thought it was *him*. I was relieved. If I could take Keaghan, I could certainly take this demon too – whoever he was. I glanced through the shattered window of my cottage. Keaghan was still lying motionless, in a puddle of black liquid.

The demon spoke again. "You have your father's spirit, I must say. A true Morelli. Shame we have to burn out another powerful light." He paused. "Of course, Morfran is merciful – sometimes. Maybe he'll make a deal with you. What do you say? Would you turn to the dark side, Angel of Light?"

"I'd rather die and be fed to the pigs than go with you."

I focused on my breathing, hoping to engage my aura, but I couldn't feel the energy rising from my chest. I was too tired and cold. Come on, Arianna. You can do it.

"That can be arranged," the demon said. "Though I'm afraid I must leave the pleasure to Morfran. You'll come with me, whether you agree to it or not."

His voice started to change. The heat that swirled around him turned to raging flames, encircling his body like a fire. His face turned a shiny red, his eyes bright yellow. His smile revealed the inside of his mouth. A forked tongue swirled around in the blackness.

My stomach churned. God help me. He looked like a snake.

"Are you ready to die, Angel of Light?" the creature growled as he moved towards me.

Quick! Do something. I looked straight into the demon's eyes and pushed enough air down into my lungs to engage my aura. I closed my eyes and took another deep breath. When I opened them again, I lifted my arms and pushed my hands forward, unleashing a beam of light. As the energy hurtled from my body, I staggered backwards, overwhelmed by its power.

He didn't see it coming. It hit him right across his chest, knocking him to the ground. He growled as he clambered to his feet. "You're better than I thought." He seemed surprised. "I shouldn't have underestimated you."

I couldn't breathe. My heart was drumming in my ears. The

blast had drained the energy from me. My human side was prevailing over the angel in me. I needed time to recharge, but the demon didn't give me a chance. His fire blast was quick and effortless. It came to me like a hot wind. I lifted my hand and blocked it with my mind, using my telekinesis to deflect the blast. It worked! The fireball landed on the tarmac, gouging a hole in the middle of the road.

Set looked at me, aghast. "You're really annoying me now, little girl."

He sprang over to me so fast that it looked like he had been launched like a rocket. I jumped to get away from him. I didn't realise how much force I'd put in the push until I found myself on the other side of the road. Did I just fly? Impossible!

"You're fast," he growled, looking even more irritated. "They trained you well."

I didn't feel fast. I felt exhausted. I couldn't concentrate. Damn you, human side.

"You're very different from the frightened little girl you were ten years ago, when we killed your parents." His words sliced through me. "Do you remember your father's face burning in the flames?" A stab of pain in my chest, followed by a flashback. I shook my head to get rid of the image. "And your mother's scream before we set her alight, limb by limb." His voice became even more harsh and guttural. His face was contorted into an evil sneer, his scaly skin shining under the moonlight.

"I'm not afraid of you," I shouted, aware of the hesitation in my voice.

"You should be," he said.

He pushed his arm forward and threw another fireball. This time it was faster. I had no time to react. The blast hit me in the chest. I flew backwards and slammed into the wall of my cottage. A sharp pain in my back. I fell to my knees. My aura had softened the blow, but it still hurt like hell.

The demon didn't waste any time. The next instant, he was

looming over me. He grabbed me by the neck and pulled me up. His fingers were burning my skin as his grip got tighter. I couldn't catch my breath. I felt as if my eyes were about to pop out, and I waved my arms in panic. Dizziness overwhelmed me. My vision blurred. I couldn't pass out. Just couldn't. I pressed my hand against his face in an attempt to push him off.

He let out a screech of pain and stepped back, releasing his grip and dropping me on the ground. I gulped for air. My vision was still distorted but I could see the agony on his face as he stared at my hand.

"What the hell is that thing doing on your finger?" he yelled. My ring? "I destroyed it when we killed that witch, years ago."

I looked down at my hand: the blue sapphire was gleaming like a star. The sight of it gave me new strength. I lifted my chin to look at the demon.

"My mother was not a witch. And you're still petrified of her, by the looks of it." I clambered to my feet, blood trickling from my mouth.

I pushed my fist forwards, pointing the ring at him. It shone bright on my finger. Set shuffled back, scrunching up his face.

"I'm not afraid of anything," he hissed, his eyes gleaming like torches. "Especially of some lousy witch's relic. That thing didn't save her then, and it won't save you now."

I gasped and staggered backwards, glancing inside the cottage as I went, desperately searching for Keaghan. What the...? He wasn't there!

I closed my eyes, feeling my aura powering again at last. When I opened them, I saw Keaghan standing behind Set. He nodded at me, placing a finger on his lips. The surge of relief gave me the strength to recharge another blast. I pointed my hands towards the demon, throwing a blast across his chest, but he saw it coming. With one hand, he diverted the blast, smashing it against a parked car.

He threw another ball of flames towards me. I ran sideways

and ducked, swerving the blast with my telekinesis, and side-tracking the blow in time.

"Aren't you tired yet?" Set muttered under his breath. He glared at me, his features twisted with fury. "Time to finish this game, little girl," he growled. "You're making me waste precious time."

"I couldn't agree more." Keaghan spoke from behind him. The demon swivelled in shock.

Keaghan's eyes were bright red. As I watched, his face changed: his skin turned to red, and his scarlet eyes glinted with gold sparks. Flames rested in the palms of his hands.

He threw a fire blast in the demon's direction, but Set stepped aside.

"Keaghan Blake."

"Evening, Set. It's been a while." Keaghan's skin-prickling voice made me shudder.

"I see you're still mingling with the wrong crowd," Set said. His heat waves turned to raging flames again.

"I see you're still Morfran's lap dog."

It didn't sound like the voice of the demon I loved. His red skin glimmered under the light of the flames he was radiating. I barely recognised him.

"I suggest you turn round and crawl back into the hole you came from," Keaghan snarled.

Set's evil laugh echoed in the street. "You haven't changed at all. You're still as arrogant as you always were."

I caught Keaghan's eyes briefly, before he turned to the demon again.

"I'm giving you the chance to walk away alive. I wouldn't throw it away, if I were you."

"It's not you I'm after. But I'll kill you first, if I have to." Set cracked his neck to one side.

They stared at each other with loathing. The flames around them were melting the tarmac on the road. They looked terrifyingly alike.

Keaghan wasn't just 'any' demon. He was a Darksider. Though deep down I always knew, seeing him in his true form was still a shock.

Keaghan was the first to throw a fireball, but Set was a close second. As their blasts crossed, there was a mighty bang, like a bomb exploding.

They were both on the ground but immediately stood, wiping the blood from their mouths, before charging another blast. This time Set was faster, and Keaghan took the force flat on his chest, throwing his body down the road. I watched, petrified, unable to move.

Set spun round to face me, pinning me with his terrible gaze. Panic ripped through me.

"Come with me, now."

"I'm not done yet." Keaghan's voice came from behind him, seconds before a fire blast knocked Set to the ground. I ducked to avoid the flames shooting towards me.

But Set was up on his feet already. "I still wonder why you're doing this, Blake. You were one of us. How could you turn your back on Morfran for this stupid girl?"

"She's worth a thousand of you," Keaghan said, another fire blast in his hand ready to be unleashed. "And you will address the Angel of Light with respect."

The blast hit Set but this one hardly fazed him. Keaghan looked tired. How was that possible?

"You're weaker, Blake." Set began walking around him as if he was prey. "Can't you see what she's doing to you? She's consuming you, drawing every atom of power from you. This can only end badly for you, Blake."

I wanted to do something, but I was frozen, my chest rising and falling convulsively.

"The only one who should be concerned is you, Set." Keaghan recharged another blast, but I could see he looked beaten.

"We shall see about that," Set roared.

They both unleashed the energy at the exact same time. The blasts hit, and both demons fell to the ground and lay still. The street was as silent as a tomb, my erratic heartbeat echoing in my ears. I heard a hiss coming from Set. He rolled onto his side and crawled onto his knees. Keaghan was still lying in a puddle of black blood, not a twitch or a sound from him. My stomach dropped.

Set looked in my direction, and then at Keaghan, before setting his eyes on me again, smirking in victory.

He climbed to his feet, dusted off his suit, and smiled. "Your turn, Angel of Light. You will come with me, dead or alive. It's your choice."

"Kill him, Arianna," Keaghan raised his chin, his face covered in blood. The pain in his eyes clawed at my gut. "You can do it. I know you can." His voice was just a whisper, but I could just about hear him.

I took a deep breath, trying to control the beat of my thumping heart, and dragged up the courage to look directly into Set's eyes as he closed in on me.

Overwhelmed by panic and fear, I closed my eyes, took a deep breath, engaged my aura and threw my hands forward. Do it. Now! A huge beam of energy was hurtling towards the demon's head. My breath faltered. The blast left my body with a violent thrust, its light shining brighter than ever before. This one felt different from the other blasts I'd created. It felt more powerful, and incredibly fast.

Set burst into flames on contact. His body turned to dust right in front of my stunned eyes. Oh my God. Did I just kill a demon?

The wind blew his ashes in my face, making me choke; the air stank of burnt flesh. I shuddered, panting. I spun round to Keaghan. His face was changing to its normal colour; his eyes returned blue.

"Arianna…" He tried to push himself onto his elbows. His eyes widened in pain and he fell back, lifeless. I gasped, bringing my hand to my mouth, my heart in my throat.

"Keaghan?" I forced my feet to take me over to him. "Keaghan?" I shouted this time, my voice shuddering with horror.

Black fluid was dribbling from the corner of his mouth. I squatted, grabbing him by the shirt and shaking him; but he didn't move. I called his name over and over. There was no heat coming from his body. No. He couldn't be dead. Don't you dare die on me.

"Keaghan, please, get up. Keaghan." I pulled him over my legs, the black fluid leaking over my dress and mixing with my blood.

"Keaghan, please, don't do this to me." I shook him again, then wrapped my arms round him. "Keaghan, please?"

Tears welled up in my eyes. I tried to shine my aura on him. I had no energy left, but I had to try. A blast of energy radiated around him and a bright light gleamed from me to him. He moaned feebly.

"I must be dead, 'cause I can smell Heaven," he murmured.

"If you were dead, Heaven would be the last thing you would smell," I said, torn between anger and relief. "I should leave you here to rot." I glared at him, before trying to help him up.

He moaned louder this time.

"I hope it hurts," I snarled, struggling to lift him.

"It does, trust me," he mumbled. He coughed and spat more black blood.

"Good." I didn't mean it. He was alive. That was all I cared about. But I wasn't going to tell him that.

I managed to get him inside the wrecked cottage, where I lowered him onto the floor, causing him to cry out in pain. The last blast had left me weak too. I felt drained.

I sank down on the burnt wooden floor of my old home,

resting my head in my hands. Now that the immediate danger had passed, the memory of Keaghan's words in the garden flooded back.

"You were fabulous back there." His croaky voice was barely audible. "Set was one of Morfran's most powerful Darksiders. You kept your cool and killed him with your very first psionic blast. I'm so proud of you."

"I couldn't care less how you feel," I snapped.

"Do you need healing?" he asked.

"I'm fine."

"You don't look fine. You're bleeding."

"I'm fine."

"I think you need Kayla to heal you, Arianna."

"I said I'm fine! Drop the act, Keaghan. I know you don't give a damn about me." I tried not to sound hurt or bitter, but my voice betrayed me.

"I'm so sorry, Arianna," he whispered, wincing in pain.

"You did your job. You saved my life. Why are you apologising?"

"You know why. I didn't mean a word I said." His voice was deep now. He tried to catch my eyes. "And you saved me, by the way."

"You're a great liar, I have to give you that," I said, my voice cold.

"I'm not lying to you. Please listen to me." He dragged himself across the floor towards me.

"I don't want to listen. I've already heard everything I needed to hear." I shrugged, pretending I didn't care. Inside I was screaming.

"Did you overhear the whole conversation?"

What? Why was he asking me that? I tried to move away but he grabbed my wrist.

"Oh, I heard you all right," I said, holding his gaze.

"Well, you're going to hear the rest now, whether you like it or not," he whispered close to my face.

It would have been so easy to fall for his charms again, but I wasn't going to let it happen this time.

"I won't believe a word you have to say anyway, so why bother?" I hoped I sounded harsh and cold.

I tried to free my hand with the other one, but he grabbed that too.

"The last thing I wanted was to upset you, and on your birthday of all days. I had to say what I did to get Nero and Bruna off my back."

Don't believe him. Don't believe him. Don't believe him.

"Yeah, right. You really must think I'm stupid. I heard you loud and clear." I looked straight into his eyes. "And for the record, I'm not clumsy. I never was. I've started behaving irrationally ever since I met you." I looked away in disgust. "And now I know why."

"I didn't mean it. I didn't mean a word of it. You have to believe me."

I hardened my heart. "Do you want to know what I believe? I believe that you need me. That's all. You need me to kill Morfran so you can get your precious soul back. You couldn't care less about me. I'm just a stupid kid with a crush, remember? Don't worry, I'll get over it."

"That's not true, and you know it." He sounded painfully sincere.

I looked back at him, my face a cold mask. To my frustration, I couldn't stop tears spilling from my eyes and I turned away to hide them from him.

Even so, I could feel it. He was looking at me with those eyes again. The look that was able to capture me in his entrancing spell. Why was he doing this to me? Don't look at him.

"I love the way you blush when you look at me."

He caressed my fingers with his, entwining his hands with mine. My lips started to tremble.

"You're so beautiful, and your eyes are so big when you're angry. They shimmer like emeralds."

He was whispering the words as if they were poetry. I felt like I was being hypnotised, and struggled to hold on to my anger.

Stop it! Stop! Don't fall for it, Arianna.

"That's what you demons do, right? You seduce your prey with fancy words."

His face was dangerously close to mine. "No, this is what you do to me, Arianna. You seduce me – you always have."

One of his hands reached around my neck, the other touched my face with burning fingers. I couldn't move. Did I even want to? My heart was bouncing against my ribs as he moved his lips almost close enough to touch mine.

"You're not just a job to me, and I couldn't care less about my soul – not unless you wanted it," he murmured sensuously. Before I could react, he released me from his hold. "Although, primarily and most importantly, my job is to protect you."

He closed his eyes and put his head in his hands, massaging his temples. "I don't know what's happening to me. Whenever I'm with you I become over-protective." It was his turn to look away. "I can't bear to see you hurt and I don't want anyone near you. It's not right. It makes me weak, Arianna. Do you understand what I'm trying to say?" He turned and looked at me, frustration etched on his face.

"You don't want to protect me anymore. That's fine," I replied, trying not to care.

"No, that's not what I meant! Gosh, you're hard work, sometimes." He grabbed my hands again. "You drive me crazy. I can't be near you without wanting to touch you, or kiss you, or put my arms around you. I call you just so I can hear your voice. You've cast some kind of spell on me that I can't shift. I've tried to distract myself with other girls, lots of them, I really have." I didn't need to know that. "But every time, you pop into my head, ruining the mood. I can't stop thinking about you, and I want you with me, all the time. It's an obsession. I'm supposed to be a ruthless, careless demon, Arianna. I've never lost control this way before."

I wanted to believe him so much, tell him that was the way I felt too. But I couldn't silence the *brainiac* in me. I had to protect myself from any more pain.

"I don't believe you, Keaghan." I looked at the floor.

He hung his head. "Maybe it's a good thing you don't, because this simply can't happen. It's wrong. I'm a demon, Arianna, made of hate and rage. You deserve better." But I didn't want anybody else. "Just having you near me drives me insane. With you, I'm... different. I feel I can be different again." He sat still, not moving a muscle.

"Good different?" I asked, my voice hesitant.

"Scary different." Transferring his weight onto his right arm, he rolled onto his knees and faced me. "When I saw you bleeding and hurt in that theatre, I felt something beating in my chest I hadn't felt in centuries. I was so enraged, I wanted to tear those demons' heads off and eat them." The remembered rage flashed across his face. "When you turned up at the Alley Cat Club, looking so damn sexy, dancing so provocatively, hell, you made me more than jealous." His eyes burned into mine. "And I was furious in London today. Do you want to know why? I couldn't bear the way they were looking at you. I wanted to rip their eyes out. I asked the Order to let me go with you to Rome because I thought that with me you'd always be safe. I'd never let anything happen to you." He grabbed my shoulders and made me look at him. "I will protect you with my life, I swear."

"Is this another one of your demonic charms?" I whispered, blinking from the tears.

"No. I don't do this, Arianna. I don't care for people. I haven't cared for anyone in a very, very long time – not like this."

He dried my tears with his fingers. I felt the heat of his body warm the area around us like a flame. He leaned over and kissed my wet cheek, drying the spot with the touch of his mouth. I jolted.

"You really have feelings for me?" I said in one breath, swallowing hard. I dragged up the courage to look directly into his eyes. He smiled in that magnetic way I couldn't resist.

"Something like that... and trust me, just the *feeling* part is a major change for me."

I was falling for it again. Can't let it happen. He would wrap me in his demonic spell once more. I wriggled, but he wouldn't let me move. He reached up and took my face in both hands, stroking my cheeks with his thumbs.

"I'm so sorry for hurting you tonight. I can't bear to see you upset."

As I met his eyes, my resistance melted. I didn't want to listen to my head anymore. I had to give in, let him hold me in his arms. "Prove it. Kiss me." My voice trembled, but the words came out loud and clear.

I needed to feel his touch. My eyes closed as his face moved closer to mine. He started nibbling my neck. I gasped. His touch was like a flame searing my skin. I didn't care about the consequences anymore. More than anything, I wanted his lips against mine.

"Do you know what you're asking me, Arianna?" he whispered, drawing back and looking directly in my eyes.

I nodded. "Kiss me, Keaghan."

His lips were half an inch away from mine. I felt his breath entering my mouth like a warm breeze.

"An angel kissing a demon? That's not allowed, Arianna, and you know it," he said, his voice croaky.

"Why?" I already knew the answer.

We were so close it was if the contours of our bodies were folded into one other. I put my arms around his waist, holding him tight. Every muscle in his body grew tense. He hesitated for a moment.

"The Order forbids it," he groaned.

"I don't care about the Order... I want you to kiss me."

He smiled, brushing my cheek with the tip of his nose. We looked at each other for a moment that seemed like forever.

"We can't," he said. "I won't let you disobey the Order because of me." In spite of his words, he didn't move away or release me from his hold.

"But if you kiss me, then I'm not the one breaking the rules, right?"

I caressed his lower back with my fingers. His muscles were tense under my touch and he pressed his body against mine harder, taking my breath away. He gasped as I nuzzled his neck, feeling a power surge through my body.

"Are you trying to tempt me, Feather girl?"

I could feel his frustration as he tried to resist me.

"I am."

We stared at each other, neither of us moving, my heart pumping. The trail of his aftershave overwhelmed me. A blend of spicy yet musky scent was firing up all my senses. Was that another demonic charm designed to tempt me? If so, it was working.

I pulled him towards me by his T-shirt, our lips finally coming together. As his mouth met mine, it felt as if fire was brushing my lips. Keaghan held my face firmly with both hands. He gently bit my bottom lip as I kissed him back, ignoring the burning sensation inside my mouth. I gulped. The intensity of the emotions mounting inside me had triggered my aura; a stabbing pain throbbing in my chest, the light shining bright above my head. His kiss was gentle at first. I felt his hand around my waist as he pulled me in closer. I crashed against his chest, gasping, and wrapped my arms around his neck. I ran my fingers through his hair and kissed him fiercely, his mouth prickling my flesh with every peck. I didn't care. It was worth the pain.

He released a deep sigh. "You have no idea how good you

taste," he said, talking between kisses. "Your kiss is everything I thought it would be, and more. It's like inhaling a cool breeze." For me it was like inhaling flames, but I chose not to tell him.

The ring of his mobile shattered the moment. Keaghan was the first to move away and break our fiery embrace. He checked the text message as he ran his hand nervously through his hair.

"It's Bruna. Everyone's looking for you. They're getting frantic."

My lips were still throbbing and I felt lightheaded. Oh my God. I couldn't believe we'd kissed. And what a kiss. I had waited for this moment ever since our eyes first met.

"We need to leave now," he said. "Before Megan senses where you are and finds us here. It would be a bit awkward, eh?" He winked as he took my hand to help me up.

We walked out of the wrecked cottage and across the road towards his car. It had started to snow. I was still in a daze as I looked at the dent in the wall and the bricks on the ground.

"I can't believe I did that." I shook my head.

"I can. I'm still hurting."

We sped off, and were outside Featherstone in minutes. Keaghan dialled as we stopped at a red light.

"Brue, I got her. Yeah, she's fine. Tell everyone at the party she's OK. I'm taking her back to the monastery for tonight." He hung up.

"You all right?" he asked.

I nodded, but in truth my head was all over the place. A wave of exhaustion washed over me. It was hard to keep my eyes open. I felt Keaghan clutching my hand and caressing my fingers as I drifted off to sleep.

30. NO DOUBT

I'd always had the dream, ever since I could remember. Every time I fell asleep, I heard a hissing noise, and red and gold gleaming eyes staring at me in the dark. I had hoped the dreaming would stop now that Set was dead. I'd killed him. God. I'd vanquished a demon. Impossible to believe, but I had. Yet, the nightmares didn't disappear with him. It wasn't Set haunting my dreams. But I already knew that. It would have been too easy.

"Wakey-wakey, Feather girl." Keaghan's voice woke me up.

The car was parked outside the monastery. To my disappointment, he was no longer holding my hand.

"Are you OK? You're sweating." He wiped my forehead with the back of his hand. I sat up, taking a few deep breaths to slow down my racing heart.

"I thought the dreams would stop now that Set is dead. Obviously not." I couldn't hide the disappointment in my voice.

"Hey, come here." He gently pulled me closer to him. A blast of heat drifted over me. "It's just a dream. No one will hurt you ever again. I swear."

I relaxed in his arms. Oh my God. We kissed. Or did I dream that too? His hand was brushing my hair, sending sparks down my back. No. I didn't dream it. My lips were still tingling.

"Morfran is still out there. Looking for me." I swallowed hard. "And he won't stop till he finds me."

"He'll have to go through me first." The glimmer of a smile appeared on his lips. It didn't reassure me. "I think Morfran is petrified of you, Arianna. I wouldn't be surprised if he goes into hiding after he finds out what happened to his fiercest Darksider." I doubted that. "You were incredible tonight. By dawn, every demon will know about what you did and what you're capable of. They have more reason to be scared of you than you of them. Trust me. And so they should be."

I looked up to meet his eyes. They were filled with admiration. I wasn't so sure I deserved it. I didn't know how I'd managed to kill Set. Luck, most likely. I tangled my fingers around his hand, ignoring the stinging sensation between the layers of my skin.

"Do you really think that this is it? That Morfran will back off for good?" If only.

"I do." He sounded confident. "I think he'll stop hunting you now. I would if I were him. He's a smart one, Arianna. If he knows what's good for him, he'll run a mile." His hand reached up to frame my cheek, and I quivered.

I wanted to believe that what Keaghan said was true. But deep down I knew this wasn't over. Morfran would never give up on hunting me.

Keaghan's phone beeped in his pocket. As he read the message a huge grin spread across his face.

"I was right." He looked up at me, then showed me the screen. Nero. "Morfran and his Darksiders have left. Every single one of them has disappeared. They're gone."

"Gone? Just like that?" Yeah, right. I didn't believe that for one minute.

"Gone." He lifted his fingers to nudge my chin up. "He knows he can never defeat us. As long as we're together, we are the key to his destruction. I doubt he'll be back, Arianna."

He leaned forward and paused a few inches from my lips, his hot breath beating against my skin. I placed my hand on his jaw and pulled him in for a kiss. His lips clutched against mine. This was going to hurt. A tingling gust travelled inside my mouth like a whirling wind. I responded to his kiss with the same urge, suppressing the yelps of pain. When the raging burn of his flesh became too much to bear, I was forced to pull away. Damn it.

"Arianna, I'll always be here to protect you," he said, totally unaware of my discomfort. "But I really don't think we'll be seeing Morfran or his demons any time soon."

A niggling thought crept into my mind like a slithering snake. It sounded too good to be true. The *brainiac* in me kept reminding me that good things always come to an end.

"Tell me what you're thinking," he said.

"You don't want to know." I lowered my eyes.

"Try me."

I sighed deeply. I might as well say it. Sooner or later we'd have to face reality. Time to burst the lovely bubble.

"There's a law in the Angelic Code of Justice…" Keep going. "W-what do we do about that, Keaghan?" Here. I said it.

"As if I could forget the bloody law," he said. His face was rigid with frustration.

"In training, I read a passage that stated a demon and an angel can't be together." I hated the sound of those words. "Is that true? Is there a way we can change that?"

He shook his head firmly. "And let's face it, Arianna. I'm not a common demon either. I'm a Darksider. There's even less hope for us." A mocking snigger escaped his pursed lips.

"What do you mean? There's got to be something we can do, right?" There had to be.

"No Arianna. There isn't." He turned to look at me, his face hardened. "The CO categorically forbids it. You could face banishment if you broke the law." I wasn't sure what that meant.

"There must be exceptions, surely." I wasn't going to give up that easily. "What if I speak to Lucius? I could tell him that you saved my life, time and time again. Convince him that you're not an evil monster. That you're good. You proved that so many times already."

I pulled his face to make him look at me. He was avoiding my eyes, but I carried on.

"There must be a clause somewhere that we can find. Another law to challenge this one. There is no way I'm giving up, Keaghan."

He grabbed my hands and held them close to his chest, his expression still beaten.

"I'm sorry, Arianna. But there's no clause, no law that can change the fact that we can't be together." His words struck me like a ton of bricks. "Although… there is one thing we could do."

My head sprang up to look at him. There was hope? Oh thank God. I was already starting to plan my suicide.

"We just keep it a secret. We don't tell anyone, and we make sure the CO never finds out." He sounded serious. "Not even your Feather friends, Arianna. No one must know."

"I'm pretty sure they already have their suspicions," I said. "I'm not very good at lying."

"I don't want you to lie." He let go of my hands. "That's why it's probably best if we end it now, before it's even started…"

I covered his lips with my hand to shut him up. "That's not an option. Don't even say it. That's out of the question, do you hear me?" I cried.

Keaghan pulled my hand down, leaned forward, and pecked my trembling lips repeatedly. If he was trying to reassure me, it was a good way to start. I nestled against his chest, breathing in the spicy scent of his skin.

I pulled back. "Then we'll keep it a secret for now," I agreed. "I'll do whatever it takes. But I know there must be something we can do. I'll find a way, Keaghan. Don't worry." Though I wasn't sure how.

"I admire your courage and determination, Einstein." He stroked a lock of my hair. "But there's no *formula* for this."

"I don't believe that. There's always a way. And I'll find it, trust me. If it takes me an eternity I will." I placed a rushed kiss on his lips.

"I trust you." He gazed into my eyes and smiled. I seemed to have convinced him at last.

"As long as we're together, we're invincible, right?" I couldn't believe my words. "I never want to be apart from you, Keaghan. Ever." I placed my head in the fold of his neck and snuggled up to him.

"We may have no choice but to part at some point, Arianna," he said.

I thought I'd managed to persuade him just a minute ago.

My head jumped up. "What?"

"Well… you have your A-levels to finish, Ms Morelli. Remember?" He winked. "Or have you forgotten about that?"

Ah. My A-levels. I breathed a sigh of relief.

"Really? I still have to take them now that I'm a fledged angel?" Didn't make sense.

"Oh yeah." He grinned. "You're still a human to the outside world. You need to maintain your cover. That would be the *brainiac*, I believe." Was he kidding? I couldn't tell.

"I don't care what I do, as long as you're with me," I said, my voice as sweet as honey.

I was back to being my pathetic-self. But I didn't care. I couldn't suppress my feelings, and nor did I want to. I'd turned into a soppy teenager, and that was OK. For once I'd let my heart win over my brain.

"Come on, time to face Marcus. This is your last night at Maidstone Monastery." Keaghan walked around the car and opened the door for me.

"I can't wait." I meant it.

"Night, Arianna." He turned and briskly strode back to his side of the car.

"Huh? Aren't you staying with me tonight?" Please say yes.

"No." There was a huge space between us all of the sudden. I couldn't feel his heat waves around me. "Must go. Bye."

Un-bloody-believable. How could he switch his mood on and

off like a lightbulb? It looked as if he couldn't wait to leave.

"Bye then," I grunted.

Annoyed, I turned and sauntered towards the side entrance of the monastery. As I pushed the door open Keaghan caught up with me, pulling me into his arms.

I clung to his waist and hid my face in the fold of his neck. He stroked my hair, nibbling behind my ear. A flash of heat raced along my skin.

"Stay with me, please?" I pleaded, my face buried in his chest. I didn't want to let go.

"Not a good idea, Arianna, not tonight."

"Did you mean everything you said before?" I lifted my head up to look at him. His eyes were so intense.

"One hundred per cent."

He held my face in his hands, looking at me with adoring eyes. I kissed his neckline, unable to let him leave.

"Don't, Arianna, or I won't be able to stop myself this time."

He must have read my mind. I was about to ask him to kiss me again, hoping he would stay.

"I must go. I don't want to, trust me, but I have to." I saw the frustration on his face. "Enjoy your last night in your prison. From tomorrow, you're a free angel." He placed his lips on my jaw, setting my senses on fire. "Night, Feather girl."

He gazed into my eyes, before leaping back in the car and disappearing in a flurry of snow.

EPILOGUE

Keaghan stared at me, tapping his foot on my bedroom floor nervously.

"Are you going to open it or not?"

I gripped the brown envelope firmly in my hand, unwilling to let go, my heart beating in my chest like a drum.

"I can't," I growled.

"You've been staring at it for the last ten minutes." He searched for my eyes, but I looked away.

"I can't."

"Let me do it, then." Keaghan knelt in front of me and gently rubbed my arms to stop me from fidgeting. "You'll have done great, I know. Why are you fretting so much?"

He placed his forehead against mine, waiting for me to open my eyes.

"What if I get B's and C's?" I frowned.

"Nonsense. All A-Stars, I bet." I wished I could share his confidence.

I sighed. "OK. I'll open it now." Come on. Get it over and done with, Arianna.

My trembling fingers ran across the paper, ripping it at the edges. I pulled out the folded sheet, my eyes squeezed shut the whole time. I felt Keaghan's lips pressed against mine. I jolted for a moment, then kissed him back.

"Come on," he whispered against my lips. "The tension is killing me here."

I stretched the paper tight, reading each line slowly. My eyes flew open. I looked up at Keaghan, my jaw on the floor.

"So?" He gaped at me, looking even more anxious than I felt.

Oh my God. No way. It's totally impossible. I read the letter again. I didn't misread it.

"Arianna, speak. Please?"

I couldn't. I was frozen with my mouth open, no sound coming out. Keaghan took the letter from my hands and read it, then looked up at me.

"What did I tell you? All A-Stars, just like I said. I knew it." He swept me up into his arms, his lips pressed against mine.

"Oh my goodness." A giggle burst from my throat. "I smashed it, haven't I?"

"You certainly have, Einstein."

Keaghan spun me around the room. I clung to his shoulders, beaming. He put me down, my breath ragged with excitement.

"You're still a geek." He pulled that sexy smile I loved so much. "You can take the angel out of the nerd, but you can't take the nerd out of the angel."

"Hey, watch it!" I jabbed him in the ribs, playfully. "May I remind you that I'm the Angel of Light, and I can vaporise you with my psionic blast?"

"I know exactly what you can do to me, Ms Morelli." He nibbled at my ear.

"Oh, can you now?"

Here I was, in the shiny new bedroom of my brand-new cottage, built especially for my Nana and me. Nearly a year ago I found out I was an angel. Hard to believe, but I was. I vanquished a Darksider and fell in love with one. The demon charged with my protection was also the demon I loved. I couldn't contain my happiness. I was holding Keaghan's hand in one hand, and a triple-A-Star letter in the other. What more could I possibly want?

I stretched up on my tiptoes, wrapped my arms around his neck and gripped his lips with mine, feverish. I pressed myself to him tightly. Although I was getting used to the burning sensation of his touch, it still hurt like hell. He let out a groan as I bit his bottom lip, causing him to smirk into the kiss. Keaghan's hands reached down the curve of my lower back, pulling me even closer.

He tilted his head back a few inches, staring at me, his eyebrows furrowed. "So, what's next for the Angel of Light?"

I shrugged. "Uni, I guess. I can be an angel and go to Uni, right?"

"I suppose. You'll have to speak to the CO about it." He tickled the skin of my back. I felt the familiar tingle. "I bet they have a list of angelic duties for you to undertake; but I'm sure a nerd like you will be able to cope with both."

"I think so too." I chuckled against his lips.

For the past few months we'd managed to keep our secret safe. No one knew about us. Though I suspected Megan had a vague idea of what was going on. I could never hide anything from my witchy friend.

It probably helped, the fact that I was constantly tied up with school, and Keaghan was busy with his fallens trying to locate Morfran and his Darksiders. They seemed to have disappeared into thin air. That meant we couldn't see each other all the time – or as much as I would have liked, anyway. But every spare moment we had, we'd spend it in each other's arms.

Keaghan placed my feet back on the floor and pulled away. "First though, aren't you forgetting something?"

"Huh?" He'd lost me there.

"Your wish?" he said. "… We could take that trip to Rome, if you still want to go?"

I'd been so busy worrying about everything else, I'd totally forgotten about that.

"Oh, yeah. Absolutely." I couldn't think of anything better.

"Are you sure? It's OK if you've changed your mind." Why the sudden hesitation?

"If it's Morfran you're worried about, Keaghan, there's no need." I touched his tense jaw. "Morfran and his Darksiders haven't been seen since the night we vanquished Set. I think you were right. He's gone. I'm safe now."

"You're safe forever." Keaghan held my face with both hands. "I won't let anything happen to you, I promise."

Holding him tight and losing myself inside the spheres of heat radiating around us, I gazed into his eyes, immersed in their blueness.

My heart was filled with contentment. There were no doubts in my mind. I was hopelessly in love with a demon, and I knew he felt the same about me.

7577641R00161

Printed in Great Britain
by Amazon.co.uk, Ltd.,
Marston Gate.